...and dreams are dreams

Vassilis Vassilikos

*

... and dreams are dreams

*

Translated from the Greek
by Mary Kitroëff

SEVEN STORIES PRESS
New York

Copyright ©1996 Vassilis Vassilikos
Translation ©1996 Seven Stories Press

Published in the United States by Seven Stories Press
632 Broadway, Seventh Floor
New York, NY 10012

First printing January 1996.

Library of Congress Cataloging-in-Publication Data:

Vasilikos, Vasilēs, 1934-
   [Short stories. English. Selections]
   —And dreams are dreams/by Vassilis Vassilikos; translated from the
Greek by Mary Kitroëff.
     p. cm.
   Translation of the French version of Greek short stories selected from: Ho komētēs tou Chalei and Hē asprē arkouda.
   Contents: And dreams are dreams—History—Stories of taxi drivers—Doña Rosita and Don Pacifico—The white bear—Three miraculous moments lived by Doña Rosita—The transplant.
   ISBN 1-888363-00-2
1. Vasilikos, Vasilēs, 1934—Translations into English.
   I. Kitroëff, Mary. II. Title.
PA5633.A46A25 1996
889'.1334—dc20   95-21663
                 CIP

10 9 8 7 6 5 4 3 2 1
Printed in the United States

to Vasso

Contents

Contents

. . . and dreams are dreams

> *"Suffocating in the chicken coop of reason,*
> *I managed to unwind by pleading the case*
> *of dreams."*
> —Aeschylus, *Agamemnon*, v. 82

> *"Life is but a dream . . . and dreams are dreams."*
> —Pedro Calderón de la Barca

There are dreams that are sold in the market, packaged or fresh, at sale price, dreams that are imported or indigenous, tax free, made locally; dreams that come out according to the seasons, like fruit; others, frozen, you can find all year round; dreams sold in farmers' markets or department stores; dreams grown with chemical fertilizers or with manure—that is to say pure dreams, greenhouse dreams, and grazing dreams—dreams sold in installments and at half price (in the flea market on Sundays you can find old dreams coveted by collectors: antique dreams, like old gramophone records or rare books); there are political dreams, propaganda for a certain party or ideology, dreams about catastrophes like those earthquake movies that make the whole theater shake (or at least that's what the audience thinks), that soak you in their drowning waters and make you wake up screaming: dreams of the frost, and the clouds, and the snow, crystalline like snowflakes, silken like hair; dreams with staircases and dreams with scaffoldings, dreams with leaves and dreams with foliage; there are also musical dreams: jazz, blues, and hard rock dreams, opera dreams with sumptuous stage scenery that seems to be three-dimensional, or the one-dimensional kind that unfurls before a plain black background; stereophonic dreams and videotaped dreams; you will find dreams everywhere, in all five continents, even in space (where they are weightless); diuretic dreams and digestive dreams, dreams of Pepsi and dreams of Coke, dreams as painful as colic and others that burn slowly:

pyromaniacs' dreams; Eskimo and equator dreams; dreams that are arranged like the Big Dipper and the Little Dipper; there are also visual dreams, and architectural ones, dreams about the art of logic and the logic of art, with innumerable corpuscles incorporated inside them like the insides of transistor radios; one can also buy metaphysical dreams, paraphysical dreams, dreams on tape, dreams on cassette, postage stamp dreams, rubber-stamped dreams, and other dreams that have as their receiver their very transmitter; dreams that you can pick up on AM or shortwave radio, FM dreams; dreams printed on one hundred-gram paper, on chamois paper, dreams by photosynthesis, in Roman characters, or Shakespearean or Dreyer's characters; Balkan, Ottoman, Palestinian dreams, Holocaust dreams; fragments of dreams that go off in your sleep like fireworks and others that go whistling by but never explode; you can buy dreams that have been cleared through customs or you can buy dreams on the black market; dreams of oil wells: petrochemical dreams, either from Europe or from colonies that have become independent; dreams of the enslaved, dreams of the free, dreams of slaves, and of Slavs and Albanians; dreams of exiles and of homecomings; migratory dreams; carbohydrate dreams that make you either lose or put on weight; drunken dreams like boats, dreams stoned on anything from Lebanese hash to opium, that is to say dreams of an artificial paradise, dreams brought on by shooting heroin, that lead you little by little to death; snapshot, Kodachrome, caffeinated or decaf, detoxified dreams; rococo, baroque, Etruscan dreams; jackpot dreams; group sex, monogamous, onanistic dreams called nocturnal emissions; slushy or granular dreams; dreams that make you go back, that reverse you or push you forward; mobilized dreams or dreams without character, anonymous, odorless, and cheap *dreams; there are volcanic dreams and dreams of boredom, of stagnation; twin dreams, Siamese twin or egocentric dreams; you can also buy two-wheeled dreams, three-wheeled dreams, four-wheeled dreams, and that's as far as it goes, because after that they take off and become balloons, gliders, Dakotas, Caravelles, multiengine, and turbo powered; there are Porsche and Maserati and Concord dreams; there are fizzy or flat dreams, soda pop dreams that explode in your sleep like champagne corks and scare you, while others have silencers and go off on the sly; crucified, Buddhist, Confucian dreams; dreams of Mao and Mao's widow, dreams of the tigress; elephantine, lionine, canine, and pantomime dreams; dreams of bouzoukis and of other smaller instruments, like the baglamadaki; dreams of rembetika, dreams like Argentine tangos; folkloric and cosmopolitan dreams, repeating themselves like Hilton or Holiday Inn hotels, changing only according to the architecture of our sleep, while essentially they are identical; perjured, empty, Leninist dreams; dreams that Trotsky would have rejected but that his descendants call Trotskyist; in China you will find Japanese dreams and in Japan granular dreams like Chinese rice; dreams of superb meals, of palaces, of dukes; incestuous and purebred dreams like the horses at the race track, where the outsider dream might just win; dreams of football fans, of tennis and ping-pong that resound monotonously inside your head since you can't see the players; dreams that win prizes like in beauty pageants; Eurocommunist dreams, gangster dreams, and dreams of poor people who see pizzas in their sleep. Finally, there are dreams of dreams that make you wake with a start and cry out: "No, that can't be true. I dreamed it."*

Precisely because they are so terribly lucid, dreams have become the objects of our waking lives and are used as slogans in advertising; dream spots often interrupt a dreamy series or adorn the pages, when they don't take up an entire page, of daily and weekly newspapers and magazines, like those dreams that recur on fixed dates. This is why there are chairs of Dreamology at the universities and why Dreamography has its dream interpreters. And this is why holders of degrees in Dream Studies are sought after by large corporations, by dream multinationals, and by the large dream trusts and consortiums. This is why the Common European Market of Sleepers obliges students, starting in grade school, to write essays based on their dreams, and instructs teachers, before starting class, to present on the blackboard or on the screen the dream they saw the previous night; and at college entrance exams, essay topics concern dream phrases by writers who dreamed not to interpret the world, but to change it.

This is why Marx speaks of the surplus value that the boss steals from his worker's dreams of becoming the boss, and the boss always fools him, just like in those dreams in which you're always on the point of having it all but you never quite succeed, once and for all. This is why the political parties play with the dreams of their voters, i.e., how to get a tax-free car or how to make their shit travel through a dream pipe to the sea, rather than amass in the garden sewer. Thus, dreams become a vital substance, the main one that keeps you vigilant in this miserable existence, in which you can't wait to run, to lose yourself in a dream film or a book of dreams or in love, where the dreams that lovers have are so often the opposite of the reality they are living; and they emerge from love rejuvenated because they were able to dream. They hate all those things that keep them grounded in life: their time cards, the rent, illness, nagging, and they live in dreams of traveling, in dream vacations, in dreamy states of cohabitation, or they might go and unwind in a football stadium dream or in a dream church. However, next to the purely individual dreams we find their collective counterparts: the nonliberating dream of the great idea; the dream of a free, independent Greece; the dream of a happy youth and a dignified old age. The swallows bring the dream each spring, hacking at the air like tailors; the swallows' tails look like miniature tuxedos and the flowers that people love transport them, with their smells, to other lands, other gardens of Eden, of dreams, where the ugliness of the wall does not exist, nor the finality of the tomb, nor the flat surface of an oblong table, because a simple vase with flowers placed upon it will transform it into an upside-down foot, and it becomes the sole of the foot of the sky. This is why, in the dreamlike state in which we live while awake, instead of the mushroom of a nuclear disaster, we offer our next nightmare a dream flower in the shape of a sunflower, which, even though it might die, will at least leave us its seeds to eat, and, since dreams are conductors of the whole, as in a hologram, we will be able, through its seeds, to keep bringing to mind over and over the flower in its entirety.

"Take my life," said the defendant to the court, "but don't take my dream. That you cannot do. Even if you wanted to."

And so, the frowning assessors thought about it over their law books, which were ossified dreams, white seashells of dreams that went away, carpets upon which dreams bled in losing their virginity, and concluded:

"If we can't take his dream, what's the good of taking his life?"

So they commuted the death sentence to life in prison. That way, the convict could dream inside his prison cell, undisturbed by the countless parasites of life.

...and dreams are dreams

We don't want to speak of Freud. We are almost completely indifferent to his interpretation of dreams. As far as we're concerned, Freud did nothing more than to lower their high frequency to a household level. The same way that Edison took sunlight and, with technical knowledge, courage, and intelligence, made it into a lightbulb. What we're saying is different: from the time man started walking on two feet, he has been dreaming continuously. The position of a biped is one that keeps pulling him higher. And this dream, that it is himself in the dream, gives him the energy he needs in his state of vigilance, in order to continue on earth his dreamless and otherwise mortal existence.

-2-

When my dreamologist friends and I (our friendship was saturated with dreams like hydrophilous cotton) decided to publish a newspaper, the *Almanac of Dreams*, in large format like papers used to be, and not a tabloid with badly printed color photographs (because dreams are black and white, and, fortunately, the cameras have yet to be made that would color them), we were, naturally, confronted with the primordial problem of all newspapers, which is the financial one. We had no capital to speak of. But even if one of us had had any, none of us would have dared suggest he invest it in an enterprise as uncertain as our own.

There were four of us in all. Zissis, a former partisan who still lived with the dream of a Greece of popular rule; Thomas, who had realized his dream of becoming an industrialist three times and three times let it slip through his fingers; Zenon, who was a dream professional (he wrote in *Dream Interpreter* magazine); and me, Irineos, a writer who had spent his life recording other people's dreams as if they were his own, or his own as if they were other people's. The fact that we called ourselves dreamologists was anything but a joke.

Then one day, we found our Maecenas: Dimitris, an acquaintance of Zenon's, who had worked abroad and returned to his country with the sole dream of investing his money in a publishing company. We were a match made in heaven. Just as in dreams sometimes, when we come across the most improbable situations and then wake up and say, "It was only a dream," so were we living our dream. But this one was real. We had found our dream financier, who not only liked our idea that "dreams avenge themselves!" but also found it very marketable.

"The *Almanac* will be a hit," he concluded, after hearing us out. "It's something that's been missing. Man can't live by soccer alone. He needs dreams and videotapes. I have found the videotape market to be saturated. Fortunately, dreams are intangible—they cannot be imported, they are not material goods—and as such, they have been scorned by the unimaginative neo-Hellenes."

Thus Dimitris was to provide the money and the machinery; we were to provide the grey matter. Our first step was to request that our newspaper be exempt from the paper tax.

"No doubt," said the clerk in charge when we handed in our application to the Ministry of the Presidency (at 3 Zalocosta Street), "dreams are tax free. But I don't know if the paper they are printed on can also be tax free. You should probably see the general manager."

...and dreams are dreams

We made an appointment with the general manager (Zissis knew him from the Association of Resistance Fighters), who received us with joy and told us we were definitely entitled to tax-free paper since we were publishing a newspaper. He only asked, without seeming too concerned with the answer, what its political affiliation would be.

"Dreams have nothing to do with politics," all four of us replied with one voice. Our motto, at the upper right-hand corner, would read, "Dreams of the world, unite." And our countersign in the opposite corner would read, "We dream in Greek." We hoped to avoid provoking any political division among our readers by eschewing mottos like "Our dreams have been vindicated" or "Our dreams are enduring,"* even though, as I suggested, "Our dreams have been educated" solved the problem, if only as a play on words.

"I see," he said. "It's really the dream of progress that you want to support. And you couldn't have picked a better time, since the state is thinking of opening the first dreamfirmary, which would be integrated into the National Health System."

He even promised us a small contribution out of the obscure resources of the Ministry. All newspapers were subsidized by the state. Why not ours?

Delighted, we ran and told Dimitris, our Maecenas, the good news. He was thrilled. And so, without wasting another moment, we got to work preparing the first issue. It was going to be four pages long, on glossy paper.

* During the elections of 1981, the slogan of the Greek Socialist Party was "Our struggle has been vindicated," while that of the Greek Communist Party was "Our struggle endures." *Trans.*

"Like the *Lonely Hearts Classifieds* paper," Thomas remarked dreamily.

-3-

There are dreams of outer space, disinterested dreams; dreams that stay for years locked in a safe-deposit box in a bank; submissive dreams, and others that are like draft dodgers, that never return to the land of our sleep but grow old far away, until an amnesty allows them to be repatriated; then they suddenly find themselves overtaken by other dreams that have grown up meanwhile, because the nature of a dream is such that it does not accept the void: the dream vegetation does not save an empty seat for the dream that's away; and there are other dreams that have been bought off, like someone paying in order to avoid his military service; bald dreams in a corrupted language; there are toxic dreams like the ones that grow inside reactors, and that, despite all protective measures, manage to expel a little of their poisonous steam and harm the people living nearby, because it is possible, and such things happen in life, that one person's dream is another person's nightmare; there are gypsy dreams, that wander around, and dreams that are centuries old, like trees; others that last only one night, that are gone before the day breaks; and also those that come out at sunrise because they need the sunlight in order to exist; dreams of the open sea, sailboat dreams, indelible as the tattoos on a sailor's skin, dreams on the waves, immured and not handmade; mosaic dreams, and dreams of Byzantine emperors; Protestant and Catholic dreams, dreams of Emperor Hirohito, fascist, grandiose dreams that disappear one day,

...and dreams are dreams

leaving their shells like fossils for the researchers of history, like a work of architecture that is empty on the inside, marking an era; pocket dreams, credit dreams—American Express, Diners Club, and Visa—dreams that can be cashed anywhere in the international market, and others, like the ruble, that are only accepted in their own country; dreams that the dreamers are eager to exchange at a rate of one to five with other dreams whose official prices keep them at a rate of one to one; there are also illegal dreams that change appearance in order to survive; scab dreams, and others that plan the big white strike called death and last as long as death does before transmuting into something else; cross-dressing dreams, that is to say transvestite dreams, amphibolous, amphigenous, dicotyledonous, frog dreams, amphibious dreams, useless like mosquitoes in the mire of sleep; dreams like seagulls that follow the fishing boats, eating whatever the fishermen discard from their nets; antiracist dreams of coal miners who dream of coming out into the light of day; computer science dreams, terminal and interminable dreams like soap operas; brochure dreams that wake you up from your lethargy; manifesto dreams; semiotic dreams that are signifiers without a signified; ostrich dreams, because they hide their heads deep in the sand, thinking you can't see them, but the dream hunters hit dozens of them, like thrushes, with their automatic rifles each September; dreams that run like rock partridges in deep ravines; sandy dreams into which your feet sink as you walk them, until a dream within the dream emerges, an oasis in the Sahara of sleep; helicopter dreams, remote control dreams, SS-20 and Hawk, intercontinental, low-flying dreams that can't be picked up by the radar of vigilance and appear suddenly before you, and make you wonder how you didn't remember them upon waking; dreams like hermits and ascetics, Capuchins, Franciscans, Pre-Raphaelite dreams. Modiglianiesque dreams, dreams of Chagall, Marco Polo, and Genghis Khan; Mongolian, Iraqi and Iranian, ironic dreams; dreams of the pyramids, Mycenaean and Aztec dreams; and also dreams of rain, of hail; lottery dreams, gambling dreams, good luck or bad luck dreams, dreams of the number 13, astrophysic dreams, blue collar and intellectual dreams, organic or inorganic, that flourish like tropical plants in our sleep; dreams of the lost homelands, Ionian, Pythagorean, geometrical, decimal, and pure wool, like hides that keep us warm; nylon, plastic, liquid gas and smog dreams, choking dreams that raise the air pollution indicator to dangerous levels; abyssal, medieval, paleolithic, nomadic, and Georgian; dreams like sheafs of wheat or like corn popped at the movie theater; dreams that burst like pomegranates and others that fall under the apple tree, dreams with apples and dreams without appeal; structuralist dreams, computer-era dreams, and barometric dreams that guide seafarers who are usually superstitious; barbiturate dreams, nepenthean, agapanthean dreams, dreams of love and loneliness, dreams . . .

All of these would have their place in our newspaper. All of these would be the material, the stuff, *the stuff dreams are made of, Dantean dreams, of Purgatory and Paradise, even though Dante himself became a synonym for his Hell; dreams of Ovid and avid dreams; screws that wedge themselves into the unprotected skin of sleep and suck your blood like leeches (it's not dreams that avenge themselves, but realities that appear like dreams and latch onto you indelibly, forever); I mean to say that there are no Dracula dreams that suck your blood, but there is a blood of dreams that nourishes them, made of the white and red blood cor-*

14

puscles of Morpheus, nothing to do with the blood that circulates in our veins. The body supports our dreams, that's true, but it has nothing to do with them (the same way bankers who support the enterprising dreams of artful merchants avoid paying taxes); there are paternalistic dreams and patronizing dreams, of the Holy Word and the Unholy Word, announcing better days to come; dreams according to the Julian calendar; monastic dreams and dreams of monasteries, Catholic and cathodic dreams, vine-arbor dreams over the ledge of sleep, offering their cool shade to the worker, the grape harvester, the woodcutter, the woodpecker; marble dreams that drip blood, bright red blood, the blood of statues; and dreams that saw away at your brain, like cerebral episodes; acupuncture dreams deodorizing the day's sweat and anesthetizing, with chloroform; cicada dreams that gnaw at the light, cricket dreams; dreams that are sweet, neat, eat . . .

All of these would be welcome in our newspaper. They would appear in a special column devoted to the dreams of our readers (a column that truly—and here I will get a little ahead of myself in the telling of my story—grew rapidly and came to occupy almost half the newspaper, since—as soon became apparent—what people needed more than anything else was to communicate their dreams, which they had seen all alone and exclusively, not sharing them even with the person lying next to them in bed). And so, little by little, through our newspaper—whose sales, I can't resist telling you, surpassed those of *Avriani*[*]—a new tendency developed, almost a trend, for people to talk among themselves of their dreams, to relate their dreams to one

[*] Populist left-wing daily. *Trans.*

another and to urge one another to share their dreams: it became the "in" thing for people to talk of nothing else all day long but of what they had dreamt of the night before, and even if they hadn't dreamt of anything, to make up the dreams they would like to have had. That way, all that had, up until then, constituted people's daily bread (i.e., politics, soccer, crimes, and the ordinary life that develops around each one of us and feeds off of us like a parasite) were replaced by the important news we would bring to the surface: the dream that Reagan had, the dream that Gorbachev had, and Ching Yu Xe's dream of modernization, since the Great Wall of Isolation has been abolished and the Chinese are now writing on the wall their most daring, even their most Confucian dreams; and they are now allowed to dream of the return of the great emperor, the same way we used to dream of the revival of the Petrified King, the last emperor of Byzantium. And so our readers got into the habit of putting their dreams in the foreground too.

The effect we were having was evident in the paper's circulation, which was increasing in leaps and bounds each week. We inaugurated an artistic column, in which actors and directors, poets and writers, stage designers and singers, would share with the public, one at a time, the dreams that had most affected their lives. Soccer stars and movie stars and big names in politics also gave interviews about their dreams, thus revealing sides of their personalities about which the public had been unaware. Thus, we found out about Caramanlis's dream of mountain climbing (he had wanted since childhood, it seems, to climb Mount Everest); the dream Papandreou had of becoming the conductor of a symphony orchestra; the dream of the general secretary of the Greek

Communist Party to take sheep out to pasture and sit in the shade playing a shepherd's pipe; Mitsotakis's dream of being a croupier at the casino; the dream of Anastopoulos[*] to be Giorgio Armani; Armani's dream of being a soccer player; and other dreams of pedestrian malls, of the Athens metro, dreams of suburbs, of ambulances, of a National Immortality Service . . . until finally, there appeared on TV a game show with dream crossword puzzles, where the contestants had to solve the clues with desires, unfulfilled wishes, inhibitions, that is to say with dreams and not with their knowledge; and all this, thanks to us, to our little newspaper.

Of course, the reader of this strange tale should not imagine that the transformation of the public was accomplished overnight. As with AIDS, it took time and hard work for the panic to spread, for the dream seed to germinate. The dream is also an epidemic but instead of killing it gives birth, instead of hurting it encourages, and it strengthens instead of weakening. Feeding the new fruit of forgetfulness took hard work, great pains, clever public relations, and the blood of many volunteers. At first, the dream lotus with which our readers went beyond themselves and revealed the other sides of their personalities, hitherto hidden away, would only emerge in secret sighs and private confidences, because, as the poet of the avenger dreams says, it takes a lot of work for the sun to turn and become the moon.

That was what we did, we five (four dreamologists and our Maecenas). We started off unsupported by any kind of substructure. Very soon, however, much sooner than even we ourselves expected, that which existing socialism hadn't achieved in

[*] Famous Greek soccer star. *Trans.*

seven decades was achieved by its utopia, which became fashionable again because it expressed, finally, the deeper desire of people to be *outis* (no one) in *ou topo* (no place). Every place ties one to a tomb, whereas the death of the soul is a utopia: no one knows where the soul goes after death. Dreams don't need land to bear fruit, or plots upon which to be built, or fires to thin out wooded areas; they need instead an inner flame. It was this flame that our fellow human beings, with our initiative, managed to develop. The notaries were the first to pay the price of this transformation, since dreams don't need to register with the Public Records Office. They don't need a birth certificate or, hence, a certificate of death.

Contracts were also superfluous. Since the egg that is a dream does not need a chicken to lay it, thus circumventing the age-old question of which one came first (matter or spirit, body, or soul), there was no chicken coop fenced in by logic. Dream railroad tracks bore trains of dreams, unloaded dream passengers; dreams were dropping anchor at seaports, taking off at airports; the farmers of Thessaly organized themselves into dream cooperatives and started managing their dreams themselves; Larissa became the dream of Larissa, and Salonika that of Byzantium; Athens again became the dream of Pericles, who descended from where his biological death had exiled him and was once more among us with Phidias. Then Pericles himself recognized the mistakes of his previous life and no longer demanded a tribute from the other cities of the Athenian league or robbed their treasuries to develop the Acropolis and build the Parthenon, or asked his fellow citizens to make sacrifices for the war; he was dreamy and peaceful, he now said that both men and women, not only illustrious men, can be fittingly buried in any land, because the earth contains the idea of destruction, whereas dreams are indestructible. Thus differences are solved in dream jousts, attacks are met with dream defenses. Two thousand one was proclaimed the first year of dreams, because at that exact time all dreams would come to fruition, would become actions, so that later, people would be able to accept successfully, with courage, having been prepared for it for a long time, their destruction; they would be convinced that they themselves were just a dream that was coming to its end. After all, it had lasted long enough—a few tens of millions of years—so there went their earthly existence, and that was the end of that.

However, things didn't happen so quickly. Things never happen as quickly as the simplifying process of our memory would like to present. Of course, in the beginning, I was so involved in the daily occupation of publishing our newspaper, of which I was editor in chief (contradictory though it may seem, dreams do need editing, organizing, and, like a nursery, they need attention and vigilance: in order for it to blossom, a dream needs fertilizing, watering, pruning), that I didn't have any time to keep notes on the side. But now that I recall the reactions of the press tycoons in this country, I don't remember them having one good word to say about our paper.

A few days after the first issue came out (number one, of the first volume, of the first year), and after the unexpected welcome it received by people thirsting for something different (that first issue, as the reader may guess, has a special value, now that the State of Dreams has established itself and the Dream Police guard the borders against any enemy violation of our ethereal space), a few days later, there came to Dimitris's printing office (located in Alimos across from the famous bakery, it was more than perfect, with the latest in technical equipment, built with the money Dimitris had made while working abroad, all of it foreign currency, the dream of the immigrant realized and our Maecenas found, given to us so our dreams too could be ful-filled) an inspector from the Ministry of Labor in order to check—or so he clamied—whether it was operating according to regulations. Mr. Inspector proceeded to observe that the cylin-drical machine, a gigantic electronic monster on which we had printed our first issue, maintained a distance of, not two meters from the ceiling, as the law dictated, but only sixty centimeters. This constituted sufficient cause for the removal of the press's operating license.

Dimitris was puzzled. Recently back from Australia, he was ignorant of Greek bureaucracy and unaware of Mama Greece's longing to draw to the very last drop the blood of any immigrant who made the faux pas of being repatriated and bringing back, like seamen do, all his foreign currency. He didn't know that this Greek state of ours, during these two hundred years since its birth, had learned to live not by blood transfusions but by drinking blood like Dracula, so he didn't pay much attention. But we knew and right away were suspicious. How much had the press bosses paid Mr. Inspector to show up out of the blue? The printing office had been operating smoothly for the past year. Why was there a problem now and not before?

Therefore, it was the very success of our newspaper—the first issue never even made it to the kiosks, but disappeared, as happens in dreams, right from the distribution vans—that had worried the smooth operators of the press business (who were used

...and dreams are dreams

to making and breaking governments) enough to send their henchman just in case, as an initial scare tactic.

"And what law is this?" asked Dimitris.

"A law of 1968," the inspector replied, and pulled out an official document.

"But at that time, these cylindrical machines didn't exist," said our friend, relieved. "This law refers to Linotypes, which indeed, for safety reasons, had to maintain a distance of two meters from the ceiling. Electronic machines are a different matter. And they weren't put on the market until 1978."

"Unfortunately, the law is always the law," said the inspector, bowing his head.

"But you're going to ruin us!" cried Dimitris. "We can't raise the ceiling, nor can we lower the machine."

"Good heavens, we don't want to ruin anyone," said the inspector. "All we are doing is enforcing the law. If only the law would change, then there would be no problem. But until then, I would advise you to start looking for another place. And do it quickly."

Of course, I think to myself now, if only they had been able to imagine the success of our *Almanac*, which became a daily paper within a few months, the press tycoons would have acted differently. That same day they would have kicked us out onto the street, thus drowning the yolk in its own shell. Dimitris would have sold everything and gone back to Australia. (It's not uncommon for an immigrant to be forced to take that road again, because of the deep hatred every wretch who stayed home shows toward the successful repatriated immigrant.)

And who knows what the rest of us would be doing now? However, progress is accomplished in life thanks to the establishment's predictable inability to deal with the threat of novelty. After all, isn't that the way it happened in czarist Russia with the revolution? If they had known of the October Revolution, wouldn't they have, before that in 1905, exterminated the revolutionaries down to the last one, the same way that the Americans, seventy years later, did with the leaders of the Black Panthers, leaving only one of them alive, a zoo specimen?

However, I'll say it again: fortunately, the old order can rarely see the dangers in something new, and that is why they let innovations take root. We ourselves were almost uprooted, but by then, dreams were too advanced in people's psyches, and whoever tried to attack us fell on his face. Meanwhile, people had started sprouting wings.

Even so, that first, unimportant little side effect we bypassed—I will tell you how—came very close to shaking us up.

Mr. Inspector showed no sign of leaving. It was as if he were waiting for something. Dimitris understood straight away.

"As you can see," he said, "we are publishing the *Almanac* not to make money, but because it's something we love to do. We are selling dreams. Not feta cheese. And not parliamentary bills. Why don't you do us the favor, if you believe our effort is worth it, of letting us get on our feet first, and then we'll move to another building. I promise."

The way he spoke seemed to be doing the trick. *Because it was the right way.* If Dimitris had mentioned something about the laws of the dictatorship still being in force, his argument

...and dreams are dreams

would have had the opposite result: the inspector was a career civil servant who had loyally served all governments. So as far as he was concerned, the determining factor of a good or a bad law was not the political background of the government that had decreed it. Rather, all laws were either right or wrong, in relation to the laws themselves. Thus, in our case, the distance of two meters could only be contested because our machine was new. The law had been intended to regulate Linotypes; he could not contest the law by the political criterion that it had been decreed under a dictatorship. If Dimitris had used the latter argument the inspector, a man of the right, could say to himself: "What's the difference between a socialist government and a military dictatorship?" However, even though Dimitris had played it exactly correctly, the inspector was not convinced.

Bribing him didn't work either. When Dimitris hinted, very smoothly, about a gift, perhaps a kangaroo from Australia, the inspector snapped that he was no animal lover. He didn't have cats and he didn't have dogs. He wasn't about to take in a kangaroo.

The boomerang effect is well known, especially to someone who has lived in Australia. So when Dimitris began to fear that all these things—bribes, politics—could end up turning against him, he chose to tell the truth about the dream we four had of publishing a newspaper of dreams, and about Dimitris's offer, which provided us the means to do it for free. And now along comes the state and says, what? That the bed on which the dreamers lay had to maintain a distance of two meters from the ceiling in order for them to be allowed to dream? With this tack, he touched the Achilles' heel of every man, harsh bureaucrat though he may seem: that is, the need to express the hidden part of ones' self, the part that dreams, while the other part acts.

That was how the inspector appeared to me: a certain gentleness came over his face, something seemed to yield. As was proven later on, civil servants, and especially the older ones, are our most loyal subscribers, since they all spend their lives sitting at their desks, dreaming. He said, with the difficulty of a man used to enforcing the letter of the law, and not its spirit:

"All right then, as far as I'm concerned, you're okay. But you'll have to take care of this matter eventually."

We don't know, from that point on, what that man went through. When after a couple of years I tried to find him at his office, I learned that he had taken a leave of absence. It seems that, during those two years, when we kept stealing readers from other newspapers, the big bosses had taken care of him.

One evening, a month after that incident, the police showed up. The reason: a tenant on the third floor had complained that he couldn't get to sleep because of the noise of the machine at two in the morning.

It was true that we printed on Friday evenings. Dimitris had his machines booked up all week long with jobs that brought in some money, and then he would turn them over to us at five P.M. on Fridays for as long as it took.

But that night, we didn't finish at eleven o'clock like we usually did. It was our fifth issue, and we had made some last-minute changes in the layout. We kept going until two A.M., and thus disturbed the tenant on the third floor. The printing office was on the ground floor of a small apartment building. The floor right above it was used as a storeroom, and then there were three

...and dreams are dreams

floors of apartments. Never before had anyone complained about the noise. The soundproofing was perfect and the electronic equipment silent. It was only when we printed posters on the two-color Roland that one heard the traditional racket of the printing press. In many respects, the operators of the cylindrical machine looked more like nurses than printers—dressed in white overalls, holding remote control boxes, they made the enormous machine move, with its flashing lights, its dials, and little screens—it looked more like a monster from the Apocalypse than a printing press. But now we had to face the charge of disturbing the peace.

This tenant of the third floor, as he confessed to us later, had been forced to call the police. He didn't say who had forced him, but we knew. When we told him what we were trying to do, he turned out to be on our side. He withdrew the complaint. He too found the kind of life that was imposed upon him to be unbearable. He too believed in dreams as his only escape from the dead end they had built for us.

All this is coming back to me, now that people are preparing to celebrate the first Dream May Day. And I recall it all, the same way veteran fighters of a just cause recall the first years, when they were still searching blindly for a way to overthrow the establishment. Because with dreams, we undermined a sham that was suffocating people. How we succeeded in achieving victory, I will tell you immediately: we worked like termites. We ate at the furniture from the inside. We filled it with holes. And when the time came, the furniture collapsed on its own. No violence was needed.

Of course, things had come to an impasse everywhere. This phenomenon of asphyxiation, of crisis, did not concern Greece alone. Man needs faith to support him. A vision. It used to be religion. Then socialism. And when that too retreated from the visions it had once proclaimed, people no longer had anything to believe in, and thus had no reason to suffer. For better days? Days would never be better; they couldn't be. People knew that. Entropy, the second law of thermodynamics, told them that their lives would only get worse. It was inevitable.

After an ideology goes bankrupt, there is always a void before something else comes along to take its place. It was that void that we took advantage of. It was that void that our newspaper aspired to fill.

From the start, we gave a very broad meaning to the word *dream*. We didn't refer solely to what people see when they are asleep. Rather, we implied that everything desirable, visionary, spiritual could, with a restructuring of the means of production, become tangible. Just as the accumulation of capital creates capitalism, we proclaimed, so the accumulation of inhibitions creates a new force that is surpassed only by the capacity of man to want something he doesn't have and acquire it. For us, a dream was every possible and impossible human desire. All was fair, since everything belonged to the realm of the dream.

Every organization needs support, so we established a Dream Bank, where our customers deposited not their money but their dreams. The interest rate was high, and the initial capital could not be touched. Soon, all mortals came running to us to deposit their dreams. Next came donations, and the first trust funds. Our profits from the newspaper formed the consolidated capital of the Dream Bank, which soon issued shares. Thus, like the diversion of the river Achelous, the Aegean bridge that connected all the islands by road, and like the satellite that was sent into space and, like an umbrella, covered the entire ancient Greek empire with television programs in our language, the first publicly financed dreamworks were built. All these works attracted more deposits and our dream credit grew in the market.

Dreams, we kept saying, constitute our physical being. Conversely, metaphysics is the life we live outside dreams, because it is beyond reality. Dreams crush death underfoot, because there is no death for a dream: one dreamer continues the other's dream, which is made the same way as a cloud: the earth emits it in the form of a vapor, the sky compounds it into a nebula, then it falls back and waters the earth, only to be reabsorbed by the attractive power of the sun. The dream and the cloud, always somewhat synonymous in the souls of the people, were thus explained scientifically, along with the deeper dream meaning of space. And we gave the dream its proper place: the dream was man's true life, and his work was simply his time to rest after dreaming.

There are dreams that are difficult to find, and others that are being sought by the International Red Cross; Cambodian dreams of the Khmer Rouge that used to be those of Sihanouk; jungle dreams and swamp dreams, fireproof dreams and firearm dreams; dreams of Saint Barbara and of All Saints, Name Day dreams, and nameless dreams; there are dreams covered in sweat and dreams that are dehydrated, salt pan dreams where the salt collects in crystals, sleet dreams and mortgage dreams; crucifix, half-moon, Star of David dreams, infrastructure dreams, sewage system dreams and campaign promise dreams, builders of bridges of a state of vigilance; feudal dreams and dreams for themselves; magnetic, miserly, playing card dreams and dreams that trap you;

evergreen and withered dreams, edible, potable like table water dreams; dreams that travel in bottles like messages from shipwrecks and those orchidaceous ones that writhe like snakes; ivy dreams that suffocate sleeping trees by growing furiously around their trunks; and dreams of contact, like the lenses that color the eyes; hormonal dreams that change the sex of the dreamer and other harmonious ones that keep pace with his life, because when life becomes a dream then the dream acquires flesh and bones. Dream skeletons, like prehistoric mammoths, are still studied by dreamologists, because the origin of dreams is searching for its own Darwin, the economy of dreams for its Marx. The dictatorship of the dream proletariat wants its Lenin and its Trotsky, but has no need of a Stalin in order to survive. All dreams have a place on earth, since the earth is a huge brain that studies the universe. No dream is excluded, no dream is oppressed by another. Dream minimalism, which was espoused by some, mostly harmed people, because the saying "small is beautiful" doesn't always apply to our dreams. There are porcelain dreams as well as steel dreams, dreams of fiberglass and plasterboard. All dreams are legitimate because they don't lay claim upon anything or anyone. All they want is to exist. Therefore, all dreams are existential. However, there are also dreams that are phenomenological and deterministic.

Dreams are us, you and I, reader, and I wouldn't go to the trouble of telling you this story if I didn't want to tell you, to make you understand that a dream subscriber who receives his dream newspaper every day can better support himself on his—and our—strong conviction that we are worthy of a better fate, in this "pocket of the Balkans," on this continent, on this earth, on this planet. And it is time for dreams to avenge us.

...and dreams are dreams

-4-

But I'm getting ahead of myself. Our newspaper started off like one of those small grass-roots movements that go unnoticed in the beginning but get stronger and stronger (like the Greens, whom nobody considered a threat and so they were left alone), little by little, with time, precisely because they represent a deeper human desire: to grow by themselves, without publicity's artificial fertilization; to take root and acquire depth. All that this process requires in the beginning is a team to join hands and cooperate, while the initiates, few but fanatical, go out among the people, until, once the appropriate conditions have been established, the explosion takes place. In this way, with our little newspaper, we proceeded to win over readers and followers, day by day, almost without realizing it.

We had rented a small office at the foot of Strefi Hill. People would come by every day, because, they said, they found in our newspaper an answer to their longtime problems and thus a sense of hope. It seems our slogan, "Keep the dream alive, don't let it die," made some sense. Then, as election time approached, the big parties wanted us to join them. They each sent a representative to offer us financial help in return for our support. But we refused every offer, because we were after something bigger: the limitless right, in the words of the poet, to dream. "What should interest you above all," wrote the poet Napoleon Lapathiotis, "is the elegant use of your life and the limitless right to dream." And then he killed himself. We left out the first half of this maxim, which did not concern us and implied a certain dilettantism, and adopted fully the second half, the limitless right to dream, which hadn't been included in any party's campaign promises.

And while the expression "I belong to the branch" took on a disparaging connotation during the first period of our socialist government, since it meant, "I'm a card-carrying member of the party in power," we rebaptized the word *branch,* returning it to its original meaning by inaugurating a column in our paper called "Branch Dreams." In this column, society was viewed as a tree with many branches, and every professional branch was given the podium. We would publish the dreams of taxi drivers, builders, tailors, umbrella makers, pastry makers, upholsterers, book binders, railroad workers, carpenters, sales clerks, printers, tobacco workers. They all had a place: the flour mills, the carpentry shops, the potteries, the olive presses, the soap works, the woolen mills, the textile works, the food factories, the shipyards, the mines. The white collars of data processors and computer scientists, video store clerks and CEOs went alongside booksellers, funeral directors, restaurateurs and waiters, florists, bakers, butchers, travel agents, jewelers, record store clerks, night club bouncers, shipping clerks, cobblers, and milliners. Representatives of all these branches of production began to pay us visits.

Around this time, we founded the first mutual aid fund, based on the cooperative model, for those who believed that dreams need support. The wheels of this mutual aid turned mainly on family ties, neighborhood and village ties; it was the fund used in the case of accident or illness. A dream is always the best remedy. It's homeopathic.

...and dreams are dreams

-5-

There are hypersensitive dreams that can dissolve at the slightest provocation, and others sprinkled with hoarfrost that will cover you like flour or cotton falling from the great pines; dreams without identity cards whose residency permit is renewed each month by the prefecture; invertebrate dreams, and dreams in small episodes, like the vertebrated films of the silent cinema; and dreams in costume where everyone runs instead of walking. Your sleep has floodproof banks to protect you when your dream rivers overflow and wet the sheets. Microscopic dreams and dreams on giant posters, raucous dreams that sound as if they're coming over a loudspeaker and you're a small unit lost in the crowd; dreams of indigestion, gossamer dreams that wrap you in magic veils; submarine dreams, in which you wear a mask and are enchanted by the world of the deep, breathing with difficulty, until suddenly your air supply is cut off and you suffocate. You want to come to the surface but your "friends" are waiting for you there with a gun to send you back to the bottom again, food for the sharks. Dreams of dolphins, in which you, another Arion, sing as you ride on their backs, while they tear through the nets, which the fishermen, in straw hats, have to mend on the piers. Silver-plated dreams and dreams of heavy lead, dreams of silver, dreams of one kilo of gold that equals 999.9 grams; tidal dreams, dreams smudged with gunpowder, wearing a muzzle, like dogs that bite; philharmonic, philosophic, philanthropic dreams of gladness and consolation; dreams about Idi Amin conversing with the crocodiles. South African dreams of blacks struggling for their *freedom; dreams in which the self becomes nobody and at the mouth of the cave you laugh at the Cyclops Polyphemus; coastal dreams, jet propelled, anarchist, and anachronistic; mastodon, chandelier dreams, transcribed from tape, literally about your fate and your generation; reptile dreams, in other tongues, of other races; waterproof dreams, plagal mode dreams; contraceptive dreams, cocaine dreams; lobed, cut in half, fragmented, lavish, porous dreams; purulent dreams that discharge their liquid as soon as you wake up, and other heraldic dreams. There are salamified dreams, eggplant and potato, tomato dreams, cucumber dreams (it's the cries of the wandering greengrocer outside your window that make you dream); stud dreams, dreams that contain ammonia, dreams that put you in front of the firing squad and others that discharge you, but which, like the army, never really demobilize you; prison dreams, entombed dreams, propaganda dreams and utility dreams that you pay for once a month; expense dreams, all numbered, which the God/taxman wants validated. There are untranslated dreams, whose riddles remain enigmatic even to the best dream interpreters; consumer dreams whose wrappers you throw in the trash next morning, and others that stay with you, like the pear inside the bottle of kirsch or the branches covered in crystallized sugar, that make you wonder how they got in there. Autumn dreams, with leaves fallen from the large trees by the river; summer dreams on the rocks by the beach with the solitary swimmers; floating dreams, boatpeople dreams, winter dreams by the fireplace, the snow outside six feet deep, blocking your windows. There are also dreams confined in cages and living in a stupor, like circus lions, and domesticated dreams—dreams of chickens, rabbits, ducks—the dream of the wild goose that you know from the fairy tale, and swan dreams, on which you cross the river Acheron with Hades as your boatman and get stamped like a cow approved by the county vet for slaughter; dreams of slaughterhouses where the blood of thousands of pigs flows into the same ditch; dreams of restaurants, their showcases decorated with wild boar and pheasant; stuffed dreams that are preserved as long as the ancient aqueducts in fields now irrigated mechanically, with water that spurts up in the shape of palm trees to the rhythm of a pacemaker; amphitheatrical dreams, in large halls where for centuries the same anatomy lesson has been conducted with interchanging corpses: in your sleep you become both corpse and anatomist. There are fordable dreams and unexplained ones like the galaxies, the ones they call universal and those that only affect themselves; dyslexic dreams, Flemish dreams, dreams with no batteries, malformed, hunchback, lame, on crutches, leaders of choruses, choirs with voice-overs because they're only lip-syncing; compassionate dreams, with stomach ulcers; dreams that have settled on the plains of your sleep like the foreign military bases you're not allowed near; exit dreams in which you walk upon your own Dead Sea; dreams as sweet as ice cream that melts in the cone, and mulberry dreams, both black and white, that fall on the ground because nobody wants them: they stain your hands, like walnut dreams with their fresh kernels, milky and not yet congealed. You break them and paint your fingers, while walnut preserves in your grandmother's ancient jars hang from the eyelashes of your sleep like laundry hung out to dry with clothespins that remind you of swallow's tails: panties that hide the dreams of adolescent girls; blue jeans dreamed of by young men from Eastern European countries; skirts dreamed of by the evzones of the presidential guard. Fugitive dreams, marble-worker dreams, trout dreams, long-last-*

ing dreams, dreams that aren't satisfied with just being dreams but aspire to become action, work; dreams of the prefecture, of the settlement, of the village, of the province . . .

-6-

"You, my friend, are living in a dream world." How these words came to mean something unfeasible, something unattainable, was the first thing we tried to explain to our readers. We wanted to transform that phrase, to change its negative sense to a positive one. So we changed it to the imperative: "You, my friend: live in a dream world!"

We did the same with the expression that implies that someone has given false information or has altered the truth: "You must be dreaming." To our readers it came to mean, "You must be telling the truth." As for "The fool had a dream and saw his destiny," we changed that to, "The wise man had a dream and saw his destiny," although that came only after we had convinced our readers that the only practical people in life are dreamers. The so-called technocrats who live in the abstract world of numbers and statistics, opinion polls and quotas, we told our readers, are actually the lotus-eaters, the fantasists, the mythmakers.

These transformations of a language that concentrated the habits of centuries, naturally, could not be achieved overnight. As with every true change, they had to first be acquired by the public through experience. And experience proved that real poverty was the absence of dreams. Every poor person was potentially rich by virtue of his dreams, whereas a rich man without dreams was forever indigent.

It wasn't easy; I'll say it again. First, the ground had to be removed from under the feet of the privileged in order to weaken their dominance, in order for a fortune not to be able to guarantee some power or other.

In the beginning, the socialist government (with its programs for social tourism, senior citizen shelters, group sports activities for men and women, European youth meetings, and the new employment organization) was eager to accept our propositions. For a while it supported such initiatives, but soon, without a dream, without a vision, it backed down. That was when our big chance came along.

Yes, the circumstances were in our favor. When the first general strikes began, our newspaper showed an unexpected increase in sales. It was as if the newly unemployed had more time to devote to their dreams. Because dreams need time and space in which to develop. They need air. A general strike makes them multiply at an extravagant rate. It allows them to take their rightful place in this life, which is otherwise so prosaic and wretched, so full of minor worries.

What was it people wanted, after all? No more repression of their dreams; no more dream cutbacks. And they hoped to use the strike as a lever to raise off them whatever weighed them down. When they realized that the best strike was not to be absent from work, but to be there and to dream wide awake, then they achieved that undermining of the system that we had envisioned from the beginning. Power in unity. Yes, comrades. The people united shall never be defeated. The people are dreaming; the government is steaming. A people that dreams doesn't negotiate its acquired rights, especially its "limitless right to dream."

During this general strike, a closing of the ranks of dreams was observed. The only scab during the strike of dreaming can be the alarm clock. A strike is expressed by workers not coming to work; dreaming takes place at the workplace but in another sphere. Because of this, it cannot be sabotaged or persecuted. There can be no absentee list of dream strikers.

So when the agro-citizens of the capital started to group dream, everything came to a standstill. In an attempt to investigate the phenomenon, journalists started asking passersby not why they were on strike, but why they were dreaming. And the answers were strange.

"I dream," said one housewife, "because that is the way I was brought up."

"I dream," answered an office clerk, "because the time has come to abolish the private sector of work, and for us all to become employees of socialized dreaming."

"Me, dream?" asked a college student. "You're dreaming the question. I have both feet on the ground. You're the one with your head in the clouds."

"To dream," said a pensioner, "is the best antidote to the poison that you, the press, feed us every day."

"Dreaming is the only thing that helps me to live," said a taxi driver. "Dreaming of going back to my village."

"I dream, therefore I am."

Finally, a cleaning woman at the Ministry of Labor replied that unless she dreamed, she couldn't mop the staircases and clean out the minister's private toilet.

...and dreams are dreams

At long last, as the reader will appreciate, our newspaper had arrived at its golden moment. It kept climbing higher every day. Like some birds that unfold their wings until they hide the sun, so that the rays of the sun must filter through them, revealing their insides. From the study of these we forecast the future: the entrails of the birds boded well for us. Surely we were going to do better as a country, as a people, as a nation, as a planet, starting at the moment when dreams became action. "Do what you dream, so you don't dream what you do" was our slogan. In short, the time of the great dreamification had arrived.

-7-

For there are indisputable dreams, incestual dreams, dreams in which you are sleeping with your mother or your father and you wake up, just when you're starting to feel good, drowning in guilt; and dreams that hatch other dreams (killing a dream before it gives birth to another one is a sin); dreams bloody with the wounds that life inflicts on you; snotty dreams that run like a nose during a head cold, teary dreams that soak your pillow; upon waking, you don't remember crying in your sleep. Vineyard dreams with crooked vines, crippled and yet with such sweet grapes; parade dreams with ten brass bands playing; ruminant dreams that chew themselves over and over; dreams with triremes, without a hearth; river dreams and others that lead you to faraway lands, in which you're always carrying the same tortoise shell; like the city, you drag it with you wherever you go, Cavafian, Solomian, Calvian dreams that surprise you with their own language; Cretan dreams, tavern dreams, dreams of large soccer stadiums in which thousands of people spell out your name on the field; always moving, fluorescent, gaseous, self-contained, self-reliant, self-propelled dreams in which you can't run away from your pursuers: they catch up with you, they arrest you, and you wake up caught inside the net of your love, with the comforting armpit at your side, the few hairs of her tenderness biting you with their toothless mouths. Futile dreams, superficial dreams with a few Calamata olives as garnish; ferry dreams that take you across without a ferryboat, dreams of Nafpaktos, of Rio Antiorio, dreams and antidreams, dreams of the Patras carnival, dreams of skeleton rocks, of Good Friday, with lots of flowers, funereal, fasting; resurrecting, triumphant dreams of life winning over death; dreams on a par with European ones, polydreams of furniture; polyphonic, polymorphous, polyhedral, polyanthic, palimpsestic, and palinodic, that recur like a curse: you are killed by a stray bullet at the age of thirty-three like Christ and you keep seeing the same dream even if you're in your fifties—oh, what harm Christianity has caused us by asking us to dream of the life to come and just let this one go by. Pastoral dreams, Visigoth, Hun, Ostrogoth dreams, chimney dreams that smoke in your sleep and stain the satin of the sky; Monophysitic, of Cerulaire, Belisaire and Narses. When a star falls, a dream is born in its place, a sea star that stalks like a crab with cloud claws. Septic, separate, sepia dreams, like old photographs from before the great fire, with Armenians, Turks, Jews, Greeks, Bulgarians, one single Greece, with all the fish; dreams of eunuchs, of the wood of the Holy Cross, of the blood, of the crown of thorns, of the lance, of the unsewn cloak; nail dreams.

-8-

We kept gaining ground, or rather sky, since that was what counted for us. "At every step, they gained six feet of sky to give away." That verse was our only strength: we didn't keep any revenues gained, but returned them to our readers and followers to make them richer. We seemed to grow taller overnight, like adolescents: we had to constantly buy new clothes. Our newspaper was growing in dream pages. Dream upon dream, brick upon brick, we were building our pyramid.

The "Architecture of Dreams" column was soon established, as was the "Cooking of Dreams." "A Dream in Trousers" became our heading for poetry. Our "Dream Culturing" column gave advice to farmers. Under "Stock Market News," we inaugurated the exchange rate between Greek dreams and foreign dreams. And since we were the most ancient country in the production of dreams (hadn't the first dream democracy blossomed in Greece?), we decided to separate the notion of the idol from that of its object. There are many idols of dreams, and they threaten to become celebrities, like pop singers. However, we insisted, each individual should be a creator of dreams; there was no point in his transferring his ability to dream to others, to dream through them. We fought the tendency to reduce dreams to mass symbols or to idols (people who would express collective dreams). In other words, we opposed the idolization of our dream lives, insisting that we would achieve our aim only when each individual, separately and by himself or herself, expressed that self absolutely. A collective dream would be one that gathered more than 10 percent of the total votes of the dream deputies. . . .

However, our newspaper could no longer adequately cover the whole of that area. Neither could the Mutual Aid Fund, nor the Dream Savings Bank where people deposited their dreams. The *Living Crossword Puzzle of Dreams* on TV and other programs devoted to us had opened up the market considerably. Dimitris, our Maecenas, never said no when it came to business. So we opened agencies and co-ops, where the indispensable condition for the acceptance of a product was that it contained dream plasma in its composites.

This plasma was extracted from a flower called dreamanthus, commonly known as the dream flower, which flourishes on the moon and in the lunar regions of our planet: the deserts. In our country, one can find dreamanthus in abundance in the Mani and certain areas of Kilkis, on plantations that the large supermarket trusts tried to have declared forbidden, as if they were plantations of hashish, but the Supreme Court beat them to it and declared the plantations protected, since the flowers did not contain any toxic substance and did not cause addiction. On the contrary, read the Court's decision, they contain the essence of life, which consists of such stuff as dreams are made of: the life-giving force of the sun.

Our coffee and tea were made of dream plasma, our oil made with dream lipids, our legumes and other vegetables grown with fertilizers of dream plasma, and our fish came from the dream Sea of Messolongi, where the plankton in the water was fortified with dream-flower plasma. Our trout, our snails, our marsh frogs, were all snapped up. People preferred our products, partly because in them they found what was lacking in terrestrial foods grown with chemical fertilizers, but especially because they could pay for them in dream drachmas, that is to say coupons that they would cut out of our newspaper and that covered the cost of production. So when the third devaluation of the drachma took place, and all goods went up in price yet again, our prices remained firm, because the ratio of the dream drachma to the dream dollar remained the same.

Our business was a resounding success. Even though I am a writer, I can't think of a better phrase to describe it. We hardly understood how we had opened such a chain of agencies, in Athens and Salonika to start with, and then all over Greece. We were competing with video stores. But as we kept growing, the business got more difficult to handle. The four of us had begun to tire. Young people had now taken over the gigantic enterprise, which made Dimitris rub his hands with glee and regard the big supermarket trusts as if they were insects.

The other newspapers kept printing embittered comments, because of the money they got from advertising the trusts, even though the journalists, as individuals, were on our side. The truth is that not one of us became rich. We didn't buy luxury cars or build villas in Ekáli. So as far as "making it big" went, there was no question of that. On the contrary, we were always quick to denounce through our paper and our weekly TV program any attempt at commercialization, starting with the key rings and T-shirts printed with the slogan, "I dream, therefore I am," and ending with the phoney stores that tried to imitate us by selling products made of dream sperm—they changed the word *plasma* to *sperm* so we couldn't sue them.

The public was on our side, because we were protecting its dreams. Whenever skits in theatrical revues tried to parody us, they were booed by the public. Whatever dream plays were dug up from the archives never made it on stage. People knew that our movement expressed serious ideas, and that these dream plays were diseased dream fantasies of the past. We raised the right to dream onto the pedestal of real life. We were terrestrial, and that is why we dreamed. We were not extraterrestrials, propagandists of a new technology or some multinational conglomerate of supermen. Our trust, if one could call it that, had to do with individualization, the way Alvin Toffler had predicted in his early books, and not at all with the turning of people into sheep, as the multinationals of the third wave would have liked. We accepted technology to the extent that it increased the potential of the dream. We did not fight technology, but neither did we contribute, in any way, to its development.

And the more the politicians went downhill with their antiquated programs, the more our movement grew among the people. Because existing political structures are like a radio station whose signal you cannot receive because, while you move along in your car, it remains immobile.

Then one day, the prime minister asked to see us. He sent one of his personal secretaries in person to invite us. We accepted most eagerly what was for us a great honor, especially since we supported his efforts.

The meeting was set for Tuesday morning at eleven o'clock. We had decided that only Dimitris and I would go. The others didn't want to go: if there were a lot of us, we would look like a union. At the entrance of the old parliament building, our names, written in the appointment book, awaited us. They kept our identity cards, and a guard led us to the office of the secretary who had invited us. He offered us coffee:

"Not your kind," he said, smiling, "ours."

"There is no yours or ours," Dimitris replied; "we are all one people."

We watched various people come through, asking for favors. It gave us an idea of how tiring the job of a personal secretary can be: answering phones, dealing with persistent requests of citizens wanting to see the prime minister in person, with powerful people trying to intervene in the prime minister's work, and others shirking their duties.

The prime minister apologized when he opened his door to let us in. The delay was not his fault, but the fault of the United States ambassador who had stayed longer than the time provided. The date was approaching for the military bases to be disassembled, so the prime minister must have had all kinds of worries on his mind, worries of a quantum nature: the foreign military bases had to go and stay at the same time.

He explained various problems to us, confidentially. Times were very hard, as always in this country, which we knew as well as he did. Then, taking a paternal interest, he asked us about our movement: where did we feel its success came from? To what did we attribute this success, and did it contain elements that he, as a governor, could promote?

"Unfortunately," I replied, "dreaming could never become an affair of the state."

"I'm aware of that," he said, "but I would like to know whether you have any concrete demands with which we, as a socialist movement, if not as a state, could help."

"Unfortunately," I repeated, "we grow in power as you lose yours. It's simple: not having any place else to go after abandoning you, people come to us, where they are given nothing more than the right to dream, which is the right to hope for better days."

I used his campaign slogan on purpose, as if to tell him that people felt their expectations had been lamentably betrayed, and that the responsibility for this failure lay, if not with him, then with his colleagues.

"They've declared war on us on all fronts," he said.

I responded that for me politics was like human relationships: unless you offer the other person a vision, a horizon, a prospect, it won't work. Otherwise, however large a gift you may give a worker, he will not respond. He will accept your gift only as a tiny bright spot in the general darkness. But if you offer him a prospect, then even a slap will seem like a caress. In this case, heavy taxation weighs on him less than a tax exemption with no horizon. That's what had happened to the movement during its second four years in power. It wasn't working, because it had no dream, no vision, no prospect. The sacks of Aeolus had deflated. Of course, I was quick to admit, as I saw his face grow dark, a lot had been achieved. Undeniably. Things that no one had even dreamt of. And yet—and I explained to him that I was speaking from my experience as a printer—the most beautiful page can seem stifling without a margin. Dreaming makes life wider, the same way a frame gives another dimension to a painting. It is the border, the shade. The depth of the world.

He listened to me thoughtfully. He was the modernizer, the renovator, the restorer, the reformer. I told him so. And immediately I added that we were not competitors in any way. We would like him to view us as complementary. My partners and I worked a system of buying and selling that didn't hurt the economy. However, like the parallel economy that thrived in our country, our system was beyond state control. As an economist (and once quite a famous one), he could surely understand that if our dream drachma was unshakeable, it was because it had a celestial clause.

There are transferable dreams, washable and exchangeable, like in primitive societies where commerce was a bartering system; floral dreams like Kyra Katina's dress; Honda, Kawasaki, Suzuki, 1000 cc dreams that explode in the corridors of your sleep; flagship dreams, fire ship dreams, and others that last for years that seem as unending as the dictatorships of Franco or Salazar: suddenly you wake up in the midst of a revolution with carnations or a regime with democratic processes but under which people are only interested in porno dreams that escape from the security of dreams. Clandestine dreams in which you have to show your counterfeit passport to pass through the security gate and you're afraid they might discover you; dreams that have failed their exams; experimental dreams, in the test tubes of your memory; fickle dreams, tousle headed, grumpy or stormy; kidney dreams, transplant dreams, with cellulite; reprehensible dreams, unvoted-on dreams, parliamentary, figurative dreams, and dreams that drop like unpicked figs and explode like hand grenades on the sheet iron, muffled; dreams of your brain damage, brackish dreams that border on the ravines of the sea, dreams that burn like dry branches, and others that won't light no matter how much pure alcohol you soak them in, until the room fills with smoke and you wake up choking. "I don't dream" means "I don't live": "I dream" means "I exist"; not I, but the legendary bunch of so many keys to doors you never opened, houses you never lived in, loves that you never took even though, at one time, they offered themselves to you in profusion. Dreams with freckles, flooded, with zebra stripes on their bodies, lashed by the sun; and dreams, caryatid, dreams of kouroi sculpted in marble, supine; dreams where you experience the anxiety of the goalkeeper before the penalty kick, strictly confidential, bottled in fruit juices, without preservatives. ("I drink fruit juices and dream of fruit.") Newspaper-eating dreams, engraved in stones; constrictor dreams; fuchsia, psyche-delic dreams, of Moluccans, flying; Siamese twins who marry themselves; critical dreams, dreams that ratify bills from the pres-idency of the republic; beautiful-ugly dreams, chained bears dragged along by gypsies, delphic; dreams from which you finally wake up richer, because they have charged your batteries with the energy of the life-giving sun.

I don't know what the prime minister did afterward, because meanwhile I died and became a dream of myself. I died on the exact date I was born; November 18, Scorpio. It was the same day that the big guys weren't able to come to an agreement in Geneva. So nuclear war was just a matter of time. What I mean to say is, I dreamed I died, since it was the date of my birth. Since birth is the death of a dream, death is an opportunity to be reborn. So at last I found myself living in my dream, from where I am writing to you, happy, because truly, when life becomes a dream, then the dream also can become life.

Postscriptum dreams and warning dreams exist; they blossom on the steep slopes of Mount Olympus; mountain climbers, tightrope walkers try to reach them without always succeeding, and they wake up soaked in sweat, screaming, as they fall into the void of the ravine that is illuminated by a dream moon that was conquered but not abolished because they still haven't been able to figure out its biocomponents. Spaceman dreams are the ones where there is no severing of the umbilical cord of communication between the spaceship and the spaceman walking on air, certain that the rope of mother earth will someday bring him close to her.

history

Plasterboard and Fiberglass

An attractive title, for sure, because we have four things joined into two: plaster, board, glass, and fiber. The same way it happens in marriage, where two individuals create a new species: the couple. Thus we say, "the Artemakises," even though the Artemakis couple consists of Yuli Prokopiou and Pavlos Artemakis. In this case, plasterboard was a new building material that could replace the old rafter or the iron tube or the brick, was serviceable and strong, even quakeproof (insisted Pavlos, who manufactured it in his factory), but which was not preferred by building contractors because they simply were not aware of its existence. But Loukia, the young architect, knew about it from England, where she had attended college. That was how she got to talking with the industrialist who, like most of his kind, was a daddy's boy.

The other members of the group traveling on Elias's yacht were listening to the conversation without contributing, since they knew nothing about construction and building materials.

The young industrialist, who until then had presented a stony face, impervious to the moods of this disparate assembly, suddenly became animated and the doctor saw that his face, normally pleasant and indifferent, blazed with an inner flame as he fixed his liquid eyes on the young woman and explained the difficulties he had come across trying to introduce this new product into the market.

50

"Of course, it's still a little expensive," he said, speaking of plasterboard, "but like all products whose price is dictated by demand, as soon as production is increased, its price will tend to go down."

The yacht, with its permanent crew (the pensioner captain, the new captain, the two stewards, the cook, and the engineer), was moored at the island port, and the passengers had gone ashore to eat fritters. That was when the conversation about plasterboard and the fiberglass insulation that goes with it began. The doctor had observed that, for the past two days they had been on board, the blond young man who was now speaking had not uttered a single word. He and his young wife had behaved like crew members, even though they were guests. The industrialist was only concerned with speargun fishing. At the table he would exchange a few words with the others about the food; he always had a pleasant but impenetrable face. Now this conversation, concerning his line of work, seemed to have awakened him, just as they were eating their fritters.

It was late September, and this long weekend cruise under the sweet light (the sun was warm this time of year, without scorching) had gathered a disparate crew, strangers to one another, on Elias's yacht, which he had offered them free of charge.

During the summer, Elias would rent out his yacht to tourists. It slept ten, and whenever there was a free place, he would invite friends to come along to keep him company. But this time, perhaps for lack of customers because the season was almost over, he had reserved it entirely for his friends. Among them was the doctor, who, without his wife, became a sort of observer of the others.

It was late Saturday afternoon when they docked at the island. They went ashore for a walk; somebody had suggested they have fritters. They would have dinner later, on the yacht. Having spent all day swimming, they now felt pleasantly tired, worn out by their exposure to the sun and sea.

It was a little chilly. The barbarous waves of summer holiday makers had passed over the island, leaving behind echoes of their money and their humming. The islanders, calmer types, considered themselves lucky that this year not a single pine had been burned. The islanders were Greeks of Albanian descent. Their island, close to Athens, was known as a resort for a certain high society that came and went on hovercrafts each weekend, almost all year round.

The doctor was bored. He found the sea tiring and the others uninteresting. He thought of his abandoned dissertation, his experiments that he would start again on Monday, the little mice he had been working with, and he tried to convince himself he had done well to come on the cruise.

Two social classes were represented on the yacht: on the one hand the workers of the sea, and on the other the bourgeoisie of dry land. The workers were faceless. They wore masks. For them, other people's entertainment was their job. But they loved their boss, Elias, just as the young captain loved his grandfather. The old captain was on the yacht illegally. He was retired and wasn't really supposed to be on the vessel. But since that was the only job he knew, and he would surely waste away on dry land, Elias had kept him on, and, to keep the port authorities happy, had hired his young grandson who had just graduated from the Mer-

chant Marine School. The same way one doesn't put a faithful
dog to sleep just because it's grown old, he kept the old captain
on board.

This yacht was an original out of the Hydra shipyards. It had
changed with the passage of time, but its principal characteristics
remained unaltered: the three masts and the long and narrow frame
of a corvette. The captain's grandfather and great-grandfather had
also been sea captains (which was why he called himself "captain,
son of a captain, descendant of captains"), on the very same ship,
which, or so his ancestors claimed, had taken part in the Greek
War of Independence. Later the ship had been used by sponge
divers; during the Asia Minor disaster, it had carried refugees from
Smyrna. During World War II, it had sailed to the Middle East.
It was only after the war, and once it was taken over by the arms
manufacturer Bodossakis, that the ship changed considerably and
was fitted with modern engines from Sweden. Just before he died,
Bodossakis sold it to Elias's father, and now Elias rented it out to
tourists and also used it himself when the opportunity arose. But
the old captain was one with the ship's hull. Just like his forefathers before him, he was part and parcel of the ship, and his grandson was getting ready to succeed him.

"But what have you two been talking about all this time?"
Persephone asked the young industrialist and the architect.

"Business," replied the former, smiling broadly. And he ate
the last of his fritters.

Persephone was the only one who had ordered ice cream
instead of fritters—she couldn't bear syrupy desserts. The others
all stole a little of her whipped cream to put on their fritters. The
two flavors complemented perfectly.

A lively conversation brings those engaged in it closer erotically. The words they speak, even if they are of dry and odorless building materials, uttered on a sweet September evening, become the carriers of another conversation that is not expressed openly, yet is implied, moving like a current under the skin, because words are one's breath modeled into certain sounds that correspond to something more vital, and when it comes to a man and a woman talking passionately and for quite some time, even if they disagree (and especially in that case), desire does not take long to pass into their breath, to moisten their words in such a way, that you, the outsider, the observer, can picture their bodies joined together, still talking fervently about plasterboard and fiberglass. That was what had come to the attention of Persephone, who had her sights set on the young woman from London and of whom she was jealous.

She broke into their conversation at the critical moment. Thalia felt relieved. She was the industrialist's wife. Sitting at his side, she hadn't spoken once during the conversation. But she could feel that the architect, even though sitting across from and not next to her husband, separated from him by a wide table, was luring him away with a web of sounds, and she could see them dangerously approaching one another. Thus Persephone's intervention, coming from the other end of the table, gave her the opportunity to say that she was cold, that she hadn't brought her cardigan, and to suggest they pay the bill and get going.

"If he's the plasterboard, his wife is definitely the fiberglass," thought the doctor, and in the way he had of playing with people like he did with laboratory animals, he asked her if she worked with her husband.

"Not at all," Thalia replied. "I work at the Athens Festival. At the Tourist Board."

She replied in such a tone that the doctor didn't pursue his inquiry.

"I wonder if you could get me tickets for Peter Brook?" sighed Lulu, a former lover of Elias's, a plump woman who had invited herself to tag along on the cruise.

The gentle evening enveloped them in its cloak. They were back on the yacht now, having passed by the coffee shops along the sea front, the souvenir shops, and the two kiosks. Aphrodite stopped at one of the kiosks to place a call to Athens. She simply had to speak to the nanny who was looking after her child.

Her maternal instinct, hitherto hibernating inside her, had been awakened by a toddler whose foreign-looking mother was pushing it along in its stroller. Greek women treated their children as if they were their only fortune, as if they supported the home, the solidity of the family. Foreign women were more detached, as if they had been charged with raising them. As if to do so was somewhat of a burden.

She waited in line for the phone. In front of her, two unkempt English women stood: they had run out of money and were calling home. By the time her turn came, the others had reached the yacht. She spoke with the nanny. Everything was fine. She felt relieved, but there was an emptiness inside her. She was moved by the sight of a cat wandering along the quay, and she picked it up and held it in her arms. They were all so alien and indifferent to her on the yacht—except for the doctor. She wanted to have some fun. That night (she had seen a poster while she was waiting to use the phone), the fantastic disc jockey Francisco would be visiting the island, only for that weekend, at the Naf-sik discotheque. There was going to be a dance competition.

"Shall we go?" she suggested to the others. "It'll be good for a laugh."

Opinions seemed to differ. Some wanted to go, others couldn't be bothered. Undeniably, all of them together, as a group, were difficult to get going. There were too many of them, all unrelated to each other.

The doctor said nothing. He was playing backgammon with the engineer and waiting for the moon to come out.

Elias had disappeared into his cabin with Madam "tag along." She had brought with her an American woman, who liked Greece so much she declared she was staying permanently. Out of boredom, once the game was over (he had lost again), the doctor thought of striking up a conversation with her. He had noticed that nobody was talking to her, and he felt a little sorry for her. Besides, it would be a good opportunity for him to polish up his English.

Night had fallen for good. The American woman had to have it, and the doctor, closing his cabin door, offered her a pound of testicles. She saw them, evaluated them, and wanted to try them. They seemed to her like quite a bunch. Muscat. The doctor locked the door, drew the porthole curtains, and watched her undress. Below her worn, inexpensive clothes, her body began to reveal its curves and swells. She had nice legs, though a little on the heavy side, a slim waist, narrow hips, and a wonderful chocolate-colored chest. He didn't care much for her face. Her eyes were like two holes.

She looked him over. He was quite strong, with a little fat around the waist, but she liked the bulk of his cocoon of caterpillars. They lay down on the narrow bunk.

history

She told him immediately that it had only been two days since she had last made love. She wasn't desperate was what that meant. He told her that he had screwed Aphrodite that morning (he indicated which one of the women she was) and that he still had her smell on him. That didn't seem to bother the American. When in Greece, she would screw as often as possible. And it was possible very often. She used a diaphragm, so he could ejaculate inside her, not to worry.

The doctor lay down next to her and touched her nipple. Right away, she put her hands between his legs and held his eggs as if weighing them. They were much more than two handfuls, and that pleased her. Then she spread her legs and told him that she was ready and wet for him to come inside her if he wanted.

He entered her, and his arms filled with raw meat. A piece of meat wanting another piece of meat in a meaty contact.

"Your friend is still doing it," he whispered to her.

"Yes," she replied, "that's why she came on the cruise."

She confessed to him that she could not live without the joy of lovemaking. She had been deprived of it when she was younger; in the States it had become a complicated affair. If it wasn't herpes it was AIDS; people had become terrified. They had become asexual. Whereas in Greece nobody cared about diseases. Like bacchic Gods, they all got drunk on its drunkenness.

Little by little she started tasting his wine. She inhaled it wholeheartedly, spasmodically, making a gift of her inner pulsations, which for her were a routine matter.

As long as he couldn't see her face, the doctor imagined he was making love to Fiberglass, Plasterboard's wife, a brunette, Raquel Welch–type temptress. Meanwhile the American had started to pant. She was climbing up the hill. At last she reached the top, and, seeing the hillside covered in flowers down below, she let herself roll down, as happy as a meatball, crying out and declaring her joy. The flowers were crushed as she steamrolled over them. When she reached the bottom of the ravine, she bent down to drink from the stream. She had him in her mouth and she was sucking him.

The doctor suggested she turn around. Not to penetrate her anally but to enter her from behind. She accepted. And she climaxed for a second time, soaking the sheets.

The ship was at sea again by the time they came up on deck. The others were already having dinner. Their plates were waiting for them. A full moon poured its silver light onto the sea. Hungry after their lovemaking, they sat down to dinner.

Persephone had heard the sighs of the American when she had gone downstairs to the rest room, and she had timed their session: it had lasted three quarters of an hour. That evening, she would have the doctor, and she already felt a certain thrill inside her. But why did these foreign leeches latch onto the domestic market like that?

At the table, even though politics was a forbidden subject, Aristotle, who had studied sociology in Paris, had tried to answer Persephone's question for her. From the time the Greek state was founded, he said, foreign powers had played a decisive role. The indigenous Greeks were nothing but extras in a play where the leading roles were held by the three great powers: the English, the Russians, and the French, whose equivalent nowadays would be the United States, the Europeans, and the Soviets. At that moment, Plasterboard was heard complaining about the reluctance of the

Socialist government to embrace somewhat more steadily the private sector. Aristotle, who had just been waiting for an excuse to show off his knowledge, quickly dropped Persephone in order to take up the industrialist's challenge. It was necessary, unfortunately, and there were no two ways about it, if one were to understand the present, to go back a little in history. Recent history, not ancient or Byzantine. In Greece, after its liberation from Ottoman rule, there was no accumulation of capital, so to speak. The War of Independence took place for ideological and economic reasons, but when in 1854, the sultan conceded to the Greeks of the diaspora the same rights as Ottoman subjects enjoyed, there was no reason anymore for Greeks living abroad to turn toward an independent nation-state that would not have guaranteed them anything more than the Turks had already, very cleverly, given them. Thus, after having helped in the War of Independence, the Greeks abroad, taking the bait of equality that the sultan had thrown them, remained in a state of diaspora. Which is why, after 1854, the Greeks who were thriving in other countries showed no more interest in Greece. Because as we know, concluded Aristotle, capital has no homeland.

The others listened to him with a certain amount of boredom, until Arion picked up his guitar. What could be better on a moonlit evening?

The islands, like tortoise shells, were sleeping blissfully, islands that had once played an historic role in the War of 1821 and that nowadays were pockets of tourism, beehives of foreigners, collecting the pollen of foreign currency to make honey and wax for the winter. These islands slipped by like a vision of huge sea turtles. Soon, the ghosts of pirates and mermaids would appear.

"I don't feel very well," Pavlos said. "Something's upset my stomach." He went to the restroom and threw up. After that, he felt better.

"The yacht is transferring its waste," observed Nikos, leaning over the ship's rail and watching Pavlos's vomit being emptied into the sea.

Horn fish shimmered. Further off, some lantern-lit fishing boats. The group's songs reached the ears of the doctor, who had gone back down to his cabin with Persephone.

Persephone was lepidopterous. She made love like a butterfly that is pinned down by the collector and keeps fluttering until it surrenders its soul, that is to say its entire being. And she surrendered by bringing her inner world out, by turning inside out the lining of her purse and pouring onto the male all her gold coins. For Persephone, that constituted giving herself totally. Her jealousy of the American increased her potential. The doctor noticed that and was glad: her jealousy was like his testicles, which got heavier with each consecutive woman who passed from his bed. Only one made them shrink. But unlike the butterfly, which, after surrendering its soul in one flutter, becomes a dead thing, Persephone, after a time of silence and stillness, returned to her drunkenness like the phoenix that is reborn from its ashes.

"Now I understand," she said, "why all the women want you."

She had forgotten about her husband and child. (In any case, even though they still shared an apartment, she and her husband had long been separated.) And she felt happy with the doctor, whose very profession gave her a sense of security. But the air-conditioning annoyed her.

history

"It would be quite a joke if you passed on some kind of disease to me from the American," she said, since she was unable to adjust the air-conditioning (it was controlled by the engine room), and she had to let off steam somehow. But the fact that she had thought of this afterward and not before was a clear sign of her remorse. The doctor handled her like a porcelain curio he wanted to keep from breaking.

"How was she?" Persephone asked.

"Thirsty, just like you," he replied. "The good thing was she didn't bring emotions into it. We had good clean sex for sex's sake. She asked for my phone number in Athens, but I gave her a fake one. So she doesn't find me. After all, it's not as if the Tourist Board gives us a subsidy, right?"

It was true that he didn't make all that much money from medicine. He did research; he didn't have a practice. And he detested the way the health minister regarded doctors. You'd think he wanted to classify them as being either factory or farm chickens.

The yacht had dropped anchor in a protected cove, near another yacht that had its light on. They would spend the night there. Aristotle was still explaining the outdated structures of Greek society to whomever would listen. Arion and Eleni were chatting with Irini, who worked as a receptionist at a slimming center. The weight-loss classes were taught to teams, she explained, and the competition among them brought results. Arion and Eleni, who were members of a musical group and had recently taken part in a concert to benefit starving Ethiopians, kept asking, masochistically, for details about how a fat woman can lose weight.

"The center is making a mint," Irini was saying. "But they're strict. If we employees put on more than one or two pounds over our original weight, we're fired. It's in the contract."

The cook had taken the dinghy and gone ashore to the island port, where his home was. He would be back at dawn. The engineer was reading a newspaper by the light of a lantern. The sailor was listening to the customs officer, a friend of Elias's, tell him pirate stories. And the old captain, on the bridge, wrapped up inside his solitude, dreamed of times gone by and glorious moments of the past. He had met so many people on this yacht . . . big names in finance and international politics.

The sea was calm. So was the sky. The full moon consoled the sea and the sky on their mutual loneliness. Like a good host, Elias made sure everyone had everything they desired. He was touchingly attentive. Then he dove naked into the sea.

Irini, who worked at the slimming center, had been without a man for a long time. Having watched the doctor's activities throughout the day, she became interested in him. The same way sheep follow the leading ram, without wondering why.

She saw him lying alone on the bridge, next to the main mast, and approached him. She asked him if he was tired.

"Not at all," he replied. "Since I gave up smoking a year ago, I feel like a different person. My stamina frightens me."

Irini was chain-smoking nervously.

"I heard your cabin is furnished in Louis XV style," she said.

The doctor laughed.

"Come and take a look. But let's not go together. I'll go down first and you follow in five minutes."

history

He went down to the cabin and waited for her. When Irini appeared, she was flushed.

"Am I the third or the fourth you're going to screw today?"

The doctor shook his head.

"The number is unimportant. What is important is that we both want it."

She was undoubtedly the most attractive. At least her body was. She was in good shape, athletic; he had watched her diving into the sea that morning like a dolphin and he had desired her. But because she was the most attractive, she was also the coldest. In order to grease the machine, he started telling her of his experiments on mice. For him, he meant to imply, a body was of no significance. He had opened up so many bodies on his operating table before devoting himself to research. What was important to him was the moment when a woman wants something more than pure love.

"You're just curious," he told her. "You came here to try what the others tried before you. But as soon as you have to face reality, you don't know what to do, like the hare that freezes in the middle of the road, blinded by a car's headlights. There are no headlights, my little Irini. You're traveling on this floating living room. You're thinking of your boyfriend or your husband. Until suddenly, pirates capture the ship and take you prisoner. The pirate will set you free the following morning, as long as you give yourself to him completely that night. Otherwise, you'll end your days in a harem on the Barbary Coast."

Presented with this dilemma, Irini had no choice. The mechanism came unblocked and she gave herself to him unreservedly, without remorse. She was struck by his tenderness. An almost paternal gentleness. But at the instant when she was about to climax, there was a knock on the cabin door. It was the American.

"I can't now," the doctor said.

She understood, and, apologizing profusely, tiptoed away.

Irini then found herself before an ancient wall. That was where the wicked witch lived. When Irini was a little girl, they had told her that if the witch saw you smile and counted your teeth, you would die. That was why even during her happiest moments, Irini kept her lips sealed, persistently refusing to open her mouth. The doctor noticed the gravity of her expression, the concentrated intensity of it, and realized that at any moment, the joints would come undone, and the fish would tumble out of the net, free.

And that was what happened. Once the net came up from the bottom of the sea and was emptied onto the deck of the trawler, it unfolded a carpet of writhing red mullet, jumping around joyfully naked in the sun. Soon, the spasms subsided, and there were only a few posthedonic palpitations from one or two sargos that still resisted.

Long after she had gone, the doctor was unable to sleep, thinking about the way one woman follows in the other's footsteps, on the same path. It was as if there were a silent understanding among their sex, to drink from the same pistil, of the same nectar. Something that simplified the process of the search. After all, he didn't consider himself a Don Juan, nor much of a ladies' man. Finally, a sweet lethargy started to come over his body. It came down from his throat through underground tunnels and made him melt.

---

* Crew member of fire ships used against the Turkish fleet. *Trans.*

The heavy bird of sleep was settling on his eyelids. It pushed him downward and made him sink to an immeasurable depth. The years were blankets. Deep tulips. And the more his body sank down, the more the galley came to the surface. He was sinking, he kept on sinking. And it was sweet. He was being transformed into a woman. He pressed down on his ovaries, where his ovaries would have been if, instead, that strange thing hadn't grown in their place. It felt sweeter and sweeter. He pressed the patch of grass that covered his annulled ovaries, until, shaken by a spasm, he flooded the sheets.

"Because the laws of development don't always produce the best results for schemers," Aristotle's weak voice was saying, floating down from the deck through the ventilator shaft.

-2-
The Captain

Standing on the bridge, wrapped in his solitude, the captain was not sleeping. *Because dreams blossom on the fringes of dreams, they react like toxic liquids that dissolve first, before recomposing themselves afterwards, into hopes that had ceased to be hopeful, galleries and calories, until . . .*

"Grandfather, tell me a story."

"Which story, my boy?"

"The one about the forest fire, Grandfather, when you would swing by your belt from one tree to another, and even the beasts of the jungle couldn't catch you. You, Grandfather, the hunter, the captain, the burlotieris* of Admiral Kanaris . . . Come on, Grandfather, tell me."

---

* Crew member of fire ships used against the Turkish fleet. *Trans.*

Standing on the bridge, leaning against the wheel of the ship that was about to weigh anchor, while here too the fire was destroying the forests, the captain, by simply touching the wheel that has remained the same all these years, was transformed into the old sailor Kanaris who, on a different night, a moonless night, had set fire to the flagship of the pasha.

"When did that happen, Grandfather?"

"When our great-grandfathers were fighting for independence, my boy, and Greece was a dog that had been tied up for four hundred years and was trying to break its chains. But three masters were lying in wait to see who would take it over. For the great powers of the time, Greece was a very useful dog. The masters wanted it to be free in order to scare the sultan's wolfhounds, but not so free that it would become a master itself. And so, the three masters, the Russians, the English, and the French, helped free the Grecian dog, but then they quarreled among themselves over who would own it. The dog didn't yet know its new masters. It would look up at them with its sad eyes, the way dogs do, full of gratitude that they had helped it break its chains. And it was hungry. It was bleeding from its struggle to break its fetters. It was a starving dog, but proud to show its ribs under its skin. Unfortunately, it didn't know people. It would run to the one who tossed it the biggest piece of meat. And the three big guys tormented the poor thing, to the point where it didn't know what was going on.

"That was when they sent the first government diplomat from Corfu, who had lived for years abroad, in the court of the czar of Russia. As soon as he set foot in the basement where the dog lived, the stench forced the diplomat to hold his breath. 'We

history

need to straighten up around here,' he said, and started to train the dog, in rather a brusque manner. Deep down, he liked the idea of a dog, though not so much the dog itself, which, having been oppressed and starved all those years, wanted to run and leap and enjoy its newly acquired freedom. 'You can forget everything you learned from the sultan all these years,' said its master, who spoke to the dog in French rather than Greek. He would say *couche-là* instead of *katse kato*. He was bent on turning the dog into a Saint Bernard, a little barrel of brandy around its neck. The very smell of the drink nauseated the dog, which was used to the wine and liqueurs of its own country. So, one day, he attacked his master and tore him to pieces. This was followed by a period in which the dog, free again, became wild and independent and happy like it used to be. It would grab every single chicken it came across, it would chase after foxes. 'That's enough,' said the foreigners, seeing that, unrestrained, the dog could become even more dangerous than its old master the sultan. Especially since it was also laying claim to other fields, crossing the Isthmus of Corinth in one bound, and devouring sheep from their pens. But neither of the three big guys would accept one of the other two as master of the dog.

"So they found a young prince, underage, abnormal, and a bit of a flake, and they told his father, Ludwig of Bavaria, to send him down to be master of the dog's country. The father accepted, and sent his son, at exactly seventeen years of age, a hippie of his time, who since childhood had been dropping acid, and the dog saw his new master coming with an army of Bavarian soldiers, fourteen thousand of them. Not one of the new arrivals spoke Greek. The dog went up to them, sniffed at them; they seemed to be

friends and not new conquerors. After all, that's what its three pro-
tectors had kept whispering in its ear the whole time it was waiting for them to arrive. So the dog didn't bark, but instead wagged
its tail with joy, because these strangers, these Bavarians, would
bring lots to eat (in the form of a monumental loan), and the dog,
having pillaged the sheepfolds and chicken coops, had been left
with nothing more to eat. So the dog was excited. But it noticed
some other dogs at its master's side, dogs of a different breed, well-
fed, ferocious, and with pretty big appetites themselves. It was
explained that these three dogs were accompanying the young king,
as he was still underage. Until he turned twenty, these three Bavarian dogs would rule the palace. The dog took a liking to the king,
because he was like a child but was afraid of his guard dogs, Armansberg, Mauer, and the other one. These three dogs then gathered
together all the Greek dogs and tried to Bavarify them.

"Up to that point, our dog had managed to escape being
barbarified, but it could see that it would be difficult to avoid
being Bavarified. And while in the beginning it thought that it
was going to get fed, the Greek dog saw that the wolfhounds
were eating its food. They would bark in a tongue that our dog
didn't understand. Everything was ruled with the military dis-
cipline of the Bavarians. They put our dog in prison, charging
it with liking its master but not his dogs. And they would have
killed it, if the good king himself hadn't intervened and begged
his dogs to spare its life.

"All this happened at Nafplion, in the fortress of Palamidi.
Then, the king's court left Nafplion and came to Athens. The dog
moved with them, during which it watched the Bavarians making the laws, the Bavarians building, the Bavarians constituting

the army. 'Who am I?' wondered the dog. 'I'm a Christian Orthodox dog. What do these people of another religion want? I had
my own Holy Virgin and my own Jesus who sustained me during four hundred years of darkness. Who are they? What do they
want?' It was as if, little by little, the dog's self-awareness was awakened. And it started exercising its jaws to bite. 'Beware of the dog,'
read the sign outside its hovel, while the foreign dogs lived in the
palace. Meanwhile the years went by, and the dog kept demanding its rights, which the Bavarian dogs adamantly refused to grant.
Until one day, the dog kicked them out. It had grown by then,
it had become strong. But with all the crossbreeding that had gone
on during all these years, there had appeared a mixed breed of
dog in our country, and the blood of the original dog, the one
they had imprisoned in Palamidi, had been polluted. Thus there
were four parties of dogs, the French, the English, the Russian,
and the dogs of the Steppe. Only the Bavarians hadn't succeeded
in grafting their breed before leaving, in order to produce
wolfhounds. And that is how, since then, my boy, we have had
these breeds. . . ."

The captain was standing, wrapped in his solitude, thinking. He could hear the conversation taking place on deck, about
the loan that the Socialist government was preparing to receive
from the Common Market ("Taking out a loan," Aristotle
explained in his nasal voice, "presupposes the devaluation of the
drachma."). Times of old came to the captain's mind, long-for-
gotten memories of that first loan our nation took out, because,
the captain's great-grandfathers had explained, "We must have a
powerful fleet. We can only fight the Turk at sea. We must have
steamships, armed with heavy cannons for the urgent needs of

the struggle." It was a loan for which our national territory was mortgaged, but we never saw the ships, and the money was pocketed by those who had given it. "We are an oppressed people, because we are indebted," Aristotle's voice could be heard intoning from on deck. And the captain dreamed on, standing on the bridge, though he did not sleep.

"But who pocketed the money, Grandfather?"

"It's a mixed-up story, my boy."

"Tell me, Grandfather."

"There were four of them in on it. A satanic foursome from the city of London. Ellis, Hobhouse, Burdett, and the Ricardo brothers, the mafiosi of that time. They started by looking for an admiral. And they found one. A 'killer' of the seas, famous for his exploits in Latin America, in Brazil. He was the one we would do business with. His name was Cochrane. 'Within a few weeks, he will arrive in Constantinople and destroy by fire the entire Turkish fleet inside the Golden Horn.' That's what they said, and that's what we believed. As if we didn't have our own fire ships, as if we didn't have our own brave warriors. But it's always the foreigner who's the coach, the technical advisor of our national team. Karaiskaki and Miaoulis accepted him in order to please the Anglophiles. The Russophiles were pleased with Capodistrias, who had not yet agreed to be governor, but who would do so presently. The Francophiles had their Fabvier. What a state this was going to be! And who were we? Kassomoulis wrote: 'It was rumored that Lord Cochrane would arrive in Greece overnight, and that Greece would be saved by his stratagems and his maritime fireworks. This encouraged us greatly.' Poor Kassomoulis! Poor heroes!

history

"But Cochrane wanted a lot of dough. He was considered an expert coach whose team was guaranteed to become world champion. So he charged accordingly. It was decided he would be paid out of the second loan, which was about £2,000,000. Of this, Cochrane would receive £37,000 in advance, and £20,000 upon completing his mission. Furthermore, he was entrusted with deciding what ships they would buy. Which meant he decided how the £300,000 intended for purchasing and arming the ships would be spent.

"Having ensured the approval of the four lenders (Ellis, Hobhouse, Burdett, and the Ricardo brothers), Cochrane went ahead and did the ordering. Having just returned from Latin America and his great victories, the killer knew what huge profits one can make from orders. His own salary was nothing compared to what he could make off the shipbuilders. So he ordered a total of five ships: two large and three small. The first of the large ones, the *Enterprise* (there is an aircraft carrier of the same name in the Sixth Fleet), barely reached the mouth of the Thames. It almost sank there and was rescued by chance by an English battleship that towed it to the port of Plymouth, where it underwent the proper repairs. It arrived in Greece, in very bad shape, in the autumn of 1828. It could not be used. It came to us simply to leave us its carcass, to die in our hands, since we had ordered it and we had to accept it.

"The second large steamship, the *Invincible*, was burned during testing. It didn't even go to the trouble of coming all the way to Greece to die like the *Enterprise* had, which, at that, had come to us like a swan and died in our arms. The *Invincible* didn't even show up. It died over there. Without a fight. Just like those French submarines with impressive names—the *Unsinkable*, the *Fearless*, the *Thunderbolt*—which would disappear from time to time, I remember, without a trace. They would disappear into the deep ocean waters, along with their entire crews, without even a signal."

"And what about the other three, Grandfather?"

"Two of the three rotted on the Thames, my boy. As for the third one, after they replaced its engine, it managed to reach Greece only to announce the death of the other two and then to die itself in our waters."

"So what happened to the money, Grandfather?"

"It was pocketed by those more cunning than us. Where else would they find such a pack of rubes, fighting among ourselves like we were? They pocketed the money, they had a great time spending it, and they sent us the cinders.

"And then, what do you think the nephew said to justify his uncle, the lord admiral? He was a Cochrane too, so he wanted to leave a pretty portrait of his uncle to the historians. He said, 'At that time (1825, 1826, 1827), I held four titles: lieutenant, private secretary, aide-de-camp, and treasurer of the fleet, and I had the keys to the safe.' (The dirty crook! The uncle gave the keys to the nephew and now here he comes, supposedly to tell us the truth, and he is naive enough to want us to believe him, because he truly regards us as rubes, as underdeveloped peasants, as thick-skulled dolts who don't know their asses from their elbows.) 'Therefore I am able to disclose the total sum that Lord Cochrane made available to the fleet,' the nephew said. 'This amount comes to only £8,000. It was this amount that my uncle brought with him from England.' (And what about the commission from the orders, teabag? What about your uncle's payment? Show us the invoices if you want us to believe you.) 'Besides, part of this amount was intended for the army,' continued the nephew, in order to whitewash his uncle, the pirate lord. 'Whereas, if £40,000 had been made available, they could have hired English and American sailors, with whose able assistance the admiral would surely have accomplished feats comparable in glory and magnitude to those achieved in South America.'

"Talk about being left holding the bag! They had taken our money, they hadn't given us any ships, and it was all our fault! Therefore how could we not go bankrupt, as we did at that time, without ever having seen a penny? Only one corvette arrived, *Endurance*, after a delay of a year and a half. Having suffered considerable damage during the voyage, its efficacy did not live up to our expectations. Ellis had kept a £10,000 commission on that corvette, which was to be built by Galloway, whose son was serving under Mehmet Ali, the enemy. Well, you can hardly expect the father to build a ship well enough to kill his son. For fifteen whole months, the captains awaited, from day to day, the arrival of *Endurance*. 'An anvil to receive the hammer's blows and to forge the red-hot ore, he, without a groan, endured in silence, like a tuna fish.'[*]

"Such were the first loans of the struggle, my boy; then everything was forgotten: we forgot who these rapacious foreigners were who had taken advantage of our nation's struggle for independence to make a profit. The only thing left was the debt. But since Greece had not received anything, what was she expected to pay?

---

[*] Aeschylus, *Fragments . Trans.*

"Our situation was like that of a poor housemaid whose masters are determined to marry her off, and who is offered to the groom with a dowry. 'More than anything else, we are in need of a Greece,' said Lord Canning (who, years later, was to be remembered by the square in Athens that bears his name). The master and mistress then ask for the dowry back (the dowry they never gave in the first place, because of course the groom is in on this too) just so she will always be indebted to them, will always be a slave.

"Yes, they wanted Greece to be a slave; ever since then she has been one, my boy: but not a Turkish slave, a Christian one. If she were a Turkish slave, they would have had to settle the eastern question with the sultan, and they had bigger fish to fry where he was concerned. They wanted Greece, as well as her Balkan sisters, to be independent so as to attain, through them, easier access to the Seraglio.

"'But watch out, servant girl!' the foreign masters said. 'Don't you ever dare raise your head. You still owe us the loan for your dowry. We've got you right where we want you.' Their only problem (and they simply could not agree on this point) was whether she would be a maid to the English, the Russians or the French. Either way, whatever they decided, she would definitely be a slave."

On board, the discussion continued among the patricians, the privileged, concerning the devaluation of the drachma that would supposedly facilitate the government's new loan. "Even though he is a remarkable economist," somebody was saying, "the prime minister did not correctly foresee the repercussions of this new devaluation, which has resulted in an increase in the prices of practically all products, since 80 percent of those are imported."

"And that's how trouble starts," thought the captain to himself, "since in the end, the Greek people are just: they have good sense, good instincts, and political maturity. They might not know exactly what their origin is, but what does it matter? They survive, under difficult conditions, and they always give a fight. They never give in, even though others have tried at times to decapitate them, even castrate them. They have a powerful instinct for self-preservation. The proof being that, the way this poor nation started off on the wrong footing completely, it should have sunk a thousand times by now, it should have buckled under all those blows. And yet it kept going. It still keeps going. It exists. It survives."

"The Greek economy has glass feet," Plasterboard was saying now. "If someone should ask to cash the state's reserves into dollars or gold, we would go bankrupt again."

"The specter of bankruptcy has haunted us since the small Greek state was first established," explained Aristotle, who was a progressive and did not like the industrialist, Plasterboard. "If the Greeks brought their Swiss bank accounts back to this country, we'd have one hell of an economy."

"But it is the specter of insecurity that makes them take their money abroad. If they knew the drachma was stable, they would all bring their money back," Aristotle returned.

"But if you don't bring your money back, and the next person doesn't and the next, how will the drachma become strong? What you describe will never happen unless somebody goes first. If, for example, you . . ."

"Don't start getting personal," Elias cut in. "A yacht is an enclosed space, short-circuited by the sea. If we start quarreling, there aren't enough cabins to separate us."

"But they're not quarreling," said the doctor, who had just come up on deck. "They're having a discussion."

"Precisely," said Plasterboard. "Besides, I don't have my money abroad. I have it here. But I know of others who . . . "

Next to him, his wife, bored beyond belief, was discussing with Irini the best way for a woman to lose those extra pounds painlessly and pleasantly.

"The problem is that as a people . . ."

"Why do you read only English?" interrupted Arion.

How could Nikos, an importer of cold cuts, tell him that he did not believe in anything Greek? That it was in fact Greek things that seemed foreign to him? Ever since he was a child he had been taught to trust foreign products. Greek writers held no interest for him whatsoever. The western European languages inspired a certain confidence he did not find in modern Greek.

And now here is the captain, this cowardly, fresh-water captain, who is transformed into a ghost, into an evil spirit, every time he thinks, because he is a captain of the mind; he's been through a lot, he too has changed employers, those ship owners who sink their old ships just to collect the insurance, not caring whether men go down with them, men with families who would be left to mourn. The ship owner has his own family to worry about: his kids, his dogs, his investments in the city of London. It's only when the Turk appears that the ship owner becomes Greek again and worries that his homeland is in danger. But as long as the Turk does not show himself, he feels like a stranger

history

in his own country, because he can no longer find cheap labor like he used to; it has become expensive, and so he prefers to hire Philippino and Pakistani and Ethiopian hands for his ships. So here is this captain, who is of Albanian origin, with Black blood on this father's side, Asia Minor blood on his mother's side, Slav blood on his great-grandfather's side, and Scythian blood. He is a descendant of the Empress Theophano, he is a suffering captain, he has been burned, a small prime minister of the mind who wants to explain Greece, from its beginnings in the epics of Homer, to the epic of Dighenis Akritas, before it sank into the catacombs of the Turkish occupation (after having placed the dome of Saint Sophia on a square base), from which emerged the song of Rigas Ferraios: "Better one hour of freedom than forty years of slavery." He, Constantine, son of Constantine Paleologue, descendant of the Paleologues, Captain Constantine son of captains, expert in massage and bonesetting, with an ivory skeleton, he knows how to defeat Mehmet, son of Bayazid.

"So then, Grandfather?"

"So then, my boy, this first loan did not end there. There was a second part to it, on the other side of the Atlantic. At that time, there was a progressive, democratic, 'by the people for the people' country, which did not want a king in Greece by any means, since it had been built itself by people who, persecuted by the kings of Europe, had found refuge in this country across the ocean and had formed a huge commonwealth: the United States.

"We had ordered eight frigates to be built in America. The decision had been made in 1824 by the representatives of the 'government-in-exile' in London. But the four mafiosi got in the way, in order to act as intermediaries; they were providing the money, so they felt they (Ricardo, Hobhouse, and company) should have a say in the proceedings. They sent their representative, a French cavalry officer called L'Allemand. In French, L'Allemand means the German. As unrelated, therefore, as his name was to France, so was this man, a cavalry officer, unrelated to ships. Nevertheless he was in on the scam, so they sent him. The American company Leroy, Bayard & Co. built the first two frigates and then waited for the money before it started work on the rest. Like any contractor, they would not continue building until they were paid. And the foursome in London was not sending any money because they'd already spent it among themselves. As a result, the Americans weren't sending us the ships. An impasse. Concerned, the Greek representative persuaded A. Kontostavlos to travel to America to find out what was going on.

"Of course, at that time one did not travel to America as one does nowadays. It was an expedition. An ordeal. Kontostavlos, a fervent and a wealthy patriot, finally decided to go. He found L'Allemand, who was furious with him, furious with the Greeks who were not sending the money, and a defendant of the contractors who were demanding the money so they could complete the order. Like all mafiosi, L'Allemand was serving the interests of his godfathers, Burdett and Ricardo, and the last thing he wanted was to see those ships delivered. The lenders' plan had been clear from the start: to spend the money without delivering the goods and then to have Greece indebted to them, so that the politicians could hide behind them and play their games at the country's expense.

"Isn't that always the way imperialism works? (Don't forget that, at the time, England was a very powerful empire.) By hiding

history

behind employers, lenders, and loan sharks, it bleeds dry an entire
people or a single worker. It's all the same, since every people struggling to break the chains of slavery is made up of many workers.
Until they bring them to their knees, at which point the politicians arrive to play their dirty game. Isn't it always a von Krupp
who prepares the ground for a Hitler? Isn't it the multinationals
of today (ITT, IBM, and so on) that claim, proclaim, and disclaim
leaders, chosen by the people, in order to allow rampant capitalism to play its shameless game?

"History provides us with very little information of Kontostavlos's actions in America. The rest is left to our imagination.
But imagination is not enough. We do not have sufficient knowledge of the period to know what he would do. All we know is
that he is a patriot and he is concerned for his homeland, which
is in a state of revolt, and which is waiting for these ships to arrive
at last so that the struggle may begin.

"First he goes to the American builders, who tell him that
if they don't get any more money they will auction off the two
frigates they've already built. They are unyielding, but L'Allemand
has given them the right to be so by ganging up with them.

"Kontostavlos is alone in New York. Emigration has not yet
begun because there is no Greek state. Emigration will start a few
decades later, when this state, for which Kontostavlos is now fighting, will become independent under such conditions that it will
force its inhabitants to seek a better future elsewhere, especially
in America.

"Kontostavlos is unaware of this. And it is just as well,
because if he had known about it, perhaps he would not have
fought with the same courage that he did then, when, upon real-

izing he had fallen victim to a gang of London swindlers, who were eating away at the money so that England would later be entitled to ask for it back, he listened within himself to the cries and pleas of the brave men who were fighting for their homeland, giving their all for freedom, going into battle with regard to everything but their lives; he listened and he took heart.

"In order to understand the loneliness Kontostavlos must have felt, we should remember that in 1824, Greece only existed on the map as a province of the great Ottoman Empire, and that in the minds of most Americans, there was only ancient Greece, cradle of civilization. In America at that time, there were no Greek American organizations, no Greek lobby to put pressure on Congress and the Senate. Kontostavlos was probably the first Greek who Sodart, the secretary for Marine Affairs; Henry Clay, the foreign secretary; and Noah Webster, the famous professor of law, had ever seen. As Colonel Benton said when Kontostavlos went to ask him for his help, 'When I studied Homer, I never imagined that I would ever, in my lifetime, be of use to his descendants.' He shed tears of joy because he was able to help. And he did help.

"So, without counting on the all-powerful Greek colony, on the archbishop of the Orthodox Church, on John Brademas or any other senators and politicians of Greek descent (which is the sole weapon that Greece has acquired since then, and which she only uses when the Turkish threat appears), Kontostavlos had an advantage over his modern-day equivalent, whether he is called an ambassador, a minister without portfolio, or a special envoy sent to negotiate military aid or the rent paid by United States military bases or the preserving of the 7:10 ratio of United States military aid to Greece and Turkey respectively. His advantage was not knowing in advance what the result of his efforts would be, of having the right to dream of an independent, strong, autonomous state, free of foreign guardianship, where those who fought in the revolution would become the leaders of the liberated nation. While he understood, because he was an intelligent man, that absolute independence is difficult to achieve, he hoped nevertheless that the Greeks would succeed as much as possible, since the name of Capodistrias had already been mentioned by the foreign protecting powers. He hoped nevertheless that that great diplomat who had helped the czar to solve the hitherto unsolvable problems of Russia in Geneva would be able to solve the problems of little old Greece. Kontostavlos hoped, the way those people at the end of World War I dreamed of a better world and fought for it with the self-sacrifice and courage of giants. The disappointment that came later in no way diminishes their glory. After all, that is the way the world goes forward: with its ignorance of what is to come. Fortunately, this ignorance allows humankind the necessary margins for it to hope, for it to struggle to change the world. If everybody knew in advance what was to come, then not a leaf would move in the human forest. There would have been no Paris Commune, no October Revolution. Thus, armed with his ignorance of what it meant to create an independent Greek state, the same ignorance that kept Kolokotronis and Karaiskaki fighting in the trenches, Kontostavlos struggled and fought all alone.

"Straight away he drew up a plan. He went to see a lawyer, Mr. Emerett, who, they said, was the best in New York. With his purse full of his own money, Kontostavlos presented the problem: they had ordered some frigates for the war. But the company they were dealing with, Leroy, Bayard & Co., was being difficult. 'Either you send us more money so that we can go on,' they said, 'or you lose the money you've already sent us, since we'll auction off the two frigates we've built.' The reason they were behaving this way, Kontostavlos explained to Emerett, was that the contractors had taken on the frigate contract as a single order: either all eight frigates or none at all. It wasn't worth their while otherwise.

"The lawyer listened, then said, 'You have no legal recourse against the merchants; hence you will have to appeal to their sense of compassion.'

"'Experience had taught me,' wrote Kontostavlos later, 'that if I had to appeal to their sense of compassion, I hadn't much to hope for.'

"Himself a merchant, Kontostavlos was a realist. He knew that there is no pity in commerce. If there were, then merchants would close up their shops and set up charities.

"This merchant Kontostavlos who was now burning with other ideals was fully aware of these realities. He went to the shipyard, where he saw the two frigates, the two dolls, waiting, as we would say nowadays, for a bottle of champagne to smash against their cheek, for their voyages to be good ones, for the waters to be gentle with them. He saw them, and in his mind's eye he saw them full of brave warriors who would have the rare fortune to fight the fleet of the pasha on board these ships. He saw them there, on dry land, in the huge shipyard in lower Manhattan, and his heart almost broke. It had taken him two months of traveling to get there. That's as long as a letter would take. There was no communication, no telephone. Whatever he achieved he would have to achieve alone.

"Desperate, he sat down and wrote to his friend Korais in France. He told him the story of the impasse he had reached. And Korais sent him a letter of introduction to the philhellene Edward Everett, who also happened to be a member of Congress.

"Kontostavlos took the letter to him immediately and, miracle of miracles, Everett opened up for him the legendary gates of power.

"'It is difficult for me to describe the obliging manner with which I was received by this eminent friend of Greece, Mr. Everett,' Kontostavlos wrote. 'Within twenty-four hours he had presented me to Adams, the president of the United States, to Henry Clay, the foreign secretary, to Sodart, the secretary for Marine Affairs, to Professor Noah Webster (whose advice I took and for which I offered him payment but which he refused), to Colonels Benton and Hill and to all the members of the Senate and Congress who could help the most. With what kind feelings toward Greece they all received me! With what pleasure they heard me tell of the exploits of our heroes! I felt an inexpressible joy as I observed the enthusiasm with which they competed to see which one of them could be of the most service.'

"And indeed, he convinced the American government to buy a frigate for Greece. All this happened incredibly quickly, within only ten days. As Kontostavlos put it, 'The committees concerned made the decisions and Congress voted on them.' At last, Greece acquired a frigate, which was named, naturally, *Hellas*. It arrived in Nafplion in 1826, and there was much celebrating. But in

August 1831, exasperated by the antics of the killer, Captain Cochrane, Miaoulis blew it up in the port of Póros."

On deck, the discussion between these "Greek residues," as the captain thought of Elias's friends, continued. But the captain was deep in his own thoughts. From the time when he was a grandson himself and he would ask questions of his own grandfather, an old sea wolf from Hydra, he came back to his present body, now the age his grandfather had been and with grandchildren of his own. The yacht pulled up anchor, leaving behind it the smoke-filled sky. One could guess at the fires raging behind the mountains of Argolis. Again this year, as it happened every summer, Greece was in flames. Fires everywhere, singing the praises of its pyromaniac God. "I imagine a modern Kontostavlos," said the captain to himself, "going to America to negotiate the position of American military bases. Where could he find the courage to hope that by sending away the bases something would change in this world governed by a network of superpowers, where the departure of one only means the penetration of another? Where is freedom today? Which independence is guaranteed and by whom? The nonaligned countries? The socialists? Nowadays the only ones brave enough for these heroics are the desperate. Those who have nothing to lose but their lives. And these are the kinds of people who fought the War of Independence. 'Better one hour of freedom . . .' But nowadays, when we know that no one in power will concede anything without getting something in return, informed as we are about what is happening everywhere on our planet, and given the complexity of the contrasting interests of east-west, north-south, metropolis-periphery, what else counts besides the struggle, the myth of Sisyphus? And yet that poor old Greek, Kontostavlos, kept hoping and fighting with beautiful illusions. That was his grandeur. That was his beauty.

"And afterwards? There is no afterwards. Along comes Capodistrias. A competent diplomat of international acclaim. He contributes money from his own pocket, 'from his very modest fortune,' so that he will not be accused of holding office just to make a bundle. But he too comes from Geneva. Just like that outrageous general and 'master builder' of the disaster of Asia Minor, Hatzianestis, who had come from Geneva. In general, the saviors of the nation always come from abroad. Usually from Paris or London. We're talking about the democratic saviors, because the others, the royalists, were all German. Starting with King Otto. But the democratic ones (Venizelos, Karamanlis) came from France or francophone Switzerland, which is where they return when the Greeks send them away, as in the case of Plastiras. But what is the connection between Switzerland and what the young people were talking about on deck a moment ago—Greeks and their Swiss bank accounts? Was it perhaps the philhellene Swiss banker Eynard who started it? Is it perhaps the banks that govern? The cash register, as the captain's old boss, the arms dealer Bodossakis used to say? And what about posthumous fame? Could money buy that also? If you're smart, you'll grease the palm of those who form public opinion. That way, when Bodossakis (who had made his first crisp dollar bills selling bullets to Franco) kicked the bucket, nobody said a word, the almighty pens laid low, and they passed him into history as an archetype, 'the man behind the scenes.'

"But there was not a single one among the mighty pens who had not received something extra. These tips were sent, even to those who did not want them, by the deceased, may he be happy where he is now, in the next world, in the company of Capodistrias, who was sent there before his time by the bullets of Petrobey Mavromichalis and his men.

"No, from the beginning, this land was not meant to progress. It was written in its cells." As he stood, the captain thought of a time in the past, of frigates and schooners, in this lake, which is enclosed by Hydra, Porto Heli, and the mountains of Argolis in flames. It was on a night like this, "a night full of wonders, a night strewn with magic," when the fate of the war was decided, at the naval battle of Navarino. Because it is we who make history go forward, not history that makes us go forward. history is a wheel in the universe that man has to set in forward motion. Otherwise, it just stays a wheel, an eternal wheel, and everything moves backward.

"I wouldn't know what to say," the old captain thinks, "but even if I did, I wouldn't say anything more than the everyday things I say, because wisdom is keeping your mouth shut, putting a lid on a lot of facts, because you know that providing information is not always a good thing. It can become a weapon in the hands of the enemy and you, remember this, are nothing but a little bug in the wheel of time."

The group on deck was now disagreeing about where they'd moor for the night. Finally, they agreed on Spetses.

"Is there a fire there?" asked Elias.

"Not that I can tell," answered the young captain.

But then they remembered that the steward had taken the dinghy to go visit his mother and wouldn't be back until daybreak, so they did not weigh anchor after all.

Irini and Fiberglass were still discussing ways of losing weight. Plasterboard was still arguing with Aristotle. The doctor, Persephone, the American, and Elias had started playing cards. And only Arion's guitar accompanied the sleepless moon.

Again the captain went back in time. He put his ear to infinity. Alone on the bridge, he was being chased by a ghost, that of Capodistrias. He would not have been angry with the governor had he not put his compatriots under quarantine at that precise moment, using the pretext of the plague that had spread on his island of Hydra, brought by Ibrāhīm's army, just like the English liberators after the German occupation had brought syphilis with their colonial soldiers. "The English," he thought to himself, "the English fought us more than the Turks." Because, in his mind, his great-grandfather was connected to the figure of the governor, but in a negative way.

-3-
The Narrator

The narrator, this person who is outside our story, outside the cruise, but thanks to whom we are informed about what was going on on the yacht and in the mind of the captain, was reading page fifty-seven of *The Political History of Modern Greece* by Spyros Markezinis. "Since they [the government] were unable to deal with this difficult situation by soliciting loans from abroad—because, after the failure of the revolutionary loans, without a guarantee, neither could a compromise be reached concerning the previous loans, nor a new loan procured—and because naturally there was never any question of a national loan, there were only two other ancient solutions left: economizing (austerity) and an increase in state revenue (taxation). The former would have to be achieved without restricting military expenses, even after the battle of Navarino, because the danger of an attack by Ottoman troops was not out of the question, and also because immediate demobilization would create social problems (unemployment). The demobilized troops would become legends."

He shut his book and went out. He wanted to go to a certain address he had been given where he could get his dose from a dealer called Elpiniki. Number 11 Maison Street. On the way he wondered, still influenced by the book he had been reading, who this Maison was. A man, a woman, or a house? The name sounded vaguely familiar from high school. But he had forgotten practically everything he had learned in high school. As for the taxi driver, not only did he also not know who Maison was (a man, a woman, or a house), he had no idea where the street was.

"It's parallel to Fabvier Street," the narrator enlightened him. "Does that mean anything to you?"

It didn't mean a thing to the cab driver, because he came from a village and had not learned the streets of Athens. He was in the middle of dreaming about the fish his brother-in-law was going to bring him.

"Well, at least let's get to Canning Square, and then we can ask."

history

But even Canning Square was unknown to the driver. The narrator was indignant.

"But don't you know the history of the place where you were born?"

"History knows me," replied the driver cockily, in that way neo-Hellenes have of turning their ignorance into a virtue and throwing the ball back at you. "I make history in bed."

The narrator, who was going into withdrawal and could hardly wait to get to Elpiniki's house, began to lose his temper. Meanwhile, the cab driver continued his monologue.

"All these people in power are in it to amass wealth. Nobody's in it for the masses, for the people. That's why I say: all these ministers can go stuff themselves."

Finally, they asked another cab driver, an obliging old man, who solved their problem: they would take Eynard Street, behind the statue of Kolokotronis, go down Miaoulis Street, across Canning Square to Kassomoulis Street, and that's where they'd find Maison Street.

And suddenly, inside the passenger/narrator's mind, which was clouded from withdrawal, there was light. Kassomoulis! Of course! He mentions Marshall Maison, General Maison, Commander in Chief Maison, liberator of Greece. He cleaned up the Peloponnese of Ibrāhîm's Turko-Egyptians, the ones who brought the plague. With a regular army of fourteen thousand, he brought the border of Greece up to the Isthmus of Corinth. Yes, that was Maison, the great warrior. Maison of Maison Street.

At last they found it.

"What number did you say?"

"Number 11."

The driver stopped at number 9.

"Never mind, I'll get out here," said the narrator and paid.

They were watering the plants on the balconies and the streets were soaking. Or maybe it was raining. You could never tell in this city.

-4-
The Captain, Suite:
The Reception

"And so what happened to Kontostavlos, Grandfather?"

"He came back to Greece, where a few years later he gave a reception at his home, '*the most beautiful in Athens*,' at the foot of the Acropolis, '*to honor the departure of Commander Maison*.' In fact, he had invitations printed (the first to be printed in Greece, according to historians): '*Mr. and Mrs. Kontostavlos request . . . to attend a soiree at their home on the evening of April 27th, which the illustrious Marshall Maison will honor with his presence*.' Everybody came, from Capodistrias to the lowliest secretary. All the foreign powers. The only ones absent were the leaders of the rebel troops. They didn't show up because they were tired of having to dance *syrtaki* for the foreigners. Given the way the revolution had developed, that's all anyone wanted them for. They were tired of being objects of folklore. The foreigners had burst upon the scene; as early on as that, they would go to Kesariani every Sunday to watch the locals dance. Not that there was anything wrong with that. But what did these soldiers have to do with dancing?

history

"Said Grivas to Chief Hatzipetros: '*If Maison wants to see Greek dancing, we'll prepare him a military dinner out in the countryside, and we'll invite him to go there. The governor can go too. If you want to attend this reception, you are free to do so. I refuse to go and be laughed at.*' The man felt he was an evzone, a tourist attraction. But wasn't Capodistrias also a foreigner? '*If the governor wishes to entertain the French commander by presenting us, that is to say by inviting us and our wives, he may do so, but we, the men, will not dance on one side, while the others are threatening our honor and laughing at us dancing bears. N'est-ce pas can take a walk.*' They called Capodistrias N'est-ce pas because up until the Fourth National Assembly he spoke in French. Even translated into official Greek, he was still incomprehensible to the soldiers. N'est-ce pas was buying the drinks and N'est-ce pas was drinking them. Of course, Grivas was married to a young and attractive woman, and to see her surrounded by those foreign dandies while he was dancing *zeibekiko* made him furious. Vayas, Hatzipetros, and the other agreed with him. Nobody was going to go to Kontostavlos's reception. N'est-ce pas wanted to show them off to his foreign friends like cattle at a county fair. The chiefs would dance to entertain the foreign guests. But who was this Capodistrias, after all? He would call the leaders of the revolution 'chief brigands,' the erudite Phanariots like Korais 'sons of Satan,' and the notables 'Christian Turks.' So who else lived in this country?"

"It's the same nowadays," thought the captain. "When ship owners bring Greek dancing trios to London, to add an element of folklore to their dinner parties, nobody bothers to find out what's behind these people. What broken dreams, what betrayed longings, what defeats—their own or their fathers'—led them to do this kind of work, to become *syrtaki* professionals, out of a deep-seated sorrow, in order to survive without being anybody's employees, without slavishly bowing their heads to anyone. And they do not sell their manliness, because it is their very essence. It was the same with those brave men in the past. . . . "

"And so, Grandfather?"

"And so, Kontostavlos was happy that so many people came to his party. But he was concerned when he saw that the chiefs weren't coming. In his opinion, everyone who had shown up had taken advantage of the courage and the bravery of these fighters, had built on their blood. And now the blood was absent.

"The music began. Maison looked around for the chiefs of war promised by the governor, but he did not see them. Next came the waltzes, one, two, three. Then the *cadrilles*. Two hours had gone by. Maison asked the governor why the leaders hadn't appeared. The governor, not knowing the reason, shrugged his shoulders and said, 'Let us wait.' Meanwhile, he sent somebody to find out why they hadn't come. 'They're sleeping.' So, in order to make excuses to his guest, he mentioned something about 'uncouthness and ignorance.' But Maison didn't buy it. He had seen these men fight with him like lions, and they had always been civil and polite to him. Therefore, something else was going on, something they weren't telling him, but which he could sense, military man that he was.

"And so, my boy, those soldiers gave one of the first lessons of national independence and pride. They refused to dance *syrtaki* and *zeibekiko* for the foreign locusts, for the Western Eurotrash. They demanded a constitution. Free elections and a

history

constitution. A Parliament and a constitution. But the governor did not want to put a razor in an infant's hands, as he said. That's how he viewed a people who had fought for liberty and won: as infants.

"*I would give the razor to the infant,' said the English admiral, Lyons, 'and then I would take its right hand and guide it so it could shave without cutting itself.'*

"*'Admiral,' replied Capodistrias, 'I did not come to Greece to end up the laughing stock of Europe. I will continue to shave in front of the infant in order for it to learn how to use a razor safely.'*

"Capodistrias wasn't especially liked by his host, Kontostavlos. His friend Korais had written to Kontostavlos that he found the governor very haughty. Korais was not wrong. But that year was a particularly important one for the land. ('Although, of course, which year wasn't important for this land?' the captain thought to himself. 'Every year was as important as a day in the life of a dying man, because this infant was born half dead, and for the past 180 years everybody has been trying to bring it to life. But let's just say that that year, 1829, counted more than the others.')

"It was the year during which the borders of the new Greece were being widely discussed. The French insisted that if '*it were limited to the Peloponnese, it would be too weak to defend itself.*' The Russians '*are in favor of imposing a solution, even if it is done by them unilaterally,*' and, having guaranteed the neutrality of Austria, they started the Russo-Turkish War to help Greece grow larger. But the English did not agree. They were afraid that if Greece grew larger, it would pass under the influence of the Russians, and then the English would lose their domination of the Ionian Islands. (One hundred ten years later, Churchill, fearing that Greece would be taken over by the Soviet Union, provoked the repression of December 1944.) *'Thank God,' cried Wellington in London. 'It* (the liberation of Greece) *had never cost a shilling and never shall.'* Besides, his orders the previous year (on October 21, 1828), to his envoy in Nafplion had been clear: *'On the subject of Greece, I would limit its borders to the Peloponnese if possible, and if not, as close to the Isthmus of Corinth as possible.'*

"It was in such an atmosphere that the Kontostavlos's reception was held, and the host was circumspect in his actions."

The captain was lost in thought again. The figure of the governor had caused him problems since his great-grandfather went into a depression because among the iron laws imposed by N'est-ce pas was one banning piracy. The captain's grandfather used to tell him pirate stories when he was the same age as his youngest grandchild was now, and he still remembered them. Because Capodistrias had his good points, but he was also a perverse man. *"Until I came along, these Greeks didn't even know how to make a salad,"* he said, showing by "these Greeks" how alienated he really was. He was accountable to a Europe that the Greeks did not know; he wanted to cure *"the illness Greece had suffered from, after four centuries of slavery and seven of anarchy,"* the same way dictators play doctor by putting a country in plaster. He wanted to make Greece into another Switzerland, but he was forgetting that the Greeks had as a model not William Tell, but Dighenis Akritas.

"So back then Greece only went as far as the souvlaki shops at Corinth Canal, Grandfather?"

"That's as far as it went, my boy. They could smell the burning scent of freedom from across the way and it made their heads swim."

"So how come it grew?"

The grandson was waiting for the rest of the story. But his grandfather remained silent. He was dreaming of his life. Oh, if only he could rewrite it!

"And what happened to Capodistrias, Grandfather?"

"They killed him, my boy, one day when he was on his way to church."

"Why did they kill him, Grandfather?"

"Because people are evil, my boy."

The grandson was waiting. He would go and watch the Smurfs video again if his grandfather didn't go on with the story. But his grandfather seemed distracted. There was something else on his mind.

"I've kept the double-barreled shotgun for you, my boy."

The young man did not understand what gun his grandfather was talking about.

"You know, my shotgun. . . . "

"And who am I supposed to kill with it, Grandfather?"

-5-
The Narrator, Suite

"Othonos Street, please. The Olympic Airways office."

"Where's that?" asked the taxi driver, hastening to add, "I'm new at the job."

"It's at Constitution Square," said the narrator, and right away he was struck by the absurdity of it. Imagine that: Othonos Street being at Constitution Square. Otto, who never wanted to grant his subjects a constitution, was now condemned by city planning to name one of its four sides. And to be forced to enter Amalias Avenue, when he had never entered his own Amalia. ("*The protocol of the autopsy performed on Queen Amalia attested that she remained a virgin.*")

A taste of videotape, sour, misleading, slippery as a banana peel, comes to the narrator's mind every time he touches upon, even by mistake, a name or an event of that period. Immediately, he thinks of the television miniseries *Queen Amalia,* starring the Greek Brigitte Bardot; and of *Mando Mavrogenous* with the Greek Claudia Cardinale: the fake dialogue, the fake period costumes, the fake scenery, the cheapness of it all. Greek history and the writers of historical novels have financed this miniseries mania, he thinks to himself. At least a novel can be read in the original. But where do you find history? It stays in your imagination, personified by its televisual models: Amalia-Brigitte, Mando-Claudia. While reading of Kontostavlos's reception earlier, he could not avoid feeling the slimy banana peel, his allergy to videotapes, crawling over his skin.

"Who was Otto, Grandfather?"

"He was our first king, the second son of the philhellene King of Bavaria Ludwig I and Theresa, daughter of the Duke of Saxon Hildburghausen, niece of the Baron Niebelhausen, and great-grandmother of Maunthausen. According to historians, her father, a ladies' man, had to abdicate the throne in 1848, because of the scandal surrounding his relationship with Lola Montez, although his abdication was probably really due to the popular uprising that year.

"Ever since childhood, Otto had been a bit of a dunce. And he was sickly too, poor boy. At the age of fourteen he was sent to Livorno, in Italy, for treatment of a neurological disorder. He had to return the following year. Nowadays, a child with such reactions would be placed under the observation of neurologists and psychiatrists."

"So why did they send him to us as a king?"

"Because, my boy, it seems nobody else was available on the market. Or rather there was one, Leopold, who wanted to come, but Capodistrias was quick to discourage him. You see, Capodistrias, who could not foresee his untimely end, did not want to have anyone else over his head. So he made sure, in his own way, by writing Leopold letters in which he spoke of Greece as a banana republic (which it was in a way, but we usually keep information like that to ourselves) so as to dissuade him from coming. And so, Leopold, who later became king of Belgium and proved himself to be a fine man, longed for Greece into his deepest old age, because he had loved it as he had loved Lord Byron. 'Belgium is only prose writing,' he wrote in a letter. 'Greece satisfied the poetic needs of my soul.' So, our good old mediators sent us Otto."

"But why did we need mediators, Grandfather?"

"Because, my boy, we were good Christians. We believed in the Holy Trinity. The Father, the Son, and the Holy Spirit. In those days this meant England, Russia, and France. But before sending us Otto, who was still a kid, they sent us a professor, Friedrich Thiersch, who hellenized his name to Friderikos Thirsios, as was the fashion back then. They sent him on the pretext of an archaeological expedition. Up until World War II the Germans always sent us their agents disguised as archaeologists. Nowadays, the English send them as journalists and the Russians as commercial representatives.

"In any case, Otto learned that he was to be king of Greece even before he had turned seventeen. He asked whereabouts that country was, and presumably he was told that it did not yet exist, but that by the time he came of age, which would be in three years, it would have appeared on the map. 'And what am I supposed to go and do there?' 'You will reign,' said his father. 'It's by the sea, and the scenery is beautiful.' (The young boy loved riding and swimming.) Besides, his father, who was such a debauchee, had given him a complex. Like Kafka. Otto kept writing letters to his father that he never sent. He only sent the ones his tutor dictated to him. And, like Kafka, he died before his father.

"So, Otto arrived, not transformed into a cockroach like Kafka's hero Gregor Samsa, but like a bridegroom, with his whole trousseau (he played the piano, he spoke French and a little Greek). One hot number, we would say nowadays. Or a stud. After all, he disembarked in the stud capital, Nafplion. He rode into town on a white horse (and ever since, young girls are said to be waiting for a prince on a white horse). But at the moment when he was about to speak in his broken Greek, he forgot everything and spoke to the provisional government and the people, who were in a way handing over power, in his native tongue. Needless to say, nobody understood a word. And that was the way modern Greek history began, in incomprehension. '*Hellenen, berufen durch das vertrauender erlauchten grossherzigen Ver-mittler . . .* ' (Greeks, invited here by the confident, illustrious, and magnanimous mediator . . .).

"Along with him came Bavarian soldiers who used the national loan for subsistence. At the time, my boy, the Greek tribunals were not able to try a foreign army man. This policy of providing immunity to the foreign military is still in force today. Bavarian jurists came, Bavarian architects, and ladies of the Bavarian court, and all that's left of them today is a dessert, the famous Bavarian cream.

"This is how a foreign traveler, the Russian painter Vladimir Davidoff (no relation to the cigars of the same name), describes life in Athens in 1834: *'We are on Ermou Street, near the entrance of the Bavarian cafe Grunen Baum (The Green Tree). We are surprised not only by the poverty of the city, but also by the absolute predominance of foreigners of every nationality over the natives, even in their own capital. In the street, the only well-dressed people one comes across are Italian shop owners, Bavarian soldiers, government employees, and the members of the diplomatic corps. The only natives we see are manual workers and beggars dressed in their national costume.'*

"It was at that time that the old man of the Morea, Theodoros Kolokotronis, decided to retire.

"*'To the extent that I was able,'* he wrote, *'I fulfilled my duty to my country, and so did my entire family. I saw my country free, I saw what we had all longed for, myself, my father, my grandfather, and all my race, as well as all the Greeks. I decided to go to an orchard I had outside Nafplion. I went there and I stayed, spending my time growing things. It gave me pleasure to watch the little trees I had planted growing bigger.'*

"But they didn't leave Kolokotronis alone either. They convicted him of being a Russophile, the same way that one hundred years later they convicted the Russophiles of being part of the E.A.M.[*] It was the Germans now, the Bavarians then. Meanwhile, Bavaria had become part of Germany."

"And what was Otto like, Grandfather?"

"He was pathetic. Not all there. He wasn't a bad guy, but he had some kind of cerebral lesion. He couldn't understand anything they told him. They would take him documents, and he would spend hours studying them, correcting the spelling mistakes and punctuation, and after he had gone over everything, he still hadn't understood anything. His last word on any subject was, 'We'll see.' As Claude Herve wrote, *I did not understand what he told me and it was obvious that he rarely understood me. . . . His hair was so flat that it always appeared to be stuck to his head. He was in the habit of passing his hand over it all the time to keep it in a state of perfect control. I never once saw a single hair out of place and I imagined that was what he desired of his subjects.'* Fortunately, he would often travel to his homeland and in his absence, his wife Amalia would conclude affairs of state and sign in his place. When he visited Smyrna, he really went nuts. He saw himself *'as the successor of the paleologues. I dream',* he said, *'of this country becoming big and strong, and I dream of my throne being there, where the last emperor of Byzantium fell.'* As for Greece, he saw it in the same way modern tourists see it. He liked going on excursions. He liked the ancient ruins.

[*] Resistance front during the German occupation. *Trans.*

100

But when the natives saw him accompanied by Armansberg's daughters, they thought it was the sultan and his harem, and that Armansberg and his aide-de-camp were the eunuchs. His case resembled that of a mentally handicapped child: you ask it what the time is, and it looks at the hands of the clock, and it tells you the minutes and seconds, but it never tells you what time it is."

"Here we are," said the taxi driver. "Isn't this Othonos Street?"

The narrator got out on the side facing Constitution Square, and crossed the street to the offices of Olympic Airways.

-6-
The Captain, Suite: And End

"It was a harsh winter."

"Which winter was that, Grandfather?"

"The one that marked the end of the first half of the century. It was very cold. Six below and even less. Even the olive trees were killed by the frost. My great-grandfather's was the last sailing ship to enter the port of Piraeus. Piraeus was small then, with very few houses. But on that day it was deserted. Outside, the ships of the English fleet had started the blockade. Just when we thought that the following year, 1850, we'd finally get going, a new life would begin, commerce and the economy would get back on their feet. The banker Stavrou wrote: *'There are three things missing from Greece: quiet, order, and money. If we wish to be useful, we should bring money.'* At the time, in the spring of 1849, the great

Jewish banker Rothschild was visiting our country. In order to flatter him, Stavrou, the director of the Bank of Greece, had the police ban the traditional burning of the effigy of Judas on Good Thursday. The Christians used to burn Judas out of love for Jesus, because he had betrayed Him. But this Judas who had betrayed the Messiah was the Savior of the Jews. Stavrou was counting on a hefty loan from the international capital that Rothschild represented, and he didn't want to hurt the banker's feelings.

"Then the English Secret Service concocted a diabolical plan: they sent their men in the guise of 'indignant citizens,' who were supposedly upset by this ban, to storm the house of a Jew, Don Pacifico, who had been born in Gibraltar, was of Spanish descent, and had been a Portuguese citizen before moving to Athens, but who was actually a British national. For the pillaging of his home, Don Pacifico demanded of the Greek state the disproportionately high compensation of 886,739 drachmas, and this demand was fully supported by Lyons, the British ambassador in Athens. The Greek state referred the case to the courts, but Lyons had the British prime minister ask for the opinion of the Council of Jurists of the English Crown. That way, the English had the pretext in their pocket and were simply waiting for the right moment to broach the delicate subject of the 'pending compensation' of their national."

"It was the English again, Grandfather?"

"Them again, my boy. My great-grandfather wrote: *'Whatever I write down here is the truth. The same way two plus two makes four. England wanted an Anglicized Greece, not a Russified one. Moreover, being selfish and most violent in her decisions, she will say one day, gun in hand: "Rather than Greece* going to the Russians, we would prefer it went to the Turks." Those are the frightful politics of England of today. Let us not deceive ourselves into thinking she has charitable feelings toward us.' At that time, the English wanted to have one of their own in the government, a certain Mavrokordatos, whom Otto had sent to Paris as an ambassador, just to get rid of him.

"In the same way, one hundred years later, in 1945, they still wanted to have one of their own involved in the affairs of the country. So they sent General Scobie, just as in 1849 they had sent General Parker and his ships.

"'It is impossible for a sailboat to leave Piraeus. An English battleship has been positioned in the middle of the section of the port occupied by the foreigners, opposite the lighthouses, and it does not allow any vessel to exit. At Spetses, the English are still seizing the vessels of civilians, and at Patras they have seized more and transported them to the Ionian Islands.'"

The captain of 1850, grandfather of the old captain of today, suffered as he saw his small homeland under seige. Of course, Piraeus was not the only port. There were Syros, Patras, and Nafplion. But Piraeus was the capital's port, and when the capital is under seige, so is the entire country.

It was only later, much later, that the grandson, who was now the grandfather, found out what the course of events had been. After the death of the Francophile Kolletis, in 1847, the appetite of the English was whetted again. But the general climate of the period was not favorable. So they waited for the revolution of 1848, which had shaken Europe, to die down before they took action.

Meanwhile, Greece was changing courtier governments as if they were shirts: Tzavellas, Koundouriotis, Kanaris, Kriezis.

Otto had been forced to grant a Constitution in 1944, after a bloodless revolution, but he kept violating it. He was still the "tyrant," the "traitor," the "hyena," the "foreign locust," and his wife Amalia the "Greek Messalina." Lyons found her *very beautiful, but also very proud of her relations with the royal family of Russia.* So where did this leave the English? How would they impose their politics on this small state that was so critical to the control of the Mediterranean? The captain of the past wrote: *"England was determined to have total influence over Greece at any cost. Any other solution would be contrary to her interests. Just as Russia exercised its uncontested influence over the Serbo-Vlach countries, England wanted to control Greece. That was what the interests of England dictated."*

One hundred years later, after the betrayal of the second insurrection, the problem would recur: instead of the czar there would be Stalin, instead of Palmerston, Churchill; the French would once again constitute a European guarantee.

But what should you do when others are fighting over your own interests? *"A wise Greek government could benefit from these pernicious politics by flattering this colossus who, thanks to his floating fortresses, held in his hands the fate of our coasts, our navy, and our commerce. But where to find such a government? For five whole years British politics had been scorned in Greece. And yet one cannonball would be enough to end it all."*

And so the new ambassador, Wise, who was to replace Lyons (whom Otto and Amalia had not wanted and finally succeeded in getting rid of), arrived freshly pressed from the Foreign Office. A sour, querulous, disagreeable man, but a lover of ancient Greece, he found the opportunity, amidst the governmental instability, to dig up the old question of the islets of Sapiéntza and Elafónisos, north of Kythira, and to claim that they came under the jurisdiction of the Ionian State, which at the time was British. But since such an untimely claim could provoke the intervention of the protection powers, France and Russia, Wise first brought up British national Don Pacifico's damage claim for the pillaging of his house by "Christian natives indignant at the ban of the burning of Judas." This claim consisted of 9,700 drachmas for money stolen; 12,000 drachmas for distress caused; 665,000 drachmas for the destruction of Portuguese letters of credit (how could one possibly verify that?), etc., etc., which came to a total of over 800,000 drachmas.

("One hundred years later," thought the narrator to himself, "in Athens, when the Italians handed over the city to the Germans, and they wanted to round up the Jews like they had done in Salonika, Archbishop Damaskinos started christening them; the chief of police issued certificates of christening that very day. The ones who did not have time to get baptized were saved by E.A.M., which issued a proclamation to the people telling them to help the Jews escape to the mountains or to the Near East. Not a single one, not even half a one, was caught by the Nazis. Only the English played their dirty game again in 1948, by not letting them disembark when Israel became a state.")

The captain of the past knew nothing of all this. All he knew was that he wanted to load up at Piraeus and set sail for Smyrna where a cargo of silk was waiting for him, and he couldn't leave. Parker, the commander of the fleet, had sent an ultimatum with a time limit of twenty-four hours. As soon as the twenty-four hours were up, he declared the blockade.

"I went uptown. The people, looking solemn, are hurrying around the markets." (That is to say they were stocking up on groceries.) *"Opinions differ. Some speak of treason, others say it is a ruse, still others say it is a disciplinary action. But everyone agrees that the English are most violent. They insult, they besiege, they obstruct, they trample on the rights of Greece. And meanwhile we expect help from Russia and France. Presently, perhaps we will see the English at the gates of the capital, and we will still be expecting help from Russia and France."*

Nowadays we say: "the blockade lasted forty-two days." But with every day that passed, the people's anxiety grew stronger and their desperation deeper.

"Oh, if only Greece were a great nation! If only we could put forward a Greek breast against the violence and, sword in hand, take revenge upon those who insult us! But alas! Greece is too small for that. That is why, in 1832, it was enclosed within such narrow borders. We are therefore forced to swallow our indignation. Goddesses of justice and liberty, look over this unfortunate nation. Let Greece survive and may we all die. Let the independence of our homeland be preserved, and may we all be sent in chains to the English penal colonies . . . ."

The blockade lasted into the harsh winter. February is always the worst time of year. It is a month that represents a certain blocking of the economy. But to have a second blockade on one's hands was too much. What was going to happen? The cold was becoming more intense. The people were beginning to suffer from hunger.

"To put our faith in Europe or to wait for Russia and France to come to our defense is consoling and heartening; however, it does not diminish the imminent danger. By the time Europe speaks

up, by the time Paris and Saint Petersburg exchange notifications, and by the time the matter is brought to the Council of London, our commerce will have been lost and our shipping annihilated."

And even so, a forty-two-day blockade isn't such a big deal, compared to other national catastrophes: wars, epidemics, civil strife. Compared to what had preceded and what succeeded it. However, it remains a question in need of an answer.

"The French steamship is expected like a Messiah. Everyone's eyes are turned to Piraeus and people keep asking: 'Has the steamship arrived? It will tell us the wishes of France. It will tell us how the action of England was received by Europe. It will tell us whether Palmerston has agreed to the two protective powers being arbitrators.' One can easily imagine with what wildly beating hearts we are all waiting for the fire vessel from France."

Because there are fire vessel dreams, and pyromaniac dreams, and self-igniting dreams, blocks of dreams and dreams of blockades, and Holocaust dreams . . .

"It was rumored today that Palmerston will only accept the intervention of France. It is an unofficial rumor. What is certain is that Europe took a very dim view of the actions of the English fleet. An article from the French newspaper Debates, *sent from Trieste, speaks acrimoniously of England. Notes were exchanged once again between the British ambassador and the Greek government concerning the islands Sapíentza and Elafónissos. But the problem of the islets is insignificant. The important issue is to have satisfaction. The compensation of Don Pacifico is a question of honor, according to the English, and for this I fear there will be terrible consequences. As an impartial spectator, I will await, with tears in my eyes, the fate of our nation."*

The captain of the past is anything but impartial. It is painful for him, as a neo-Hellene of unknown descent, to accept destiny "in the Greek way." "If it be destined for this land to be enslaved again and lose its independence, then let us prepare to suffer this ordeal 'in the Greek way.'"

It was precisely here that the problem was posed, thought the narrator. What did the captain mean by "the Greek way"? This adverbial phrase had acquired a particular significance concerning the man's feelings. Would a Frenchman ever say, "we are suffering this new ordeal in the French way"? It was only concerning divorces that the phrase "Italian-style" stuck, and that was because under the Catholic Church they were forbidden. So was it forbidden for one to be a Greek in Greece? Or was Greece simply an idea and not a reality, in which case, as an idea, "in the Greek way" takes on the meaning of "in a respectable way"? But what does it mean to be Greek? If we believe Fallmerayer: *The destruction of the ancient Greek world started under the reign of Justinian, when the enormous column of nations between the Danube and the Baltic, shaken by the great historic events, dragged itself over the Greek soil like a dark cloud propelled by a raging storm, and there was not a single valley, mountain or ravine that it did not devastate. The first act of this invasion lasted three centuries. This fact finally sheds light upon why in the* Greek Chronicle of the Morea, *the mountain range of Taiyetos is preferably referred to as the Slavic Mountains. And the localities of Plátsa, Statsa, Loutsaina, Chloumitsa, Levetsova, Zitsova, Vársova, and Polonitsa attest to these invasions. In act II of the drama all the towns and villages of Greece were persecuted and stripped of their population. A new race of people settled in, into*

*which, every now and then, there slid, like foreigners, the small
remnants of the ancient masters of the country. Until, at last, the
rejuvenated Byzantine Empire, strengthened by the addition of the
vital barbaric power, once again subjugated a Greece that was now
Slavic, and, by grafting her with the Christian faith and the modern Greek language, created a completely new Greece."* (He meant
in relation to the ancient one.) *"Nowadays [1844], the Albanians, ancient neighbors of Greece, constitute the majority of inhabitants of the new kingdom."*

Therefore, concluded the narrator (and psychoanalysis can
take a flying leap), could it be that the words *to suffer this ordeal
in the Greek way* take on a much more complex meaning in the
captain's mind, a meaning that contains all these ordeals, invasions, insults, and deteriorations that the foreigners brought to
our country? And the captain of the past cries out the ever-top-
ical slogan of national accord, which is always used during the
nation's difficult moments: "For the sake of our nationality, let
us forget for a moment the crimes of the past."

"And how did the story with Pacifico end, Grandfather?"
"He was finally given a small compensation, instead of the
800,000 drachmas he had asked for. Ambassador Wise returned
the 150,000 drachmas that the Greek government had given as
a guarantee, and the settlement for the Portuguese letters of credit
was assigned to Louis Beclar, the French charge d'affaires in Lis-
bon. The settlement was completed, and instead of the 665,540
drachmas he was claiming, that is to say approximately 26,000,
he received as compensation 3,750 drachmas, approximately 150,
in other words practically nothing. And in order to whitewash

the English, Lyons wrote from Geneva to our compatriot Dragoumis: '*I cannot easily forgive him* (Lord Palmerston) *his decision. For four months Europe was in an upheaval because of Pacifico and a small state was oppressed, a state created, no less, by the oppressor. I too was obliged to protect Pacifico, but I would be ashamed to incite such protection.*' As for Palmerston, he gave a speech at the Council of Communities that went on forever, invoking Cicero, who said that Rome protected any Roman who was able to say, 'Civis Romanus Sum' (I am a citizen of Rome). And that, Palmerston affirmed, went for all citizens of the British Empire. He received a standing ovation."

The captain feels stifled by that longing people have for a happy day in their lives, a decent, carefree day, as the yacht approaches the port of Piraeus and he sees, outside the port, all those ships anchored in bundles of immobilized iron, reduced to inertia, while maintaining them in the water is costing a fortune. He sees the other ships tied at the jetties: Russian, English, French, from Liverpool, from Odessa, from Marseilles, the three great powers. And while his own vessel moves slowly along, with an official air, through the still waters that take on the color of honey from the rising sun, he thinks to himself that things have indeed changed from the days of his distant ancestor. Now he has radar and a telex on board, now he keeps informed, he communicates, he signals immediately and everywhere. And yet the people are still left out of the game of power. They will only find out much later what was said during the meeting between the Soviet ambassador and the prime minister or between the United States ambassador and the president of the Republic. When the burning interest of the same day has died down, when there is no longer an immediate demand, like the one he has to respond to now: he must decide where to moor the boat, and at the same time he is watching out for the Flying Dolphin hovercraft, which usually makes a tight turn at the breakwater without worrying about other vessels coming into the port.

Years from now, when today's events are history, when the boats will be moored on dry land, much later, people will find out the why and the how: what happened with the Cyprus issue, what was said about the United States bases, what was the truth behind the smoke screen the media put up to confuse people. And of course nowadays, he thinks to himself, "there is no 'Moussouros affair.'" But still, as they were at the time of Moussouros, our relations with Turkey are severed. Even though people no longer believe that the capital of Greece will move to Constantinople, the Greek islanders who live across Asia Minor still feel threatened. There are three great powers again, and we don't fit in with any of them. Still we wonder: which is the best road to follow in the long run, so that the people are not betrayed once again?

He moors the boat next to the other yachts. At last, he has found an empty space! He throws the ropes ashore. The guests begin to disembark. It is Monday morning. Their businesses will be opening soon. Plasterboard will go back to his factory and the doctor to his white mice; Persephone, Thalia, Irini to the slimming institute; Aristotle the sociologist to his research center. The architect will return to her tracing paper, the American and Madam "tag-along" to no one, Niko the importer of cold cuts back to his knockwurst and salami. They thank their host Elias and the crew for a lovely three-day weekend. One by one they walk along the gangplank, carrying their gear. The last to leave the vessel is the grandfather-captain with his grandson-captain. But even after them, like a ghost, last of the last, the narrator slips out of the story.

stories of
taxi drivers

Everything's fine. Everything's wonderful. Monday morning and the world is open, a meeting of sunshine and strength. The city is bursting with health and life. And I am bursting inside like the city.

This summer, having lost my car, which was registered abroad (unable to afford to clear it through customs, I was forced to sell it for a song to the state), I got around quite a bit by taxi, which, in Greece, is hardly a luxury—in fact, I would say fares are still scandalously cheap, compared to other countries in Western Europe—and so came to know that amiable class of people, taxi drivers, who believe, and rightly so, that they are performing a service by substituting for a deficient public transport system. The capital has no metro, and traffic limitations, combined with bus and trolley strikes, have made moving around "within the city walls" problematic.

Taxi drivers, I was to find out, are a class unto themselves. They are often talkative and they form, for the most part, public opinion, as if they constituted a newspaper, which (like certain laws) is not printed and yet is heard, and which yet has a circulation, in Athens alone, of 600,000 copies a day.

I am a man, I must say, who generally likes to chat. I am literally fascinated by other people's stories. My own story bores me. This is why I have a knack for making other people talk to me: I lose myself in their words and forget my own problems. Taxi drivers are, by definition, talkative. Those who, like me, were once immigrants are also dreamers.

Stelios and His Lost Tomatoes

For Stelios, the tomatoes in his garden were a consolation. He owned a small plot next to his house, in the suburb of Pefki, where he grew his tomatoes, some zucchini, a little clover, radishes, and a few sweet potatoes. But his tomatoes were his great love. He would see them every morning growing red, like the cheeks of young girls.

It was summer. The deep of summer. July. His wife and daughters were away on vacation, if one could call it that, in Oropos, visiting with an aunt and doing some swimming. Stelios was left on his own. He worked in his taxi and enjoyed his work. He came in contact with people. But his consolation, amidst the smog and traffic jams, was his garden, a substitute for his village, perhaps, which he had left while still a child in order to emigrate first to Belgium and then, a few years ago, to Athens.

He hadn't regretted coming back to his country. There were the children to consider. He was afraid Belgian society, with its drugs, would corrupt his girls. With the money he had saved up all those years he worked in Spa, he built his little house in Pefki and got his own taxi.

Next to the house (built without a license) was his little garden. He had bought the land with his wife's cousin, since he couldn't afford to buy it on his own, and the cousin had built a house next to his. They were separated by the garden.

But the garden belonged to him. That had been determined from the start. Since then, two years had gone by. He didn't have much to do with the cousin, who had turned out to be a man of bad faith. Misunderstandings over a few meters of land, while they were both illegally building their homes, caused a rift between them. But he was Stelios's wife's cousin, not a stranger. Stelios swallowed his anger. Which is why he started having stomach trouble.

"We don't always get along very well with the neighbors," he would explain.

But it gave his wife a sense of security to have a relative nearby. His wife, sweet Merope, had worn herself out in Spa all those years, working at the mineral water bottling plant. It was hard work for her and for Stelios too, who had worked at a factory that made car parts.

In any case, things weren't too bad. But today there had been a disaster. And the taxi driver vented his anger on his unknown customer. Namely, me.

"I got home in the afternoon. I had been working all morning. All morning I had been dreaming of the salad I was going to make myself, since the old lady and the girls are away at Oropos, with the tomatoes from my garden. They had ripened to perfection. I was going to fry myself a couple of eggs and have a snack. So I go home, and I find they've been picked. It made me mad. It still does."

"Was it burglars?" I asked.

"Burglars? Since when do burglars steal tomatoes?"

"Then who stole them?"

"Who? Even if I told you, what would it mean to you? But it makes me mad. And it makes me even madder because I can't tell him. I know who it was. It was him that did it. My wife's cousin. My neighbor. Only *he* could get into my garden."

That was when I learned about the house, about their not getting along, and all the rest of it.

"And why don't you just go straight to him and tell him?"

"And what good would that do, my dear man? It's done. The tomatoes are gone. But I tell you, it made me mad. I couldn't wait to get home to go into the garden and pick them, they were so red and plump, like little watermelons, organically grown, and I didn't find a single one. He had picked the exact four that I was going to pick. The others are still green."

As he drove me to the offices of my newspaper (*The Almanac of Dreams*), I could see that the man at the wheel was truly suffering. I was filled with pity for this "pavement ship owner" (as they mockingly refer nowadays to taxi drivers because of their meager earnings), and I wanted to show him my compassion.

"Listen," I said. "To keep it all inside is no good. It doesn't set you free. You have to let it out. You're only human, you need to get things off your chest. You told me about it, but I'm a stranger. Soon I'll be gone, you may tell it again to someone else. I don't want it to stop there: I want you to do something about it."

From what I gathered, if he were to mention the tomatoes to his cousin, the discussion wouldn't end there. It would spread over into other things: their old feud over the land they had bought together, the disputed two meters of land ("which is exactly how deep they'll bury us both," the taxi driver had remarked wisely). And it might even have gone further—who knows—to the village, to the family affairs of his wife, to the fields that her relatives looked after while she was away in Belgium (perhaps the famous cousin was among them), and to her not having been able to claim her share and feeling wronged over it. The tomatoes were the hand grenades that would explode, and their seeds would destroy the good relations of the neighborhood once and for all. Also, Stelios did not want, as he told me frankly, to pick a fight when his wife was away, that she should come home all tanned and renewed, only to find the house turned upside-down.

I began to picture the innocent tomatoes that knew nothing, poor things, of the problem they had caused; that had surrendered themselves without protest to the hand that had stolen them; and that could even have become the cause of a murder. How can one blame a tomato, grown in a garden with affection, turning red with shame like a young girl (in Stelios's case, his own daughters, who grew more and more embarrassed in front of their father as their breasts swelled), and then along comes a vengeful hand and steals them away from the one who raised them with his own sweat and tears?

The street was full of cars. We were moving along with difficulty. It was terribly hot. Like all taxis, this one didn't have air-conditioning. There was ventilation with, supposedly, fresh air, but that too was burning, like the air in the street.

Stelios, lean faced, was smoking at the wheel. I sat in the back seat; we communicated with our eyes through the rear view mirror. I pictured the scene: he comes home to Pefki dripping with perspiration around 3:30 in the afternoon, after earning a hard day's wages, living with the dream of his tomatoes, to have a bite and then lie down, closing the shutters and leaving the windows open to let in fresh air. And then, as he enters his garden, the vegetable garden of his dreams, which he would water and weed in order to relax after a hard day's work at the wheel, among drivers who knew nothing of driving, who were daring, inexperienced, and impudent, waging a battle every day just to avoid being crashed into, he finds among its branches, instead of the red orbs he expects, freshly cut stems.

"The dirty rascal didn't even leave me one single tomato as a consolation prize."

"Couldn't it have been someone else?" I asked.

"There's no way. Nobody can get into the garden or the house, the way I've fenced it. One can only get in from the inside. And from the inside, only my cousin could have done it. He pulled the same stunt on me last year, with two avocados. But my wife covered for him. And I didn't care about the avocados."

How horrible life is, truly! To be condemned to live under a metal roof that is being scorched by the sun, and to dream of a fresh salad, and then for someone to come along and steal it from your plate! But as our discussion progressed, with me in the role of the calming influence, to help the man get it off his chest, I began to discern that the problem was not so much the tomatoes as it was Stelios's fear for his daughters.

This cousin was a bit of a satyr, as I surmised from what Stelios told me about his life and times. The father, who loved his girls, wanted, like every father, to be the first to taste their fruit (which, of course, would never happen, so, to make up for it, he would find them husbands who wouldn't make him jealous). Stelios had come to fear his cousin, his neighbor, who had designs on his girls and wanted to devour them. He had noticed that the cousin was already hungrily eyeing the elder one, who was seventeen and would be finishing high school the following year. He caught that leer of his one afternoon: Mairoula was in the garden hanging out her wash, mostly panties and socks, and the lecherous cousin (a man of thirty-five, swarthy and unsavory) watched from his balcony and undressed her with his eyes. Stelios was weeding his garden and pretended not to see. But as he stooped down, he caught his cousin's eyes lusting for his daughter; as he bent over, the blood rushed to his head. At that moment, he could have taken his hoe and split open his cousin's thick, vulgar head like a rose. But he restrained himself, and he swallowed his anger like he swallowed everything else.

Now Mairoula was almost eighteen, while his younger daughter, prematurely developed, also had the body of a woman, and the cousin surely had his eye on her too. As for Stelios, whether he would lie down with his wife for the kind of love-making that had long since been made out of habit and not passion, or whether he would unwind with some low-class prostitute in a brothel, the image of those girls of his dominated his thoughts and made him climax. He would have his girls on his mind, and as he would struggle to chase those thoughts away the girls would come to him and caress him tenderly with their hands. At night, before going to bed, they would beg him to be the first man to sleep with them, which would disturb Stelios terribly and make him ashamed in front of his wife; he thought everybody knew about his fantasy and so he would ignore his daughters, and his wife would reprimand him for not being an affectionate father. His daughters thought he had stopped loving them, even though they hadn't done anything to upset him.

Mairoula was a serious girl and a good student; she was going to study physics and math at the university. The younger one, with the nice figure, was a talented dancer and attended a ballet school in Pefki (one of the many dance schools that shot up like mushrooms when *Fame* started playing on TV every Sunday evening). They had never caused him any trouble. Born in Belgium, having lived there for fifteen years, they stood apart from their Greek-born classmates, who were vain and precocious, who wanted to be "cool" and rebelled against their families. His daughters were serious. In fact the elder one had joined the Communist Youth, where the kids were almost puritanical, growing up with principles in the face of the triple enemy: capitalism-imperialism-Americanocracy.

Yet Stelios's soul had succeeded in discovering the Devil in the face of his wife's cousin, who would bring home the occasional nightclub singer. Many times, toward daybreak, Stelios and his wife could hear the moaning of these women in their very own bedroom. "I have daughters," Stelios would tell his cousin. "At least have a little respect for us." But he, Mr. Tough Guy with the pencil-thin mustache, who, before coming to live next to them, lived in the boondocks, did not share their sensibilities.

I came to realize all this, little by little, as the line of cars moved along with little hops (I was already late), until finally (what an abyss the human creature is!), the significance of the tomatoes acquired within me its true dimension, and I saw that even if it were true that this man, Stelios, had a weakness for his tomatoes, and even if it were true that for him, his garden was a dream amidst his dangerous, paved, polluted life, it was equally true that these tomatoes, in relation to the cousin, signified something else, something much deeper, something that not even he himself realized, and that, were I to reveal it to him, he would have taken me for a lunatic and kicked me out of his taxi without even letting me pay my fare.

But he was suffering, I could see that. The blow had been mortal, and what was worse, he couldn't get it out of his system. The important thing in life is having an escape valve for all poisonous gases. That's all that matters.

Finally, we arrived at the offices of my newspaper. I invited him to come up with me. He wasn't familiar with the paper, but he said he would be glad to subscribe to it, since he might be able, through a dream, to find some temporary relief for his problem.

But Stelios's problem, as the reader must have realized by now, was of the virtually insolvable kind. His being at odds with his neighbor was a constant threat to the serenity of his family. Only if he put up a fence of dreams between the two houses could he find peace. And he would not be able to put up a fence like that, unless it was . . .

"What?" he asked.

"A vine arbor. Nobody will know the real reason you put it up, it will offer you the protection of its foliage and its shade, and it will make it safe for your girls to wander around and your tomatoes to ripen."

The idea appealed to him.

For there are vine arbor dreams, and dreams on crutches. There are dreams that isolate our spiritual tranquillity inside their immaterial walls, like the noise-absorption walls along busy freeways passing through populated suburbs.

-2-
The Lost Woman and the Bed Full of Dollars

"I met her through my job. She was looking for a taxi at 3:00 in the morning. When I asked her where she was going, she said she had no place to go. So I took her back to my place, where I live alone. She went into the bathroom, undressed, and came back wearing only a pair of black panties. Her body was much younger than her face, which was quite wrinkled. At the sight of it, a shiver went through me. I too undressed and lay down next to her, my body very white compared to hers, which was deeply tanned by the sun and sea. She was crying. I let her cry to get it out of her system, without asking her what was wrong. She liked that. Then she looked deep into my eyes and invited me inside her. I entered a flooded cavern. I tried to hold onto the walls, but they were also soaking. Then, like a blotter, I drew out her waters and as she began to dry out, I steadied myself inside her. This sweet rowing lasted a long time. In the morning, I woke up to find the bed flooded with dollars. I sat there dumbfounded, staring at the miracle. She slept on, cleared from the fog of her pain. Her face now had the tranquillity of a lake."

According to this taxi driver, this woman had the ability to produce dollars, just the way bakers turn dough into sweet rolls, or chickens produce eggs, out of a machine that must have been in her stomach and caused her pain. Every time she was about to fill the bed with dollars, he would see her straining, making

a superhuman effort, like a medium communicating with the spirits, with such tension, and such an inner rumbling, like a "one-
armed bandit," which greedily gulps down your coins until
suddenly you hit the jack-pot and its metal apron fills with a noisy
cascade of the coins you had fed it. It was somewhat like that, as
I understood from what the young taxi driver was saying: this
woman, this unknown customer, would produce, at the moment
of her liberation, shiny, wet twenty-dollar notes, one after the
other, with the speed of a sewing machine. Authentic dollars, that
the bank accepted; he never had any problem, he said. Just the
way one squeezes sweet oranges and gets seeds instead of juice,
that's how he would see the bank notes spilling from the fork of
her legs, as if he kept winning the lottery and no longer needed
anything or anyone else.

The dollars were the isotopes of the sweetness that she drew
from within herself, from within her own body, self-sufficient in
its food and water, its energy sources, with its secretion and dis-
cretion, a sweetness that was self-absorbed and transformed, as
in fairy tales, into the green hope that gave him joy and security,
without the anxiety of earning a daily wage.

He congratulates himself on finding her while she, proud
and vulnerable, always asks him: "You don't only love me for that,
do you?" In a word, he had stumbled upon the woman-legend,
the woman-liberator, and he had to protect her, so that nobody
else would find out their secret and steal her away from him.

She was afraid she'd suddenly go dry and he would stop loving her. "Don't talk nonsense. I didn't know you had so many talents hidden in you," he would say. "It's only with you," she would
reply, "that it happens so simply." A gift of God, mysterious like

His ways. "One would think you were Christina Onassis," he would whisper sweetly in her ear, and, with the help of money, all his dreams could at last be realized. "But then," she would answer gravely, "they will cease to be dreams and desires: your true riches lie in wanting and yearning for things—not in having them."

Her own wish and desire was that they always remain together. And she would draw strength from him, and sweetness, that would pass through her like lightning, with thunder and rain that would keep getting stronger, then disappear. Then she would transform herself into a money generator. Until finally he started to be afraid. He would hide her. He knew that those who used to exploit her were out looking for her. And while she rarely spoke to him of her past, she led him to understand that it had been traumatic, that she had suffered much because of her ability to make men happy, and that everybody envied her. They would beat her until she dried up and then she would become unhappy. Because her talents remained buried, they would make things worse for her and she would run off, with difficulty, just like that night he had found her in the street, looking for a taxi, with no place to go, in tears. She had just escaped again, with the help of the cleaning lady, from her last prison. But she didn't want to be imprisoned by him. She wanted to be able to go out, to dance, to laugh, to go to the beach and to restaurants, and not to see the sunlight only through closed shutters.

That's why they decided to go abroad. Even though the Mafia's tentacles spread everywhere, tracing them in a foreign country would be difficult. So they left. They lived, free and happy in Düsseldorf, without anyone discovering their secret. He would give her more sweetness than she could bear, and she would return it with more money than he could spend.

"And then what happened?" I asked, as the story was drawing to an end and we were approaching my destination. "The truth is," he said, turning around for the first time to face me, "that love is an elusive bird."

"I don't understand. Can you elaborate?"

"The truth is that suddenly one day she went dry on me. Like the wells in my village. You keep drawing and drawing for water, but there isn't a drop."

"And how did it happen? Out of the blue?"

"Completely out of the blue. I had started seeing another woman. A blond German woman, Ursula. When my girlfriend found out, she didn't say anything, she didn't make a scene, but she stopped putting out dollars at night. And one day she left, she disappeared. I even had Interpol look for her. She was nowhere to be found." The woman-legend, the woman-liberator, the woman with a capital *W*, was finished.

"But please tell me," I said, as I paid my fare. "There's something I don't understand: you told me you had saved up a lot of money. So why are you working as a taxi driver?"

"I didn't tell you the most important part. When she went dry, all the dollars she had produced and that we had put in the bank also disappeared. I went one day to withdraw the money, and they told me there was no such account."

"Could she have taken it when she left?"

"No. I had my own separate account. It just seems that . . . how can I explain it? By losing the absolute of love, I was left with the relativity of passion. Love is an elusive bird."

stories of taxi drivers

I got out of the taxi. The young taxi driver was looking at me intently. Suddenly, I realized how much I resembled him.

"And what was her name?" I asked him.

"Doña Rosita," he said.

-3-
The Story of the Immigrant Who Worked at the Düsseldorf Zoo Before Coming Back to Athens and Buying His Own Taxi

"The story I'm going to tell you will seem like a fairy tale. At one time, I was working as a guard at the zoo. There were all kinds of animals there. But Rosa, the young tiger, was different. Born of a tiger-mother and a tiger-father, she began very early to feel stifled by the prison in which she was forced to live. It seems that memories of the freedom of the jungle, transmitted to her genetically through her chromosomes, made her nostalgic for open spaces, the same way babies born at sea will grow up nostalgic for it. From the moment she became aware of her surroundings, in the same cell as her parents, she would involuntarily watch their courting games, which were hindered by lack of space. She would see her tiger-father's desire to run and throw himself on her tiger-mother, but he was unable to in the narrow cage. She would see her tiger-mother's desire to growl with pleasure, but she was unable to because the animals in the neighboring cages would make fun of her, imitating her cries. As for Rosa, the little tiger, she had always wanted to run away—to the jungle where her ancestors had lived happily in the wild—to find the freedom she had in her blood.

"Our attempts to mate her with a young tiger at the zoo failed miserably. Seeing her always sad and listless, yet of unrivaled beauty, the director of the zoo decided to give her to a circus. Even though she would remain in a cage, she would lead a completely different life, moving from place to place, country to country, train to train, camp to camp. And perhaps someday, during a tour in Africa, I thought to myself, she might manage to escape.

"That was how I ended up losing Rosa, the little tiger, even though I loved her very much. After she went to the circus, I made sure to keep track of how she was getting along. In the beginning, Rosa didn't do very well at all. Then one day, a new animal tamer arrived, who they say took a strong dislike to her. He would beat her savagely.

"Initially, Rosa took this violence very badly. The animal tamer was the first who had ever dared go against her, fearlessly, even in the face of her fiercest roars. One time, she even tried to attack him from behind and tear him to pieces, but he, quick and supple like a wild cat, evaded her, they say, and then, throwing himself on her, managed to grab her and force open her mouth with his plierlike hands, then blow into her with such force that she almost suffocated. From that day on, Rosa blindly and fearfully obeyed his orders as if they were cracks of a whip. He would always start by looking her deep in the eye, which would make the tigress restless and troubled, something which, because she was a virgin, it seems she had never felt before.

"Rosa's love for the animal tamer was common knowledge among the people of the circus. Whenever he wasn't around, she would languish inside her cage and refuse to come out and do her numbers. The first time he went on leave, she went on a hunger strike. They kept her alive with injections. Then he returned, all tanned after a month by the sea, and Rosa came back to life.

"One night, they say, he went into her cage, coming out the following morning. Nobody knew what happened in there. But after that night, the tigress began turning into a human being. Little by little, she started becoming a woman. The circus employees were horrified each morning to see her changing shape. This transformation lasted a few weeks and was also observed by many doctors. It wasn't a change of sex. She had always been female. It was a change of species. At the end of one year, she was a full-fledged woman. All that remained of the old tigress were her nails, which she was unable to hide no matter how red she painted them, and that flame in her eyes that reflected her jungle origins.

"They were married and lived happily. The animal tamer taught her human speech, and in the street, at the market, everybody desired her: she was a real volcano. A sex bomb, as they say. Rumor had it that they kept her husband's old whip hanging on the wall above their bed, like a cocked antique rifle. She gave birth to two children, irrepressible and wild like tiger cubs.

"One day, I saw her shopping in Kuhenstrasse. As soon as she saw me she recognized me. She ran to me and hugged and kissed me. We reminisced about old times. I told her how happy I was about her transformation. She said she might stop by the zoo and see me one day, but that she was afraid of how she might react to the place where she had suffered in captivity. What can

I say, my good man? I was tempted. I wanted her like crazy. Everybody wanted her."

"And then what happened?" I asked, as I saw him staring into space, when he stopped at a red light.

"Ah, then, you don't want to know. A sad tale. One day, they found her husband dead of a snake bite at the circus, where he still worked as a veteran animal trainer. At that very moment, they say, sweet Rosa started to turn back into the tigress she once had been. At her husband's grave, her family and children looked on with amazement as she started to change, to grow smaller and longer, her black clothes becoming fur, her hands dropping to touch the ground, her nails sinking into the soil of the tomb. She became a quadruped again.

"The doctors came running, and so did the TV cameras. I saw her that evening on the news: she was a regular tigress. When the camera zeroed in on her face, I saw the figure of the animal trainer reflected deep within her gaze. He was still alive in those green eyes, standing upright with his whip in the air, just like when he used to order her to jump through the flaming hoop. The same way they say it happens with the old, useless TV cameras, on whose cylindrical mirror there remains, indelibly etched, the last shot the camera took before being put away somewhere, never to be used again." The taxi driver stopped talking, moved by the memory of his story.

"But tell me," I asked, "have you regretted coming back to Greece?"

"Have I ever!" he said. "At least in Düsseldorf, animals are kept in cages. Here, they roam around the streets free, on wheels."

stories of taxi drivers

-4-
Where for Different Reasons,
Another Immigrant Taxi Driver Regrets
Returning to Greece

He saw them coming from a distance, like two scarecrows. His burned property still smelled of smoke. The few tufts of green that had survived on the trees seemed absurd reminders of what had once been there. "Why were they the only ones to survive?" he asked himself. "Why?" He wanted to climb up and chop them off.

He appeared immersed in his sorrow. "So, Mr. Irineos, where were you when the fire started?"

"Are you still asking about that? I was at my beehives. They're gone now too. Nothing but ashes." He seemed not to want to talk to them. Entrenched in his bitterness, he became completely inscrutable. "If only the planes had arrived sooner. . . ." was all he said. "They couldn't get here. The wind was blowing like the devil."

In the village, they were burying the victims. He would have gone, but he was afraid they'd lynch him. They were wrong to suspect him. He would have to leave now, he had lost everything; he would sell the taxi and go back to Canada. That's where he would leave his bones. In a foreign land, a foreign continent. Greece was a heartless mother, always chasing you away.

"The almond trees won't flower next year," he said.

"On your way back from your beehives, you didn't see anything, you didn't notice anyone?"

"The workers were coming back from the mines."

"There are no mines anymore. You're thinking of the years before you emigrated. All the workers left the island, just like you. And just like you, they all came back loaded with dough." (The truth is, he had come back last. He had taken too long, far too long. He hadn't had time to build like the others.)

The two periods of his life began to merge in his mind: first was the social despair. And now, in full bloom, ruination by fire. Always, albeit for different reasons, the same disaster. "There were cars going by. With boats in tow, and caravans. How would I know?"

"Is there something or someone you could indicate to us?"

"The donkey crapped and its steamy dung set fire to the dry pine needles," he said finally. Impenetrable, immured in his silence. "Here," he said, extending his hands. "Handcuff me if I'm a suspect. Don't torture me anymore with questions." The two visitors, the police sergeant and the representative of the court, were forced to leave.

His property had become a vacant plot full of ashes. The seagulls had turned grey from the smoke. In the dry stream bed, the partridges no longer cackled.

Old legislation is like an old hat: it does not fit well on the head of a man who evolved according to technology. So it was that Irineos (who was telling me this story while driving cautiously through the jungle of the city) could not get into his head the reason he couldn't build on his own property. "Because it's designated a wooded area," he told me. "What does this mean, designated a wooded area?" he asked the officials. He had lost touch with the way things were in his country, which he left when just a young man, in 1955, with great difficulty, because he belonged to the left, and even then he was able to leave only thanks to the tricks and bribes of a travel agent who managed to get him a passport. ("And don't you ever come back," the agent had said, "or I'm done for.")

"A wooded area," they explained at the local office of the Forestry Department, "means it has pine trees, and trees are protected by law."

"If there weren't any pine trees, would I be able to build?" Irineos asked the first time he spoke with the forest ranger, who, like most civil servants, seemed to enjoy the confusion of the man who had become a stranger in his own country.

"Only if it were rocky, arid ground. Even if there were only brush, you still wouldn't be able to build."

At first, the taxi driver's story went, he had gone to Belgium, where he worked for five years as a coal miner. But when the dust started bothering his lungs, he went to Vancouver, Canada, where he started off working in a car factory, and then he opened his first used car lot, which was soon followed by a second and then a third. Business was going well; he married Eulalia, a woman from his village, the daughter of immigrants; he had children, he put them through college, he married them off. But his dream—*because there are dreams like Christmas trees, covered in ornaments, in the middle of town squares, trees that make you daydream when you look at them, that support our existence, dreams that are enlarged under the magnifying glass of sleep and of being in a foreign land*—was one day to return to his village, to his island, and to build, upon the land of his forefathers, a home, a cottage for he and his wife, a sweet little cabin in which to rest their weary bones. He would have his rowboat, his beehives, and his goats; and friends from Vancouver could come and visit.

"If only you could thin the trees out on the sly," was the advice of an engineer, a fine young man who took pity on him. "Perhaps then you would be able to get a construction permit. Of course, if you had the right connections, that wouldn't hurt either."

The seed began to germinate in his head. And one night, he secretly cut down several pine trees with a chainsaw. But it seems that a fellow villager squealed on him, impelled by one of those ancient, inextinguishable hatreds that one finds in villages. So not only did Irineos not get the construction permit, but the Forestry Department sued him for destroying trees.

"You don't have to continue, I get the picture," I said, for I could see he was getting upset.

But Irineos wanted to tell me all about it. I was a dream specialist and a journalist; to whom else would he tell his story, if not to me?

So he got mixed up in the Greek court system, where one needs to be a magician to get one's rights vindicated. Accustomed to the Canadian way of life, in which bureaucracy is unknown, in which people aren't always trying to poke each other's eyes out, and in which everything—work, licenses, permits—obeys other, faster rhythms of development, his dream to build fossilized. But the idea of setting fire to the place never once dawned on him.

That summer, the whole of Greece had been in flames.

"I know," I said, "I was here."

Everywhere, during July and August, fires were breaking out as if nature were protesting the pitiless drought of the sky. Fires that would turn entire areas to ashes were started on the eve of

stories of taxi drivers

the day when strong winds were expected, or on the day itself. Only a fire would get him out of his dead end, Irineos thought to himself, as he watched the news on TV

"But it was only an idea, mind you, because I was so exasperated."

And, indeed, there was such a fire on the island that August. Violent, relentless, infernal. It destroyed everything, including his land. It burned down their prefabricated house; he and his wife barely made it. The fire cost lives, since in their effort to put it out, both locals and foreigners fought with great determination. The wind was blowing like the devil. Irineos and his fellow villagers found themselves in their rowboats out at sea, watching the savage spectacle with mixed emotions. But the others kept glancing over at him suspiciously, because he was unable to conceal in his face, illuminated by the reflections of the fire, an absurd air of satisfaction.

"Where were you yesterday afternoon, Irineos?" the police sergeant asked him first thing in the morning, while they could still smell the horrible odor of burned wood. By an unfortunate coincidence, Irineos had been at his beehives, the area from which the fire had started, near Kynira. It seems he had been overheard at the cafe, saying that only if he burned the wretched plot of land would he be able to build on it.

"I'm not the one who set the fire, Officer. It was the wind that brought it all the way here; and nobody knows which way the wind is going to blow."

Others had lost their goats, their sheep, their fortunes. Mitsoras, who was going to marry off his daughter on the fifteenth of August and was offering seven hundred lambs as a dowry, didn't have a single animal left. Aunt Lissava, who looked after the chapel as if it were her own, found only the stone walls and the belfry left. Flames had devoured the sculpted wood icon. And the son of the resistance fighter had burned to death fighting the fire. Because the flames danced around like Salome. You didn't know where they'd pop up next. And that brave young man had found himself wrapped in their veils without realizing it. He had believed in a new Greece.

Thus, it was not long before Irineos found himself in court again, since he didn't have an alibi. Or rather, his alibi placed him in the very spot where the fire had started that afternoon. And that was incriminating evidence.

"As to who the arsonist was, we have no knowledge," he told me, as he had told the court. "We can't know who it is. It might have been one person, or it might have been many. Then again it might not have been anyone."

"How can that be?" the court asked.

"I'll tell you how," he answered. "There exists within nature the elements of its entropy, as in thermodynamics. It's the famous second law. That's how trees catch fire on their own and burn up."

"Yes, but, as a court of law, we have to examine every possibility. That's what we're paid for. Whatever you might say, the fire was started by certain people who wanted it. Who could those people have been on that Thursday, the day of the fire?"

"First of all, there were two yachts moored in the natural port of Kynira. There were tourists who had set up camp on the beach, under the pine trees.

"The tourists disappeared like birds at the sound of a gunshot, frightened from the forked branches of trees, the whole flock taking to the air and darkening the sky as they flew off elsewhere. As for the yachts . . . "

This seemed to be a cue for the rest of the members of the court to offer their own candidates. "There were a couple of shepherds, Lazos and Sotiris, and the refugees at the settlement of Ano Karya."

"And let's not forget the wandering monk, with his knapsack over his shoulder, telling everyone 'Repent! The time is nigh! The fire will burn you all!'"

"He disappeared. Either in the flames, or he returned across to Mount Áthos. In any case, the priest pronounced an anathema on him in church, because the monk was a heretic. But the priest's beard didn't escape from the fire either. He had to shave it off, and now he looks like a Catholic priest."

"So then the monk is also a suspect?"

"Everyone is a suspect, I admit it. But Irineos is the prime suspect. The fire coincided with his third and last visit to the Forestry Department, where he was given the final 'no' by the forest ranger, and which he left muttering dark threats."

"Count him in. But you and me, too. You've put on weight recently."

"I've been overeating. I gave up smoking, so now I'm overeating. And do you know why I gave up smoking?"

"Because you're less of a suspect if you don't smoke."

"Exactly."

The great culprit had to be found and hung in the village square. "Who had reason to set the fire?"

"The Israelis, using the Turks as intermediaries. Everyone knows their secret services collaborate."

"Before examining the macrocosm, let us examine the microcosm. Before we look outside, let us look inside ourselves."

"The arsonist is wandering around among us, a free man," said the mayor of the village, who wanted to keep his title at the next election.

Irineos was finally acquitted, but meanwhile he had become very embittered. How vile of them to suspect him, instead of each one of them looking inside their own souls to find the culprit. And so he started thinking of emigrating for a second time, in his old age. He would sell the taxi and go back to Vancouver. His homeland had hurt him again. The first time was when it wouldn't let him leave because he belonged to the left. And now again . . .

"I only wept for the son of the resistance fighter," he said. "His father and I started off together, working in the coal mines in Charleroi. He stayed there, married a Belgian woman. His son had come back two years ago. He was the first and the finest young man in the village. Along with the other young people he founded the cultural center and the popular art museum. He never stopped working for the good of his country. And, because of our family connection, I was the one who was chosen to notify his father. But I didn't know if he would want him buried here or there. Meanwhile nobody would take charge of the body. The hospital would only accept someone who was alive. 'What if they're dying?' I asked. 'In that case, yes. But not dead.' He was beginning to smell. The heat was unbearable. There was no cold storage area available. I took him to Kavála. . . ." Indignation filled the smoke-stained breast. The struggle, the sacred struggle for justice and the equal distribution of wealth. *"Where are you youth, you who predicted I would become another?"*

"What do you mean *another?"* I asked.

"That verse of Varnalis's became a reality for me: I changed my name in Canada. Nobody could pronounce it there. Since in Greek it means *pacific,* I changed it to Pacifico."

Doña Rosita
and
Don Pacifico

Doña Rosita is a vast woman. Because she encompasses the dream. That is to say damp expanses, planted with trees, with gardens where birds can live. Doña Rosita embroiders. An embroidery into which she passes all the uncomplicated thread of her love. She has eyes that call you to become a seafarer, to explore it all, right and left, right side up and upside-down. Doña Rosita is irrigated by tributary dreams. Since, as we already said, dreams constitute the center of our existence, Doña Rosita materializes dreams, as when she bends down to collect autumn leaves with which she composes large tableaux. She has them framed at her neighborhood frame shop. Or when she catches birds' cries, passes them through her, and then exhales them in the forms of song. Snail people, suspended from their windows, come out of their shells to listen to her.

Doña Rosita is a vast woman. She also has a vast wardrobe. The two rows of dresses that hang in it are not enough for her. She has a rich collection of outfits of all kinds and she changes them with the frequency of dreams. Never has Don Pacifico seen her wear the same dress twice. "I'm empty, empty," he cries to her. "Empty."

"Fill yourself with water. Fill yourself with dream," replies Doña Rosita.

"But what will the water reflect? An empty sky?"

"No, it will reflect my face."

Doña Rosita's face is made from the soft dough that fritter dreams are made of, *because there are fritter dreams as there are napoleon dreams, and chocolate cake, and cheesecake, and angel food cake, and Black Forest cake dreams; half-eaten and half-baked dreams; dreams with almonds, with walnut and cinnamon filling, covered in syrup; chocolate eclair and caramel cream dreams, lollipop dreams, ice cream dreams—Baskin-Robbins, Ben and Jerry's, strawberry sorbet, lemon and lime sorbet—sugar cone and popsicle dreams, boutique, batik, and Calvin Klein or cotton candy dreams.* Doña Rosita is a vast woman. And Don Pacifico is too narrow to accommodate her entirety.

But if Doña Rosita is the dream, then Don Pacifico is the implied arsonist. Even though he himself never set the fire that logically he could have set, considering his lack of logic. (The suspicion that the arsonist was a Jew caught on easily among the mistrustful islanders.)

By burning the hinterland and transforming it from a wooded expanse into a barren wasteland, they reasoned, he could then build his home. "As an arsonist, I bear my guilt in full. As a builder, I pass this guilt through the building materials, the plasterboard and fiberglass that are words."

On the horizon of Doña Rosita, mistakes are marked in the words she makes out of clouds. When Don Pacifico burned down one of her wooded areas, Doña Rosita (the land of Doña Rosita) grew poorer by a few acres, but she had boundless expanses inside her to withstand the devastation of his fire. She was annoyed that he had filled her sky with smoke, but a different sun shone down upon her undamaged expanses the following day.

"Why did I do it?" Don Pacifico asks himself. "Or could it be that I didn't do it? Could it be that the fire started by itself and that I had nothing to do with it? Could it be that the joy I draw from this cleared land, where I am finally able to build with words, is a guilty joy, drawn from the Talmudic scriptures and the Old Testament, while I am anything but guilty?

"It hadn't rained since April. And then in August, that terrible month (I always hated August), the pine needles caught fire by themselves, those pine needles whose presence burned us, pricked us, and aroused our senses without us being able to resist them, because they would drag us along every day into a conflagration, after which we never knew where to hide the ash and cinders. Could it be that because they were not allowed to burn Judas in effigy, Christian fanatics and fifth-column activists set fire to the entire land of Judea? No, it is not me who is guilty."

-2-

Doña Rosita has overcome her crisis, and Don Pacifico is leading her at a steady pace where he chooses to go. One, two pictures come to her mind: it was midday, on a hill overlooking the sea. The pine trees were small, gnawed by the salt. On the ground, pine needles. Inside her, a dense heat, with no outlet, made her want him very much. . . . Now he is reviving that scene for her. He is talking to her of dry brushwood, of pine needles, of the burning of the sun, of her own burning. And of his burning. He takes her by the hand. He leads her to a vestibule with heavy red drapes. She identifies with the picture in her mind. She gives herself to him. It all happens in the mind. He covers the weakness of his body with the power of the word. He dominates her. He takes her there where she becomes a sea, a lilac, a flower, a vision, a tree.

He leads her and she lets herself be led because she loves him. Because she trusts him. Because she admires him. Because she respects him. Because she wants him, she wants them to be together, to share the joys and sorrows. She doesn't care whether he'll be rich or poor. As long as she sings and he builds. And she shall sing and he shall build when they are together. That's for certain. But that's not the point. That's not where the problem lies.

So he leads her down the path on the roller skates of his mind. With his mind, he does with her whatever he wants. And she wants him to do with her whatever he wants. She lets herself go. He describes scenes to her: he sees her, he says, naked on a road in the midday sun. He waits for her, hidden among the jasmine. She's coming, she's approaching. He sees her having difficulty; an evil neighbor came to her window and gave her the evil eye, he tells her. Yes, he sees her coming, she's getting closer, he's among the jasmine. The jasmine calls to her. She falls finally, naked, into his arms.

The little girl she becomes in his arms rejoices in love, she proclaims it and shouts it out. She likes to hear her own cries. The poor vulnerable girl feels protected in his arms. She believes that he loves her. This love reinforces her faith. And her faith reinforces her love. Should one of these two supports break, she will come tumbling down. And he doesn't want her to come tumbling down, does he?

She hurts him. He hurts her. That's what she says. What she believes. She is happy. Her entire body overflows with joy. It is a tortured body, he should never forget that. Often, she wants him more than her body can stand.

"I'm strong," she says. "I'll survive separating from you." But she only says that when she's angry. When the ancient anger deflates, she feels vulnerable, helpless. "I'm helpless," she says, "because, as you yourself say, I haven't two faces, but only one. I've abandoned myself completely to love. To my love for you. And I love the whole world too. I love everything in the world. You are the only one I ever let into my solitude. To pillage all that I kept, hermetically, for myself. Now there isn't a place inside me that isn't also yours. I want to share everything with you."

This young woman that he leads with a sure hand along the path of joy, he also loves. Because she is tender and good and joyous and pure. He tries to instill evil in her, just to give her a taste of bitterness, not to make her truly bitter, but she resists him. Her space is marked out with clear borders. There's nothing mixed up inside her head. She wants love. And love is both of them together, predestined to meet by God, or whatever exists beyond them, because there is a force greater than themselves.

A million attempts to seize her castle, to undermine it, have failed. He tries to put a worm in her that will eat away at her, making the fruit rot. It's impossible. The ripened fruit is offered to him, that and none other.

She gives him the gift of her sweetness, and he grabs it greedily and keeps it in his safe. Why? Deprived of sweetness all his life, he craves it. The sweetness of the other. For this he has trained her to walk in her sweetness. By now the path is taken without difficulty. One and two. The sweet road strewn with the honeys

Doña Rosita and Don Pacifico

of the world. Honey everywhere. Sweetness everywhere. Everywhere pleasure. Joy. He rejoices. He rejoices.

He leads her. He possesses her. Like a marvel-of-Peru, her face opens and closes according to his mood. Oriented toward his sun, she turns like a sunflower. Her gaze follows him as soon as they part. It annoys him to have her gaze follow him everywhere. But there's nothing she can do. A liquid, like mercury in a thermometer, attaches her to him. As soon as he touches her, her temperature rises. As soon as he leaves her, it drops. Her needle moves, like a magnet, toward his north. He draws her to him; she can't say what it is exactly that attracts her. She's never known such a pull. This is the first time. She tells him so. That "first time" makes him giddy. As he has never deflowered a girl before, "the first time" is like a balm for him. He keeps asking her: "Is it true?"

"I don't know how to lie the way you do," she answers.

He lies due to the excessive secretion of his imagination. She is more grounded. She functions differently. Everything comes to her from below, rising from the earth. She is a tree with deep roots into the soil of the centuries. With him, it's as if his roots are in the sky. He comes downward. This is how they were paired, by intertwining their branches, they both believe.

He leads her. He teaches her words she doesn't know, which, by repetition, become familiar, sweet. As far as she knows he doesn't say them to other women. Now she knows, she tells him, that he's faithful to her. That he hasn't another. Because he doesn't need to. He has found in her, he tells her, and she believes him (it would be terrible if she did not!), the woman who encompasses all women. She herself becomes, is, so different. She changes face, skin, hair. He tells her so and he believes it himself. And she too believes him. It intoxicates her. His tongue in her ear, his voice in the shell of her ear, envelops her in a cloud. She needs this cloud so she can take off. And with him she takes off. She travels. She tells him: "With you I take my most beautiful journeys."

The landing is always a success. Always dangerous, like every landing, but never an accident. They're both proud of this. Touchdown is always good, both on land and on water. The passengers always applaud. He's a good pilot during their journeys. He flies her well. Air turbulence, whenever there is any, obeys the laws of the atmosphere. Before, he loved trains. Now, he refuses to travel without his personal airplane. He leads her. Sometimes to a field of daisies. Sometimes to a stone terrace, bleached white in the midday sun. Sometimes to the glistening sea. Sometimes to the jasmine garden. Sometimes to the hill covered with pine needles. He takes her by the hand. And she gives herself to him. He asks that she give herself. As a condition of their relationship.

And the days go by. The weeks go by. And the Easter of the massacre is constantly postponed. She waits, like a good little sheep. But the confidence she gains each day helps her cement a foundation. It's fundamental. She tells him so. Before, he used to tell her stories about other women. Now he's cut down considerably. She feels as if she is him. The two have become one, a curious union. She is interested in Siamese twins who never separate. He asks her about her twin sister.

Her world is infinite. She experiences infinity. And each day is a nail that fastens the blue of the sky to the frame of her horizon. Her knowledge is deeper than knowledge, because it encompasses the fall of man. They have said everything; all the harsh,

Doña Rosita and Don Pacifico

near-cynical words he has said to her. They have explained everything. What she wants. What he's after. At times, she's called him every name in the book. Put all the world's curses on him. They didn't work. Nothing works in the realm of the word. The depth lies elsewhere. In this elsewhere, it's something else that counts. What is it? Every popular song contains a truth about love. In every verse hides a life story. That's why people love songs. Because they express their feelings. "There are thousands, millions of people like us," she tells him. "Write."

He is her poet. That is the only way she will accept him. She wants poetry. She wants expression. Her own porno video is the "Song of the Songs."

He leads her steadily along a road. Abyss Street. Number 0. For Doña Rosita it's a new life. She gathers twig after twig, wherever she finds them, and builds her nest. For Don Pacifico, these are weights hanging from his wings. Roaming all day around the wild edges of word, he hunts, like his grandfather before him, for rock partridges, will-o'-the-wisps. Days go by, time goes by. On television, the disasters continue. First in Colombia, where the dormant volcano erupts, causing twenty thousand deaths; then the earthquake in Mexico City, soon replaced by a concert to benefit the victims. Just like for the children in Ethiopia or for all of Africa.

"It's not necessarily bad," she says.

"No, it's not. They're raising money for charity. And that's good."

And yet there is, deep down, a certain deception. Deep down, a shipwreck is replaced by a floating stage upon which famous stars sing. At the site of the shipwreck, of course. For the victims of the shipwreck. But the shipwreck does not exist. Only entertainment exists.

Days go by. Time goes by. The leaves fall from the trees. But they grow back. Governments fall, others take their place. The price of gasoline goes up and back down.

"We're used to watching scenes from Dachau while calmly eating our macaroni and cheese."

"The image, in contrast to active memory, has a debilitating quality about it."

"What's the latest on Nicaragua, anyway?"

"It's been a while since they gave us any news on the Iran-Iraq war."

A coup d'état in some African country awakens that country from the lethargy of the map, only to let it sink back again into the nonexistence of the white world, the white news, the white madness. Because it will be whites who will meet with whites in Geneva to agree, if in fact they do agree, on nuclear arms. Those with black, yellow, and brown skins are out of the game. "White *gentlemen*," she adds. "Because the white ladies aren't going to agree on anything of the sort. They will visit museums or fine clothing stores, or they will attend a charity ball."

"Whites have done a good job of dividing the world into capitalists and communists."

Time goes by. Days go by. The seasons change their shirts, one after the other. He persists in not changing his. He likes grime. He feels more comfortable in filth. As for her, she likes order; she's obsessive about cleanliness. Days go by. Time goes by. November is a very sweet month.

Doña Rosita and Don Pacifico

He smokes. Before he even looks for it, his lighter is in his hand. Before he even has time to desire something, she gives it to him, having guessed it. They have everything. But something is missing from their relationship. What could it be? "It's like last night at the theater," she says. "From my seat, I could only see half the stage. When the singers sang on the part of the stage that I could see, everything was fine. But when the action took them over to what was for me the dark side of the moon, I could only hear their voices. That was agony. I had to imagine them. And however much I bent down, I was still in a disadvantageous position. From that box, with those two lesbians in front of me who would not let me squeeze into the front row, I couldn't enjoy the show fully. I felt as if half of me was also missing. It was as if my destiny was showing me, at that moment, my situation. Because that's how I am, my darling, without you. A half. With the thirst of the whole. Listening to the voices and imagining the movements. With two lesbians lying in wait like dogs. Besides, if one should bend over too much, throwing up is just a matter of time."

Yes, what was missing was perspective, that which keeps people alive. Without it, even the most permanent things in life seem temporary. The best things become bad. The most bearable become unbearable.

She leads him. She opens up horizons for him. She helps him understand himself. Who he is. What he wants out of life. He writes and thinks of her in her pensive moods. He writes: "The word belongs half to him who speaks it and half to him who hears it" (Montaigne). "Every door has its nail" (popular proverb).

But how to find the halfway point, the golden rule of cohabitation? How not to encroach upon each other's land? When a woman, by nature, wants to share everything with the man she loves, and a man, by nature, when he loves a woman, wants to share everything with his friends? Or with other women whom he doesn't love? When the home is the woman's natural environment, and everything outside the home (the ballpark, the bar) is the man's natural environment? When the void seeks to be filled, because the void does not accept itself, and woman has such a void, by nature (Bellotti), while man has a protuberance that can fill the void?

He builds guns, cannons, rockets, all phallic extensions of this protuberance. While woman lives surrounded by holes: drains, wells, bidets, buttonholes. The void dresses up in fine clothes to cover itself. But it's always lying in wait, gaping, under the clothes. Thus the problem remains. And the soul is the void within the void. That's where it's based. And it gives off a foul odor when nothing fills it. By contrast it is calmed when something fills it. What would be the reason for having doors if nobody came in through them? (Windows are no more than breasts. They can only be aroused.) A tomb is a door that closes because nobody can go through it. However, things become more complicated from the moment that man himself realizes that he is half woman, since at the base of his penis lies the canceled female sex.

Suddenly, he is attracted to the shag carpet, to its provocative, fiery red. He tells her of a secret source of pleasure, at the root of his tree. If she presses down there . . . It is the remnant of the female, which, when gender was determined in his mother's womb, decided to become male. That is where the roots of his pleasure lie. She presses down on it. And then he, sweetly, upon this red shag carpet, explodes like an overripe pomegranate.

Doña Rosita and Don Pacifico

He leads her along paths, not at all certain at first, to the source of her ancient joy, where as a little girl, an adolescent, she tasted that joy alone, in her lonely room, in her lonely bed. And as he leads her, as they trace together the paths, the musical roads of pleasure, she attaches herself to him, she becomes a barnacle on him, a limpet on his rock. Any attempt to unhook her has the opposite result: she hangs on even tighter. The limpet begins to spread and gradually covers the entire rock. By then, the rock has taken on the limpet's shape, like a Chinese hat.

"Weaning is impossible. We have reached the point beyond which there can be no separation," he writes.

-3-

He leads her, he takes her into depths that even she doesn't know, into unexplored regions, but she likes sinking with him, tied to him, their bodies tightly bound, with their exchangeable temperatures, where the current circulates, comes around again, where the force leaves her to gather in him and pass back into her, two bodies like suction cups, one upon the other, four absorbent hands, his on her chest and the nape of her neck, there where all the pathways of the nerves converge to pass through, and he with his hand, controlling the tollgate of the nerves, as if he dominated them; and she is quiet and dominated, because her head has the pedestal of his hand to lean on, her beautiful head, as he says and she knows it, while with her hands she massages his back, feeling the bones, his silken skin; bound this way, one on top of the other, he carries her with him to the tunnel, so he can bring her out into the light on the other side, so they can keep going, passing through another tunnel, another light, until a field appears before her, the field of daisies from her childhood years, where she becomes a child again, during the time she snuck out of the shack without her mother knowing, ran through the daisies to meet her lover and lie down with him on the sweet-smelling soil among the daisies that would break their fingers on her, just as she is now breaking hers on his back, until little by little her hands abandon him, becoming wings, or at any rate trying to become wings, because she wants to fly now, or rather she is flying, carrying under her back, stuck to her, the red shag carpet; he sees her hand quivering like a wing and he lets his hand take hers, their fingers intertwined, without rings that hurt; they are now in ecstasy, they move, they fly together, and instead of soaring, he takes her lower and lower, to a premythical, forgotten time, where, as a little girl, she would see around her an alien, treacherous world, lying in wait for her, tempted by her beauty, but now she does not fear it because he's there, and in this inverted position, her eyes, their eyes, fixed on one another, communicating almost desperately, their panting, and time is folded over, like a crust, a pastry crust that envelops her, like the cream puffs her grandmother used to make and bake in the oven just as she now, as if burning up with a fever, is baked with him in ovens, crematoriums, from which he escaped but to which she offers herself in a holocaust, and she gives herself to him and he gives himself to her entirely; she is in a deep, hidden corner, from where as a little girl she now sees herself becoming an adult, for what she was always waiting for, love without terms, without limitations, without borders, without stopwatches or dos and don'ts,

Doña Rosita and Don Pacifico

the kind of love that nourishes you and makes you beautiful in your own eyes, giving him everything that is she, freely, selflessly, generously, while he whispers sweet words in her ear: "I love you, I'll always love you, I want you," sees her opening the bolt to where she keeps her treasures: "Take them," she says, "take them all," and relieved that she has given him everything without asking for anything in return, she reaches, finally, her fulfillment.

He leads her, takes her down, dark and brilliant goddess of another world, supine like the dead Ophelia, he holds her tightly for fear that she might fall, but their descent is slow as coins sinking into blond water, and the wider they are, the more they dance as they sink through deeper and deeper layers, through beds that become clear, sparkling lakes, beds that are different each time, in other rooms, in other countries, some narrow and some shady, with springs that are revolutionary or revolutionized, at time with strained nerves or orthopedic boards, but everywhere, no matter what the latitude or longitude of the country, it is imperative, in order that she may be lulled, that the light be turned down low at night—the light irritates her eyes, just as during the day, dust irritates her throat—and she is in this position, on her back, when he comes and plops himself down, like a prince, on the other pan of her balance, which, balanced with great precision on the scales of the sensitivity, begins to sink, moving through the successive layers of water that dry up or rise, and it's the same thing, air and water, consubstantial, up and down, one and the same path, and as he bends down to embrace her, he resembles those who climb up telephone poles with safety hooks around them, or climb down, listening to the mystical hum, where it's coming from or where it's going to, it's the same thing, a distant homeland, lost in flames, that she never knew other than through the stories of her dear grandmother, whom she would ask, when she was little, in order to find her roots, which would lead her to other roots of another life, the one she had lived before she was born, while with the horizon of his body on top of her, a horizon she loved, she is bound to the shape of his tenderness, always in front of her, a few centimeters away from her mouth; she is confident that she will not be startled, that she will not fall, that she will never be left hanging in the air, and indeed she has not, during these two years that they have always been coming together, not like the first time (then they had hardly come together at all, they were still strangers), but like the times after that, as the force of their bond grew, and, feeling secure in his embrace, protected, she would tell him that, liberated, she could fly very high or reach great depths, which was the same thing, it meant the same, since they were in a place with no pressure other than that of sweet juices (one cannot tell whether they come from the earth and climb up to the tips of the branches, or if they come down from there to be spilled and lost in the soil, because the tips of the branches suck up the light of the sky), and that is why, if she can't see his eyes, it is almost impossible for her to find the sources, which were, up until now, unknown to her, the joys that have laid hidden inside her like ores, waiting all their lives for this moment, for him to mine them.

And he, he watches over her, he is intoxicated without getting dizzy from her fall or her ascent, like a bird clutching his prey in his claws for fear he might lose it before he reaches his nest where he can tear it to pieces at his leisure; he understands by her glance, that flashes and clouds, by the fog that comes upon

Doña Rosita and Don Pacifico

it like a gentle mist in the splendor of the morning; he understands by her breath, by her mouth that seeks his own, by her
little tongue, at once sensual and impertinent, licking his palate;
he understands what stage she's going through, so then, bending
down, he plants landing kisses, hand grenades, with his teeth at
the root of her neck, on the nerve of the "Song of Songs," on her
neck, necklaces of loving teeth marks, and higher up still, in her
hair, on the electrified skin of her skull, and in this way he
descends with her, he finds his own childhood memories that
never hit their target, hitting the dark womb of the earth, the
point of darkness from which life emerges, into which he disap-
pears only to rediscover himself intact, and there's something
about this baptism very much like the ceremony of Epiphany,
when the cross is thrown into the water, followed by the diver,
and they become, for an instant, cross and man, one and the same,
the symbol of the faith and the believer, while the bishops, standing on dry land, along with the ordinary people and the digni-
taries, applaud this union taking place in the water, by singing
beautiful hymns—in rooms that understand nothing, on beds
that can't feel, in countries that mean nothing—everywhere,
they're one and the same, the same submersion, the same anticipation, the same sweetness that will express itself afterwards, on
her peaceful face.

Clocks make unbearable hands turn. Bells toll. Airplanes
take off and land. It's nice when the fruit becomes like honey.
"The room becomes sweeter when you're near me."

Space, as an element necessary for a wider garment, when
one's clothes are tossed onto mentally deranged chairs, expands.
Space as time of joy. The joy of space makes time a tenant. "And

yet you have still not sung of love." Time, which is money for others, does not count for them. Money is for those who know how to make a profit, who know how to use it. For them, money is the dream.

She would sing arias for him, which, in the past, she had sung on stage; now she sang them only for him, and he enjoyed them, sole audience of a voice that once moved so many people. "When will she move those people again? Why does she no longer sing for them?" he asks himself, while she, searching for her voice, finds it growing increasingly stronger under the veils that almost suffocated her. "What is a voice," muses Don Pacifico, "as it passes under the guillotine? A guillotine can cut a throat, but it can't stop a song. Her voice could be a gold mine, and yet here I sit, despairing, struggling with words, while at my side this Pactolus keeps flowing, untapped."

But it is difficult to get a mechanism back in motion. Public relations count more than private ones. And that's where things get complicated. The ancient canals would have to be rediscovered for the babbling water of Doña Rosita to flow through them again and irrigate the thirsty plains. Wherever they turned their gaze, they could see that the new irrigation was functioning perfectly, but that something was missing from the impetus of the water that carries off leaves and soil in its eddies. The new technology of the irrigation canals was definitely irreproachable. At no point was there a leak, at no point was there the slightest malfunction. Perfectly designed and constructed, all parts converged toward the final goal, without leaves or soil to impede the flow of the water, which was itself well protected in reservoirs. And yet something was lacking in this whole system: that which used to make the plain intoxicating. Technology had, to a certain extent, wiped out the art of irrigating, the art of singing, and television, which reproduces the irrigation of the plain on small screens, gave all the peasants the opportunity to participate in the process of irrigation, but deprived them of the unique joy of only a certain number of them—and not all of them, as was now the case in their homes—being earwitnesses to the musical event, in a small room perhaps, but stripped of the technology that will inevitably weaken the torrent of a voice, the explosive presence of a personality whose errors are also inseparable parts of its makeup.

"We live in a time," reflected Don Pacifico, "where man is pitted against the perfection of his machines. And that turns him into a machine, depriving him of the possibility of remaining human. Since voices need microphones and transformers, since a computer will soon be able to produce an aria impeccably, where is that element that, owing to its particularities, humanizes great art?"

Henceforth everything obeyed an initial nucleus whose message was increasingly altered each time it was reproduced. From that moment on, no one much cared about the origin of all this: a human being, a cry, a pain, an effort. And even if they came to reproduce this singularity, so many other singularities would come long afterward to annihilate it that the average viewer, listener, or reader began more and more to resemble someone who, remote control in hand, jumps from one channel to another (among the fifty or so available), creating a new film of his own composition that impoverishes him instead of enriching him, because it is incoherent, shapeless, fragmented, a mosaic that won't hold together, and it is only in his sleep that he can, by renouncing everything, find his own truth, which is the dream, if indeed he dreams.

Because dreaming is our self-defense against the bombardment of counterinformation and updating that accomplishes nothing except to make us aware of the tragedies of the world upon which we are incapable of having the slightest effect, except by putting our hands in our pockets.

Because there are dreams that torture, on racks, there are dreams that are altars to the Thermidors of sleep, endless dreams made longer by expectation, guillotine dreams . . .

So she would have to start singing again. But how? How does one catch hold of threads that have been cut? Which one of all these threads that lie jumbled in your palm leads to the big hook? She worked alone, she prepared herself, she didn't seem hurried.

It was he who was in a hurry. He didn't know how difficult it is to sing. How the throat, this channel, this canal of the voice that brings forth the melody, can very easily become blocked and cancel itself out. He didn't know about the thousand and one threads that make up the embroidery of the voice on an ethereal canvas that then ceases to exist. With the exception of recordings, which immortalize it in its temporary and changeable eternity. He did not know that everything hangs upon one instant, is born and dies in this instant, in this instant where everything flows, where everything is but an instant. But for this instant to arrive the human being does not need the calm found in the eye of the cyclone, but the tranquillity of the ocean that is never disturbed by cyclones.

Because there are floating dreams, suspended, where everything walks on air, with no other prospect than to continue as such; dreams in which the present, the future, and the past all live in the imperfect and the present tenses, being imperfect, in the dream,

Doña Rosita and Don Pacifico

becomes horrifying, nightmarish; dreams that torture, on racks, in Thermidors of sleep, endless dreams made longer by expectation.

Doña Rosita is a vast woman. At last, we rediscover the breadth of Doña Rosita's soul. She has just returned from the audition, tired, but not exhausted as she had feared. Doña Rosita is deeply in love with Don Pacifico. All day long on days she doesn't see him, she makes him live in her mind. In her mind, his picture is indelible. Doña Rosita's hands communicate with a source of energy that lies outside herself. With these hands she kneads his body, she besieges it, she overwhelms it. He sleeps in her arms, almost against his will.

He feels that time is limited. There isn't enough of it for him. "The time it takes to eat, to sleep, to watch the news, to fall in love, to go out, to finish work, and, the most time-consuming of all, to write. How can one get all that done? It's raining. I like the rain. Rain is a blessing from God. The sun is a curse."

"It was four o'clock," she says, lying next to him with a turban on her head. Across from them, embracing dolls hang from the ceiling. "It was four o'clock and I had finished the housework; I was happy to have gotten through it quickly, and it was quiet inside the house and out. The construction next door had finished, and they had taken down the cranes, when it started to rain again. My relaxed state of mind and my bodily exhaustion predisposed me to receive the message of the rain, inside the empty shell of the house. It was against the large bay window, the one with no shutters, that the rain was making the greatest racket. The rain was supernatural. It was the first time I had experienced it this way in this country.

"I would like to be able to describe how I felt. I would like to speak the language that the rain used to speak to me. Because she told me many things. She came from somewhere else and acquired a voice as soon as she touched the glass. A polyphonic voice that I began to pay attention to, in order to catch her meaning. I knew there was something she wanted to tell me. And coming out of myself, I heard her. As she fell and spoke to me with her watery keys, little by little I grasped her secret melody. She spoke to me of elsewhere. There, beyond our bodies, exists energy, God, the almighty eternal cycle. Since I was alone, perhaps it was easier for me to understand what she was trying to tell me. She spoke to me of the impossibility of composing her substance into a form or a face. Indeed, I could see, as I watched her, an image, a body, trying to form itself on the windowpane but failing. The drops wouldn't stay on its vertical, slippery surface. They fell into the drainpipe; from there, following their own course outside the gutters, they would surely end up on the sidewalk, where the gaping mouths of the sewers would be unable to swallow them all up at once.

"Had I opened the window for her to come in, she would have formed puddles on the floor, and perhaps there I could have better studied her meaning, but this way, she was like a man speaking to me from behind the closed window of a departing train, while I, standing on the platform and unable to hear, can only see the desperate opening and closing of his mouth as it forms words I cannot interpret, being in a confused emotional state. I don't know if his absence will be long, short, or eternal. He could be saying, 'I love you, I'll always remember you, I'll miss you,' or

Doña Rosita and Don Pacifico

perhaps something much more mundane, like, 'Don't forget to pay the bill,' or, 'I forgot to turn off the switch.' It is only by his worried expression (since I can't hear his voice) that I can assume he is saying the opposite of what I fear. I can assume he's saying that he is coming back tomorrow or in a few days.

"And so it was with the rain, speaking to me in her own language, underlining key phrases with claps of thunder, as if to tell me that all this was of no importance, because, beyond our feelings there exists another reality, that of the higher world, home of the clouds that send us the rain and watch us all as if from an airplane, tiny lost insects, caught in the web of a spider city, with our small, insignificant problems that we make immense. It is only the torrent of the water that is immense, the pelting rain that accentuates our solitude.

"'Which isn't solitude, my dear rain,' I replied, 'when love is burning its logs in the fireplace. Nothing matters compared to the power of love that springs from within me and obliterates everything else. I exist to await his return, or to go and meet him, to touch him and he to touch me; I exist solely for the moments when we'll be together. Suddenly, nothing else matters. I am happy to love. I feel complete, fulfilled.'

"And as the rain tried to compose the face of the unknown God on my windowpane, talking to me in a solemn language, consumed by her passion, and at the same time angry that her liquid whips couldn't touch me, she was like a woman trying to tell me to protect myself from pain, from suffering. But love does not know what will dissolve it. Within love, the antibodies that would destroy it cannot develop, for, if they did, then love would cease to be what I call nourishing, or liberating, or capable of raising you to other heights, and would become anxiety, lamentation, pain. The inability of the rain to articulate its speech, to compose itself into an image, was due to its falling against the window I had opened inside me, protected by the crystal glass of my faith in love, which is a window open to the world that lets in the exultant light, the first sun, and turns out the rain's bogeyman with his claps of thunder. 'You're wasting your breath, my dear rain,' I said. 'As soon as you stop I'll hear the key to my door turn inside me, and it'll be him. You'll see, rain, you'll see. As long as you stop.' In fact, the rain stopped soon after. The greatest of silences fell over the city and the house."

Lying down, Doña Rosita was beginning to get groggy. (Her hair, covered in an oil that she would later wash out, was still wrapped in a turban.) She heard the key in the door, as if it were turning inside her, unlocking her own deepest, seven-times-sealed door. She heard his steps, then felt him lying down next to her, with his soaking head and cold feet: he had in fact come to meet her as soon as the rain stopped. She wept, so as to join her tears with the raindrops that still covered him. All of her became a trembling tree of tears. Then, having calmed down, she washed her hair with a dream shampoo, filling the bathtub with dream bubbles.

Obeying Doña Rosita's call, Don Pacifico had rushed, as soon as the rain stopped, to carry out his duty, which was to provide water for her mill, so that it might open its beautiful wings and the wind might rejoice in its blowing. *"A fine, virtuous mill, made by angels"* (Rilke). But the wind is diabolical. It blows furiously on Mykonos in the summer, just as it blew on his own island when the fires started, at the time when he was accused, indirectly, of arson. Which he had not committed. Only in his mind.

Doña Rosita and Don Pacifico

But suspicion regarding the Jew caught on easily among the mistrustful islanders. So, as things were going from bad to worse and no decisions were being made concerning matters of import, the horses wallowed, destined never to race.

Because there are turn-of-the-century dreams that face the great changes, like vultures beaten by Visigoth winds; syndicated and unionized dreams, condemned to be put into practice, and other, aphasic, unenlisted, internationalist dreams, like hymns with a musical refrain; leitmotiv dreams that recur; Saint Simonic, routine, railroad dreams, idle, centripetal, hard of hearing, vengeful dreams; centennial dreams, constructivist, domesticated or wild, with interest, interest-free, usurious, CIA, and KGB dreams, dreams that have escaped from prison guards; productive dreams that multiply for you, or dreams that, like governments that have lost their base and cadres, dissent from sleep; and others, hypnotic ones, that are outlined by the Grand Interpreter of Dreams; dreams of the Central Committee, of the Executive Office, of sections, of cells; dreams of extreme clandestinity and dreams that are reinstated at Party Conferences long after the dreamers have died; ivory dreams, aphrodisiac dreams that overflow like the froth on glasses of Bavarian beer; dreams without ornaments and others from Susa, made of heavy gold, of Darius and Parisatis; dreams that set fire to the aprons of young girls like magnifying glasses gathering the rays of the sun into one; outdated dreams, narrow dreams that limit the economy of the bed and dreams with sesame seeds that are sold, like jasmine, for a penny; dreams that are tear drenched, teargassed, tearjerkers.

His heart, torn in two this way, was unable to achieve balance. Outside, the rain completed his inner misery. "Since I have nothing left other than this light well through which I receive the tenants' garbage, in order to acquire a plot of land to build on I have to burn the land I inherited. I have to set fire to the forest to make a dreamport where flying words (my grandfather's pheasants and my aphasia) will finally be able to land."

With a mind as sharp as a razor, he shaves the beards off his dreams, and finds himself with naked cheek, scarred, face to face with the grooves of his pain. They both sink into a gigantic sleep. And while prudent people cook before they get hungry, they, lost in a hunger that sometimes reached its peak, gnawed, for lack of anything else to eat, at their very flesh. The brain, that great invalid, was not programming the questions correctly. Thus, they were called upon to give answers to erroneous questions, and the words of the oracle kept coming out wrong. Meanwhile the money was running out.

In any case, a writer's job is difficult. But her job was even more difficult. "Human beings can live without the word, but not without music. Music is the most profound form of human expression." And as he watched her, she seemed like a huge, beautiful bird whose wing had once been broken. It would be difficult for the bird to rise again, to take to the sky. And yet it would. Every door has its nail, but every nail opens a hole when you pull it out, what the Christians call the *eye of Judas,* through which you can see who's knocking at your door. If it's not the north wind. And so, climbing up high, he saw down below his beloved city with its irregular development and violated town planning. "This city is without a heart," he thought to himself. "Somebody ought to give it a transplant."

Doña Rosita and Don Pacifico

the white bear

*"The idea of a novel cut me like a knife. . . . Mentally,
I was killing a bear."*

Yiannis Skaribas, *Figaro's Solo*

How a White Bear Ended Up in Athens

The white bear was wandering around the streets of Athens, searching for its lost master.

Who is this white bear? Who is its lost master? That is the topic of our story today.

But let's start with some background information. Which Athens was it wandering around? What did Athens of that period look like? That period of crisis, of inflation, of renewed devaluation.

Do economic terms, terms that are detached from the action and the character of its heroes, have their place in a story? What is the difference between the myth and the mythified?

All questions that demand an answer. But we, readers, are not about to mythologize. We are enlisted in the struggle for a better tomorrow for the world and for ourselves, we are fighting for better days to come. And they are bound to come, there's no doubt about that. All bodes well in this better-than-all-possible worlds.

But before we even start, we have to obey a narrative convention that wants the bear to be of neutral gender, because since childhood we are used to referring to a bear as "it," unless it is specified as a Papa or a Mama bear. In any case, we have no other choice but to work with the materials available. And these materials are, for the most part, determined by chance.

Let us not try to make head or tail of something that has neither. If we had an organized life, a timetable, a position that gave us precise authorities, whether constitutionally guaranteed or not, we might proceed according to a gradual, well-thought-out method. But when everything is on the verge of chaos, when everything marches on in the dark (inside power, in the center of its center, in its main core, there is a dark nucleus), everything is possible, every beginning is good, nobody is forcing anyone: I am not forced to tell the story of the bear that got lost in Athens during the holidays, nor you, much less you, reader, to listen to this story, which, alas, is in danger of becoming a boomerang coming back to hit me in the gut, making me, once again, throw up all the disgust and joy I get from life.

The important thing is that, up to this moment when I am sitting down to write, even though I smoke a lot, I have yet to suffer a heart attack, which would scare me and make me give up or cut down on my smoking, roll up my sleeves, and start writing only about the important events of my life, leaving a sort of heritage testament to posterity. I am still now (knock wood) perfectly healthy. I have not burdened others with insurmountable worries. When Aliki and I broke up, we both cried a little of course, but this took place within reasonable, human limits. She flew off to stay with a friend to alleviate her solitude, while I buried myself in the anonymous crowd that was traveling by plane, in order to retire into my own solitude. Of course, I am still damp from Aliki's touch, from her virginal freshness against my cheek, her lust for life that nothing could injure. I think of her, I want her; that girl tore me to pieces. I'm like a schoolboy when I'm with her, but I like this state she often put me in.

On the whole, therefore, I am well. Amidst the general misery of my country and my people, I am still behaving relatively optimistically. Proof of that being that I'm still in the mood to type. The required amount is at least three pages a day. Let us get to three pages to start with, and then we can move painlessly to five, eight, sometimes even ten, on those days when inspiration fills my sails, a wind that tears itself against the riggings and masts, a nor'wester, as it's called. A moment will arrive, during this digging up of feelings, when I will identify with the universe, with the deeper path of life, when I will surpass myself and then, as gambling people say, I will have hit the jackpot. I will feel like a writer worthy of his mission. But until then, I must walk a long, joyless, monotonous road, overgrown with nettles and thorns. The peaks are few. And precarious. And the road that leads to them seems interminably long!

It was from such a peak that our friend the bear descended. It had been living free in the mountain when its lair was discovered by some topographers who were taking measurements for the digging of a tunnel through the mountain—that of Ahladokambos to be precise—in order to shorten the road leading into the interior of the Mani. They took the bear and brought it to the town of Kalamata. That way, while it was still a cub, the bear associated with people and came to know their peculiarities. It lived as a domesticated animal until the day when, the daughter of the topographer having gotten involved with a gypsy (the one who had relieved her of the little gold chain around her ankle), the young bohemian spoke to his father about a bear that lived, if you please, in the backyard of his girlfriend's house. The gypsy's father went and asked the girl's father not for his daughter, but for his bear. In order to sell, the topographer would have to get permission from his daughter, who had become attached

the white bear

to the animal. His daughter, Aliki from Kalamata (four *as* in a row: Kavála has but three, Patras, two, and Tziá a single one), in accordance with her friend the switch-hitter, told her daddy that he could give the bear to the man who wanted to buy it. The young gypsy, who was turning her on, had made this a condition of their love affair continuing.

The topographer was gladly rid of the animal, which had caused all kinds of problems in his garden and had made him the laughingstock of the neighborhood. One neighbor in particular, Manolis from America, had suffered an accident in Chicago and was not all there, poor man. Every time Manolis saw the topographer, whether in the street or the cafe, Manolis would ask him, at the top of his voice, how his bear was doing.

And so it was that, from the mountain heights of Ahladokambos, after a brief sojourn in Kalamata, the bear found itself in the hands of the gypsy, who took it to Athens for the Christmas holidays, obeying that ancient custom that dictates that gypsies with bears should wander through various neighborhoods collecting money by making the bear do certain tricks. Now, how the bear came to get lost in the concrete city of Athens and how it was picked up by the traffic policeman at the junction of Third of September and Alkouli Streets and handed over to Police Lieutenant Livreas, we will see presently.

But first, a few words on the sexual attraction between Aliki and the young gypsy who had relieved her of the small gold ankle chain; and a few words also on the consequences that the disappearance of the bear might well have had on the cultural life of Kalamata.

I should point out that it is purely coincidental that the young girl in our story has the same name as my friend, from whom I am expecting a tender phone call at any moment. It is one of those coincidences that occur both in life and in fiction. Nothing more. No further symbolism or thought association intended. Aliki from Kalamata is a high school senior with an acne-covered face. She goes to the cafes in town, where she sees the boys sitting around talking about motorbikes and soccer, but she avoids coming in contact with them.

On the outskirts of Kalamata, as almost everywhere in Greece, lies a semipermanent gypsy camp, which provides the town with vegetables, Nissan pickups, seafood, fortune-tellers, witches, songs by Manolis Anghelopoulos and Jehovah's Witnesses. As she strolled by the cafes with their plastic chairs and ice coffees, and the discos with their video clips, the young Aliki had decided to strike back at her *acne vulgaris* and cure it—something no dermatologist had succeeded in doing so far—by surrendering to a vulgar entanglement with the young gypsy. This assignation took place one evening that May as her grandmother was in the garden, killing a chicken for the feast day of Saints Constantine and Helen, which also happened to be the names of Aliki's father and mother. The young gypsy was stealing plums when Aliki saw him and said: "Wait, you don't have to steal them. I'll give them to you." The gypsy couldn't have asked for more. The household seemed like a privileged one. Aliki gathered lots of plums in her apron and took them to him just as the chicken fluttered in the old woman's hands, breathing its last. As she lifted her skirt, the gypsy saw Aliki's pretty legs and became flustered. Twilight was falling, nobody could see them. Thus it came about

the white bear

that, amidst the intoxicating fragrances of spring, Aliki gave him the gift of her first sigh, her first spasm, that coincided with the chicken's last one. From then on, every evening at six o'clock sharp, at the bottom of the garden, she would meet her friend, who was in no danger of compromising her in the cafe where her friends hung out, since gypsies were not allowed inside. Besides, her swarthy lover was very sexy.

It was during that summer that her father, Constantine, who had a thick mustache and was a militant supporter of the Socialist Party, was awarded the contract for the digging of the tunnel that would shorten the national road between Athens and Kalamata by two whole hours, and, having come across the white bear in the mountains, had brought it home as a gift to his daughter. And it was during the same summer that the young gypsy, fancying the idea of a bear, had spoken about it to his father, the chief of the gypsy camp. All of which led to the bear, aged only a few months, walking around Athens during the Christmas holidays.

As for the cultural life of Kalamata, no, the bear was not missed at all: a very active mayor had turned this town into a little Paris.

On the other hand, the bear had been something of a consolation in Athens, first cultural capital of Europe, until the moment when it got lost at the junction of Third of September and Alkouli Streets and put itself obediently into the hands of the police officer, who led it, according to regulations, to the traffic police headquarters nearby on Saint Constantine Street, as the bear had been obstructing traffic. The usual circulation restrictions in the center of town had been lifted because of the holidays, and the traffic was absolute chaos.

-2-
Whereupon in Athens, First Cultural Capital of Europe, the Sight of a White Bear Still Draws People's Attention

We are not among those who doubt that whatever was done was done well. However, our gypsy started off from Kalamata in his Nissan pickup with Aliki the bear tied on the flatbed amidst wishes for a bon voyage; like another Zampano, he took his own Strada. He made his first stop in Nafplion, first capital of the modern Greek state, before Athens. The summer Lotharios were resting up in the wintry square below the fortress of Palamidi, listening to the latest Harry Klynn[*] tape at full blast. The sight of the bear excited them. At Corinth Canal, where he stopped next, everybody was eating souvlaki and listening to the same tape. The gypsy listened carefully to find out what people were laughing at. He heard about how different politicians acted in Parliament, about soccer players, and about well-known entertainers. During the next few days, he taught all these things to his bear, who would mimic them with an acting talent as great as, if not greater than, that of the movie star who was also called Aliki. The bear would mimic the top Socialist minister speaking in Parliament, the goalkeeper Sarganis diving to save the ball, and the president of the republic embracing his wife.

[*] Greek comedian. *Trans.*

Having thus trained his prize pupil, he would set out from working-class neighborhoods and march upon suburbs where, the summer before, the culture hounds had flocked in their Mercedeses to converted quarries to attend performances by Peter Brook and Peter Stein. These events had been successful beyond expectation. Children gathered round the gypsy and the bear; so did grown-ups, who hadn't seen such an old-fashioned spectacle in a long time. The gypsy was raking it in. The poor man dreamed of sending his own son to school, so that he might escape the wretchedness to which society would condemn him for being the son of a gypsy. The people laughed at Aliki's antics, and, with the holidays drawing closer, having spent their Christmas bonuses, they amused themselves by watching the bear make fun of the neo-Hellene who was forced to tighten his belt, when for him, a big gut had always been synonymous with prosperity. This act was not part of Harry Klynn's tape, which had been recorded before the devaluation of the drachma; the gypsy had added it at the urging of a greengrocer friend of his.

At which point he decided to march up to the more distant suburbs to the east. However, although on the map this journey looked simple, in reality, most roads were closed due to the digging of sewers. Just as it was in Kalamata. However, he made a decent living, thanks be to God, and had nothing to complain about. Not like when he was a boy and he had to sell flowers in the taverns. He even appeared on a TV show about occupations that were dying out, in which he said that his bear made the most money at the lines formed by the unfortunate Athenians waiting for a bus or a trolley. As he spoke, his gold teeth shone on the TV screen like a corporeal treasure.

-3-
Whereupon a Gang of Junkies Decides to Dope Up the Gypsy's Bear

They were just sitting around doing nothing. Each one had become the other's snitch. One would pretend to be friends with the other until he could squeal on him to score a hit. Nothing else counted in their relationships. Although relationships, the way most people perceive them, did not exist among them. Their only reason for living was to score a hit. The area was perfect for it, because of all the retired military officers. There were no cafes, no pool halls like one would find in other neighborhoods. There were no political party youth organizations, not even any kiosks. In other words, there was nothing reminiscent of a traditional suburban neighborhood with its video rental shops and funeral parlors open all night.

Here in Papagos there was nothing. Only wide roads where solitary types walked their dogs, where Philippino housemaids and gardeners pruned the trees at a distance from one another. The kids growing up here had nothing better to do than commit the odd burglary, siphon gas out of cars, and harass the local cops, who gave them the same fossilized bullshit as their parents. The appearance of the gypsy and his bear could only cause their pinball brains to tilt. They convened and decided to drug the bear. The leader of the gang, son of the "commie-eating" General Vorias and a former prison inmate (a fact that rendered his power over the others indisputable), suggested they first daze the animal with their motorbikes, irritating its master, and then, when the gypsy wasn't looking, slip the bear a spiked pastry.

But the clever bear did not fall for this trap. To begin with, it had not liked this area, because it was full of barking guard dogs. Then, the bear had looked into the eyes of those young people as they surrounded it. It searched for those dreamy eyes that would gaze at the bear in order to escape the misery of their lives, eyes that Aliki had often come across in the center of Athens, on the faces of passersby who held two or three plastic shopping bags; but here it did not find the eyes it was seeking. As a result, the bear showed no interest whatsoever in the pastry it was offered, while its master the gypsy, thinking he had hit on an aristocratic neighborhood, passed the hat around, only to collect stones and dried shit. They even slit one of his truck tires and he had to change it in the freezing cold. He left, cursing and swearing, while the junkies, furious that their devilish scheme had fallen through, followed him, revving wildly and popping wheelies, all the way to the suburb limits on Mesoghion Avenue.

-4-
At Traffic Police Headquarters

The officer on duty, Lieutenant Livreas, was taking a statement from a lady, Doña Rosita, who had just escaped death in a car crash at the junction of Mesoghion Avenue and Hypoxinou Street, when the traffic policeman came into his drab office to report the arrest of a stray bear. Next to the lieutenant sat a young traffic policewoman, who seemed to find the story amusing: "A bear found unaccompanied in the center of Athens? That's a good one." Lieutenant Livreas looked up from the lady's statement and asked the officer where he had put the bear.

"In the basement, Lieutenant," he replied. "We're waiting for its owner to come and claim it."

"It'll probably be a gypsy," said the lieutenant, and turned his attention back to the lady, who was still shaken by her nighttime collision. In his head, he was trying to figure out where the hell this Hypoxinou Street was; he had never heard of it. He concluded that it must be a side street, in which case the lady who had been driving along Mesoghion Avenue had had the right-of-way and therefore the person who had crashed into her was solely to blame.

"But there wasn't just one, Lieutenant," insisted the woman. "Two cars crashed into me."

"Two? What do you mean two?" the officer asked, puzzled.

"I told you: I slowed down, I flashed my headlights at them to show that I would keep going since I had the right-of-way, and even though I saw they had stopped, suddenly, I don't know why, they both crashed into me."

Lieutenant Livreas was hunched over his report, trying to summarize the statement of the beautiful Doña Rosita in the conventional language of police reports, when the lottery ticket salesman walked into the office, his pole covered in tickets like a leafy tree. Both Livreas and his secretary berated him for their bad luck at the big New Year's drawing and refused to buy new tickets.

"What are we going to do with the bear?" asked the officer for the last time.

"Bring it here," said Livreas, sounding official.

the white bear

"But it won't fit in the elevator."

"Then bring it up the back stairs."

The officer left the room.

"Were you serious, sir?" asked his secretary, as she stood up to welcome some colleagues wearing civilian clothes who had come to announce the glad tiding that they were finally leaving work.

Meanwhile, the officer went down to the basement, took the bear by its chain and started to lead it up the stairs, but on the first floor he ran into an unusual congregation of young motorcyclists, probably motorcycle messengers who had been forced, because of a new law, to re-register their bikes. The hallway was packed solid outside the registry office, but the appearance of the white bear had a catalytic effect. Where it had been impossible to get through, panic and terror soon opened a space; the officer and his animal passed through easily and continued up the stairs. Both officers and civilians laughed at the unusual spectacle; the bear, who had never been in a public building before, did not seem perturbed by anyone or anything. Upon arriving at last at the lieutenant's office, the bear came face to face with its boss, the gypsy, who threw himself on it sobbing woefully, like a poor man who has lost his sole possession. Unmoved by this display, the bear sat down and proceeded to follow what was being said about it, as if the discussion concerned another: did the bear have a license to circulate? Had the gypsy paid for a bear registration? Had the bear been cleared through customs? Since the bear had been imported, it must go through customs. The gypsy thought he was losing his mind.

"It's from Ahladokambos, Lieutenant, it's not imported. This country has bears, doesn't it?"

"Bears come from the Soviet Union, from up north," the white bear heard one man say.

"It's Greek," insisted the gypsy master. "Come on, Aliki, show them what the Socialists do in Parliament."

And so, while the office filled up with more and more policemen, the bear did its usual routine, then it pretended it was a goalkeeper diving for the ball—it didn't dive as far as it should have of course, because the space was limited, but in its desperate attempt to prove it was Greek, it did whatever it could.

"And how come it got away?" insisted the lieutenant.

"I had gone, with all due respect, Lieutenant, to relieve myself. I left the bear outside the municipal restrooms, and when I came back out it was gone."

"Okay, get going," said the commissioner as he marched into the office. He had heard that there was a bear in the building and was afraid the tabloids would get wind of it. "Get lost!"

The gypsy, glad to have avoided a bureaucratic odyssey, declared he would take better care of the animal, took it by the chain and walked out. Outside on the street, he breathed with relief. "You better not disappear on me again, you fleabag, or I'll wring your neck."

-5-
But Where Do I Fit into This Story?

I bought Aliki the bear from the gypsy at a disgracefully low price. He had wanted to get rid of the animal as soon as the holidays were over. He could no longer afford to feed it. This suited me fine, since I lived in a small villa in Halandri with a garden, and I wanted company. In this house lived people who had nothing to do with me—in a way I was putting them up by default—and I wanted to have an animal of my own, since I didn't have a person of my own, or rather since I didn't want to have one. People generally have a lot of problems, whereas animals only give you their devotion and love. At night, I would take the bear to my room and we would sleep side by side. I always intentionally present it as my companion.

All it needed was a few caresses. It loved me very much. It would look into my eyes, its eyes concealing the unknown land of its origin. And I would dream of arctic steppes or distant retreats where man had never set foot.

In any case, when you circulate with a bear, just like with a dog, you discover things that were not evident at first. Many places are forbidden to you, and moving around in general becomes difficult. An animal, of whatever kind, imposes upon you the circle of a powerful spotlight. You cannot go unnoticed. People in the street will stop and stare. Women and children are fearful. They react atavistically to the sight of the animal that, very long ago, was their enemy.

During winter the bear did not suffer. But in the summer it seemed to have trouble with the heat. So I decided I would take my vacation time. I was going to show the bear Greece, but a Greece different than the one it had seen with its old master, the gypsy. "Tomorrow we leave for Nafplion," I announced one morning as I awoke.

It had been years since I had been to Nafplion, and I was amused at the thought of returning and seeing all my old acquaintances, accompanied by a bear. So we got into my Toyota. At the tollgate, I got my first snide remark. The bear was sitting next to me in the passenger seat, with its seat belt tightly fastened, perfectly behaved, and ignoring the mustachioed man who looked over at it mockingly as he handed me my receipt. At Corinth Canal I fed it ten souvlaki and from there we went straight to the new Xenia Hotel in Nafplion. I requested a room for two. Fortunately, there was one available.

"Two beds?"

"No, one double."

But at that moment, the kids who had been playing outside came in and got scared when they saw the bear. So did the clerk at the front desk. He was just about to say, "It is not allowed," when he recognized in me the former general secretary of the Greek Tourist Organization. He immediately notified the manager whom, by a strange coincidence, I had appointed to this post before going into the army to do my military service. "I understand your situation," I said, "but there's not going to be a problem. The new cable car elevator goes directly to my room." That way, I wouldn't even pass through the hotel.

The bear was very happy with all this luxury. Later, we went for a walk on the back side of the mountain and watched the sunset together. I found my acquaintances at the harbor, walking around the polluted soil. They were astonished to see me. In the evening, upon returning to the hotel, I found out that the top minister of the Socialist government had arrived in town. "Now you'll see who you've been mimicking all this time," I told Aliki. Aliki was also the name of the minister's wife.

the white bear

Next day, on the road to Kalamata, after Tripoli, the bear kept asking to be let out. I let it drag me, for the first time, like a dog following a scent. It took me to its old haunts. To its lair. It wanted to live there. I let it. Until one day, when it is found by a topographer who takes it home to his daughter Aliki who's involved with a young gypsy; the gypsy tells his father about the bear, and the story starts over. But where do I fit into this story? I am waiting for a phone call from my own Aliki. And while I'm waiting, I'm writing. And so on and so forth.

-6-
Conclusion or Narrative Ending

For the informed reader, I must say that there is no relation between my bear story and the poem "The Sacred Road" by Anghelos Sikelianos. I don't have it with me at the moment, but I remember that in his poem about a bear (a species faced, sadly, with extinction, like the spinning wheel), the poet of "The Lyric Life" gives symbolic extensions. For Sikelianos, the bear symbolizes the history of a people (the Greek people, of course) bound with the chains of slavery and not wanting to dance to the beat of the tambourine played by its master; but in my case there is no symbolism. There is no hidden meaning to my story. It was simply my need to describe Athens during the holidays—that reflection of misery and horror—that gave birth, in the little room of my mind, to the white bear, whose wandering around this sad setting amused me because it gave it a different touch. In front of the piles of clothes on Athinas Street; and in a shop on a small street behind the National Theater, which sells herbal teas, salep, and aromatic herbs from Chios, with an old publicity poster in English for the island's mastic, dating back fifty years, when there were neither any telexes nor any automatic telephones, and when going to America was not simply a matter of hours and when the Chiotes who had emigrated to the United States would sell the products of their native island in their new home; in front of a *Politis* (the journal), which reminds me of a woman without a lover becoming hysterical; an *Anti* (the magazine), which also reminds me of a woman, but one who sleeps with a different man each time without enjoying it; a *Commentator*, who seems to be taking pleasure in himself; and a *Reader*, which is a Lothario preying on foreign tourists. That is to say, full of translated texts, amidst the vomitous daily press, I suffer the same kind of depression as in the center of Athens, and I search my brain for white bears that will enrich me with their presence in this downtown civilization that reproduces the cultural Kalamata (four *a*s in a row: Kavála has but three, Patras, two, and Tziá only one).

three miraculous
moments lived by
Doña Rosita

n her mind, full of fruit trees that never bore fruit because their flowers had been struck by an angry frost, while she is lying on the pavement, having hit her head, feeling dazed, and while she can hear above the roof of her skull, shaken by the unexpected collision of the two cars, which would surely have injured her more seriously if, as though by magic, the left car door had not been flung open by the force of the crash, throwing her outside, so at the very moment when she notes the deep alienation among people who live in a city that differs little from the jungle—except that there, the beasts surely would show more compassion for a fallen one of their species—at that very moment, in a half faint, but with all her faculties intact, Doña Rosita can hear the anxious voices of the drivers who hit her. They are talking overexcitedly about insurance, no one offering her a helping hand to get up; on the contrary, she can hear through the fog of her mind phrases like: "What's the point of calling an ambulance? Can't you see she's all right? She isn't even bleeding." Phrases that denote the fear of the two drivers who had both crashed their cars into the right-hand door of her Mini Morris, throwing her out through the left-hand door. These two unknown drivers, talking among themselves, are joined by their common infraction: the second had accelerated because he saw the first doing so. And as she lies there on the pavement, the speakers in Doña Rosita's head also bring to her the phrases of people who are taking her side, contrary to the police officer who insists that it's no big deal, and the sooner we wrap this up the better. Doña Rosita, wanting to grab onto something, onto a pleasant memory in order to survive not her death so much as her deeper desolation, her abandonment on the pavement by her fellow human beings who seem concerned only with the damage to their cars, with their insurance, with everything except the damage to the human being (that was the horror of this sudden realization in the middle of the night, under a light rainfall). And while she lies immobilized on the pavement, Doña Rosita projects into her cloudy mind, in the form of a consubstantial trinity, in order to save herself from her present misery, three beautiful moments she spent with Don Pacifico during their recent travels over the Christmas holidays in the vicinity of three monastery chapels: three Holy Virgins, three mystically interconnected experiences. Inside her shaken mind, they spring up more vivid than ever before, like three secret flowers, and reveal to her their deeper meaning, their secret charm.

She was in Salonika, the city that had known such sorrow, where her friend Don Pacifico had his roots, and where he was showing her around, trying to find within his own mythology the nonexistent traces of his origin. Very little survived of the city's Jewish heritage. Everything had been devoured by a barbaric construction boom that had wiped out the few remaining old houses.

Finally, after stopping at a bookshop to visit Mr. Molkhos, a distant uncle of Don Pacifico's, they took a taxi up to the old ramparts, and from there ended up at the Monastery of the Vlattades, where they found the church door closed. They watched the peacocks, waiting for one of them to open the fan of his tail. No luck.

The day was foggy, the kind of weather that, like a wedding veil, suits this city we call the Bride of the Thermaic Gulf, the once-glorious cocapital of the Byzantine Empire. They had been sightseeing all morning and hadn't found a single place open. Apart from his own disappointment at not finding a trace of his heritage (except for the bookseller who had remained, as if by a miracle, unchanged over the years), everything else he wanted to show her happened to be closed that day: the restored White Tower; the Archaeological Museum with the treasures from Vergina; the churches—Saint Sophia and all the others—except for Saint Dimitris, the mosaics of which Doña Rosita had seen when she had passed through Salonika on another occasion.

And now, after coming all the way up to the ramparts, they found the Monastery of the Vlattades closed as well, and the peacocks refusing to display their tails. But as they prepared to leave—the taxi waited for them at the entrance of the monastery with its meter running—Doña Rosita noticed, in the small darkened church, the figure of an old lady, which at first she took to be a shadow, something incorporeal. They knocked, and the little old lady opened the door. She was wizened and bent over, but she began straight away telling them the history of the monastery, and how it was named after "vlatti," a fabric of wool and silk that the monks used to make and sell all over the known world. The church was tiny and could barely fit all three of them.

The memory of Saint Peter's of Rome, with its marble luxury and metaphysical barbarity, was still fresh in Doña Rosita's mind. Thus she was relieved to find herself inside the shell of this church, which, were she to slightly raise her wide shoulders, would envelop her like a snail and keep her under its protection. The walls were blackened, and the fragmented mosaics looked like shards of pottery that experts had stuck back together, leaving the missing parts painted in ocher. There were ancient and more

three miraculous moments lived by Doña Rosita

recent icons; telling them when the monastery was built, the old
woman led them to a smaller enclave, where the foot of the apos-
tle stopped and formed, along with the other stones, the sign of
the cross. It was forbidden to step there. The old woman was from
Constantinople, and she assured them that with the courage of
faith, one can fall into the fire and not be burned. They left her
a small tip and went out into the courtyard.

Doña Rosita had been completely immersed in the experience; she remembered now, as she lay sprawled on the pavement,
the drunkenness that had come over her as she had looked into
the intense eyes of the old woman. She remembered the fulfillment
she had known, her soul finally quenching its thirst, as she listened
to the old lady talk of the lost grandeur of Constantinople; the Patri-
archs; and the last king of Byzantium, who had turned into marble, with all the reverence inspired in her by that little church, lit
by the flickering flames of two candles, its lamps burning constantly
with the oil of faith. The metaphysical prolongation of this place,
none of whose joys she had tasted, since everything that day was
closed, made up for all the ugliness she had seen.

Everything that was being built around the little church
was ugly. The blocks of flats that had overrun the Upper City
were ugly. The cars that buzzed unnecessarily around the old
castle were ugly. But the little old woman had saved the day.
She had communicated the shiver of faith. The history of the
monastery became linked to her own distant past, which had also
been lost, mummified somewhere in the lost homelands of Asia
Minor. Just as Don Pacifico, once he had seen Mr. Molkhos,
found the strength to continue to live in this city, which, during
the eighteenth century had been the birthplace and home of the

last prophet of his race, so did Doña Rosita, by virtue of the thread handed to her by the old woman, find herself reconnected, in the shell of the church, with her own past—that of a Byzantine empress—and fortified by the power of faith, that unknown power that will keep us from burning should we fall into the fire. The eyes of the little old woman burned brightly as she spoke, and Jesus Christ, Son of God, our Savior, was the ichthus, the fish she would have for lunch. After all, He had been the first to give her that right: "Take, eat; this is my body. . . . "

The second scene, following on the heels of the first, took place in Nafplion. As soon as they arrived, before they even checked in to the hotel, in the dusky light just before nightfall, Don Pacifico took her for a walk along the path that starts after the port, twisting around the mountain above the sea, where, in the distance, they could see a ship slowly approaching, cutting silently through the water's satin surface, measuring time at its own pace, that of the daylight draining from the sky. They took a vegetation-choked offshoot of the path, and found themselves at a chapel that was above the main path and offered a better view of the open sea and the waters of the gulf. There was no one in the chapel; its icons were unguarded. They each lit a candle, Don Pacifico more in order to accompany her. There, too, appeared a woman, a sacristan, to collect the candles and lock the door for the night. They didn't speak. The icons that had been stolen by lowlife tourists and antique smugglers had been replaced by cheap paper replicas.

Doña Rosita prayed to the Holy Virgin and then they went out to the courtyard, where an upper gallery over the white stone terrace looked out onto the sea. The sun had long since disappeared behind the mountains of Arcadia, leaving the clouds to keep alive its memory; they too would soon become ashes. The slow-moving boat was gradually entering the gulf. It was the kind of moment that brings on ecstasy. And, as she breathed in deeply the sea air, Doña Rosita felt a wave of happiness swelling inside her: the location was beautiful, the hour belonged to her. This hour when the day burned out like a firework and when everything invited her to return to her deepest nature, which was intensely romantic.

She remembered that it was there, in that idyllic place, that she had thought that all she was missing to make the dream perfect was a white rose. The face of the Holy Virgin of the chapel, exactly like that of the sacristan, appeared to Doña Rosita like a slide projected on the firmament, and, as she saw the Virgin looking down, full of compassion and beautiful sadness, she took the hand of Don Pacifico who had been smoking next to her, and its warmth made her shiver, the same way the breeze sent a ripple over the honey-colored sea, forming pirouettes and arabesques. And then, as if by a miracle, in front of her and a little to the left, next to the ledge of the terrace, there where the dry pine needles formed a brown cover over the white stone, there where the white had started turning darker as evening fell, a white rose appeared before her, on a delicate stem with its leaves spread out. Had it been there before and she just hadn't noticed it? Had it been born of her strong desire? In this honey-sweet hour of the evening, with the ship as the only moving object in an otherwise immobile tableau, everything was possible. Everything.

Shaking from a happiness she had never before felt, that penetrated and tingled inside her body, she bent down and smelled the rose. It smelled as strong as one hundred concentrated roses, as if the saltiness of the sea air had tormented it, causing it to smell even stronger. Letting out a small, inarticulate cry, the cry of a happy bird, she picked the rose with trembling hands. As if she had discovered a treasure, she brought it to Don Pacifico's face and offered it to him.

The ship was getting closer and closer to the axis of her gaze, as unhurried as if it were being pushed by the invisible hand of the boy Jesus playing with his little boat. Finally, it dropped anchor. The noise, echoing in the empty shell of the landscape, at the same moment when the lights came on on the islet of Bourdzi and in the Acropolis of Árgos on the mountain facing them, brought her back to reality and she started telling Don Pacifico, who hadn't been aware of what she had experienced, that she was happy because her deepest desire, to have a white rose, had been realized by the will of the Holy Virgin.

For Doña Rosita, such moments constituted happiness. That's what she lived for, and now, as she lay stretched out on the pavement, the strength this memory gave her made her sit up and remain deaf to the cries of her alienated would-be murderers.

The third episode that completed the first two took place in Póros, during that desperate effort Don Pacifico had made to show her, in only a few days, the hidden beauties of Greece. It was again in the evening. They arrived via hovercraft, and after dropping off their few bags at the hotel, before night fell they took a taxi up to the monastery. It was windy. They went through the gate and up the wide concrete steps. Something was being built here too, resembling a church, but outside the enclosure of the monastery. As they reached the top, they saw the door was closed. At their feet, over the stretch of sea between the island

and Galatás, the dusky light of evening was slowly fading away, planting passionate kisses on the full lips of the land that demarcated the narrow stretch of water. The mountain facing them projected its mass onto the water below, like a Visigoth warrior standing at ease.

Doña Rosita was enchanted by the view and the light. Soon, she overcame disappointment that the monastery was closed. Its inner wall protected them from the harsh wind. The cypress trees descended like exclamation marks to the sea; the slope rustled in the northwest wind. To the right, the pine forest shivered like the skin of an animal fearing the onset of treacherous night. Once again, Doña Rosita felt intoxicated with the beauty of the day ceding its place to the darkness; she had trouble keeping her scarf wrapped around her neck, as the wind kept snatching it away.

Then Don Pacifico, having pushed open a door, found himself in a courtyard and saw, beyond its fence, lemon trees heavy with fruit. He put his hand through an opening to pick a lemon for her. But as soon as he reached his yellow target, he heard a gentle voice coming from one of the monastery windows: "Why are you stealing?" He turned and looked up. The face of a young man was framed by the dormer window, his hand on the shutter.

"We are not stealing," he replied. "We are only picking a lemon. We wanted to come into the monastery to say a prayer, but unfortunately it's closed." The young monk didn't see Doña Rosita leaning against the wall, her scarf standing on end, under the light that kept being swept away by the wind. Nothing else was heard. But soon, a young monk with Byzantine eyes, dressed in blue jeans, appeared at the door and held it open for them to enter. "The miracle is happening again," thought Doña Rosita, impressed by the young man whose liquid eyes, under this meta-physical light, excited her, as she later confessed to her friend when he kept asking her, insistently, whether she would have slept with the young monk.

"Yes, I would have slept with him," she admitted, choked with a shame she was not ashamed of, because, within the sacred space of the monastery, everything was sanctified by a power that was not of this world, this prosaic, explicit, crawling world, but that sprang from other forces. These forces keep us suspended like puppets from invisible strings, making us act out our earthly comedy until they decide to pull us upward, where playacting has no place, since we are rejoined with the whole from which we were only temporarily detached.

Walking in the courtyard of the monastery, Doña Rosita once again felt that shiver of sacredness run through her body. Inside the church, she stood before the ancient, heavy icon stand, which, like a mirror leaning against the wall at a thirty-degree angle, let her see her reflection from head to toe. Its carvings impressed her. The icons were worthy of the best Giottos. The miraculous icon of the monastery, the Virgin Mary Source of Life, stood outside the icon stand, on a wall to the left. That was where she bent down and prayed, while the young monk kept silent watch. And once again she was overwhelmed by her communion with the divine, as she had been at the Monastery of the Vlat-tades, and at the chapel at Nafplion. For the third time in just a few days, she felt the gift of tradition. She felt faith laying its benevolent hand upon her.

Everything was mystical in this isolated monastery, far away on the island. In none of these three places had there been any other secular people. The people were in the jungle of the cities, where, at this moment, hit by other people's wheels, she lay, having miraculously escaped death. The jungle was people. God had long since abandoned them and withdrawn to his shelter, where only through prayer and fasting could man find him.

Having dropped a generous donation into the monastery's collection box, Doña Rosita bought two reproductions of the icon of the Source of Life, one for herself and one for her mother, and thanked the young monk for letting them come in at such a late hour. As she was leaving, the inner courtyard of the monastery did not remind her in the least of *The Name of the Rose*, which she had just finished reading, the same way Orthodoxy had nothing in common with Catholicism, which frightened its faithful instead of appeasing them.

The taxi was honking impatiently in the dark. She stood one last time, gazing upon this other Bosporus (the other Galata, that of Constantinople, she knew of only from her grandmother's descriptions), breathing in the wind and taking in all the beauty of the hour and place, when suddenly, obeying her deepest desire, not one, but dozens of white roses sprouted on a bush behind the fence, which not even the nimble Don Pacifico could reach, and she simply gazed at them, happy that the miracle had taken place here too.

Wherever she went with her love, wherever there was a white stone ledge, at once white roses would bloom among the pine needles. With what joy, what force, what yearning and passion she rode downhill in the taxi, moving along the winding road through the woods, while she held the lemon he had picked for her tightly in her hand, breaking its skin with her nail and inhaling its unique, refined perfume.

Now, lying on the ground, then sitting up, she wonders whether it was she who caused the miracle, or the miracle that caused her. But our life is so prosaic, so flat. She took courage from this triple memory, while Don Pacifico, the man who had been next to her and through whom she had understood that these miracles had happened, at this critical moment was absent from her side. And that killed her spirit more than the accident that had almost killed her body. Not the fact that he wasn't with her, but that he did not know that she was in danger, or rather that she had just escaped danger. And as she couldn't make sense of the shouts and noise around her, she took refuge once again in those moments when she had partaken of the mystery, when the miracle of ecstasy had gone right to her soul and lifted her up to the sphere of that irrational faith, the only place where she felt complete, the only place where she could say that she touched the limits of her being and attained fulfillment.

She was a woman alone in the heart of the night, a victim of the violence of two men, without anyone else around to support her, except for some kids who had seen the accident happen and said it was the fault of the other two drivers. Doña Rosita couldn't tell which one of the three Holy Virgins had saved her: whether it was the little old lady at the Monastery of the Vlattades; the sacristan with the face of the Virgin Mary at the chapel in Nafplion; or the Source of Life at the monastery on the island of Póros. There, later that night, she was remembering strolling up and down the steep streets with Don Pacifico, under the sur-

three miraculous moments lived by Doña Rosita

veillance of the odious TV antennas, which sprouted in the gardens like sterile trees, she had come across a fairy-tale baker, solitary, bent over his magazine, short and bony like Charles Aznavour in the role of a French peasant during the war. As soon as he saw her face up against the windowpane of his darkened bakery, he thought it was the beautiful moon that had come down and was beckoning to him, so he got up as if in a trance, opened the door and asked her in. Doña Rosita went in alone. Don Pacifico purposely stayed outside so as not to ruin the baker's vision. Afterwards, she told him of how the baker, tired by an especially hard day's work, because he had to provide people with enough bread for three days in view of Epiphany, saw the beautiful woman at his door, and, as he was sleepy and still covered in flour, but calm, telling her that there was no more bread, suddenly 2 + 5 = 7 loaves appeared out of nowhere on the bare shelf, where an empty pan awaited a receiver of stolen goods, and the baker was as surprised as she was by the miracle. Then he watched her leave, looking toward the sky as if trying to see where the full moon had hidden itself after coming to visit him. Doña Rosita, meanwhile, was walking down the hill arm in arm with Don Pacifico who was telling her, an avowed Orthodox Christian, about the Jewish quarter, when they came upon a church that was just then being opened by a couple, a man and a woman, holding plastic bags. She went in, and discovered an icon of the saint after whom her father was named— her father who had died just a few months earlier.

On the way back, looking out from inside the hovercraft onto the colors of the sun setting into the sea, into the waters of the Saronic Gulf, she had Don Pacifico by her side, keeping time with her happy song, her overflowing joy that sprang from a Greece she did not know but wanted to get to know, a Greece that was inexhaustible and full of beauty, far away from the evil city of Athens, the murderous, concrete, heartless city that absorbed like blotting paper the feelings and emotions of its otherwise good people.

Finally, her adventure ended happily. The ambulance arrived, despite the protests of the two men. She was taken to the hospital. All they found was a slight concussion that would be gone in a few days. They took a CAT scan of her brain, which she showed her friend the next day, and he saw, with amazement, how his darling would look once she was dead, without her lips with which she would kiss him passionately, without her nose, a beautiful, rounded, heavy egg, still beautiful in the nakedness of the X ray. Even if he had first seen her this way he would have fallen in love with her. They reminisced together about those moments of their trip: the old lady at the monastery, the white rose on the white stone ledge, the lemon whose peel she had punctured with her nails, releasing its perfume in the taxi that had smelled like a male locker room, the beautiful liquid eyes of the young monk in blue jeans. Meanwhile, the night lowered her veils, eternal mistress of the moon that came out from behind the mountain with the radar and stuck to the windowpane of the baker/Jesus, while the bony ladies of Avignon, the TV antennas, inside abundant gardens of tangerine and orange trees, brought messages from the outside world to a world that still lived in prehistoric times.

Everything can always be either better or worse, but nothing is better or worse than waiting, when the loved one waits for

three miraculous moments lived by Doña Rosita

you with love, a manifest liquid, the liquid fire of the Byzantines; the secret of which was well kept by the emperors. It spills all over and burns up the space you can no longer see. "What is love?" Don Pacifico had often asked himself. The truth is, he hadn't caught any of Doña Rosita's messages, when she had her car crash and then found herself all alone at the hospital, having her beautiful head CAT scanned to see if there was any damage. If love is a thing that leaves one person to go to another, like a carrier pigeon with the message around its little leg, then shouldn't he have been reached, that night, by her desperate message? But nothing had reached him. Trying to recall what he had been doing at the time of the accident, he saw himself in the company of a noisy young group, eating a huge pork chop in an Albanian tavern somewhere near the city. "Therefore," he thought to himself now, "love (which was something he had never quite understood) was not simply a question of emitting, but the receptor also had to be on the same wavelength in order to catch the hertzian message. Therefore, it is only when we love that we can know love, and not when we are loved."

He felt truly mixed-up the next day, when he went to see her and found her in bed, still having dizzy spells from her accident the night before. And he admitted to himself that clearly he didn't love her as much as he had thought he did, since something as serious as the near loss of her life had hardly touched him. Then he began philosophizing: "What does our life hang from? A thread. Dozens of people are killed in car crashes, as if in a time of war, only no one remembers their names, and the main cause is bad roads." With thoughts like this, he sank twice as deep inside his remorse: once for not having been near her at

that critical moment to help her, and a second time for not catch-
ing anything in the air.

"But how did it happen?" he kept asking her. "Tell me, how
exactly did it happen?"

"What's certain is that it wasn't my fault," replied Doña
Rosita. "I was going home, it was ten o'clock at night and there
was a light rain falling, when at the crossroads of Hypoxinou Street
and Mesoghion Avenue, where the traffic light has never worked,
I saw two cars come up the side street and stop. I flashed my lights
to signal to them that I would keep on moving since I had the
right-of-way, but I slowed down just to be on the safe side. I don't
know what they were thinking, but even though they were at a
standstill when I entered the intersection, suddenly they both took
off and crashed into me. You know the rest."

She was still dizzy, she said, and she ached all over. It was
a miracle she had survived; of that she was convinced. It had been
quite a crash. Hadn't he seen her car downstairs? Visibly shaken,
Don Pacifico went downstairs immediately to look at the car and
estimate, by the damage, how severe the crash had been. The body
of the car had indeed been hit in two places. He came back to
his darling and lay down next to her. He caressed her tenderly
to assuage yesterday's pain.

"Where were you last night around ten o'clock?" she asked,
her voice weak and not at all reproachful.

"I had business to take care of with the contractor," he said.

That reassured her. Then, she told him that what had sustained her through her pain and abandonment were the three
Holy Virgins, the three monasteries; in other words, the three
excursions they had taken together a few days earlier.

three miraculous moments lived by Doña Rosita

It was a grey day. The central heating came on only in the evening and early in the morning, so it was cold in the room. They turned on the electric radiator that emitted, besides its heat, a honey-colored light. In the apartment next door, someone was trying to play the piano. But he was too much of a novice to give them the pleasure of a melody, even by a fluke. Then they dove into silence, a silence full of secret messages.

Don Pacifico couldn't get over the thought that his darling could have been killed or irrevocably mutilated. That was what angered him: the injustice inherent in life itself, whereby it can be interrupted without any warning, without any ceremony. It's only when you expect it to be that it isn't interrupted. And he started weighing all those cases of people who hadn't been given long to live and yet, fortunately, lived for many years, against those who were given no warning of their sudden end, and he concluded that the latter cases numbered more than the former. Life is a sweet self-delusion, he thought to himself. That's why there's no point in fretting and worrying. Life is a miracle that is given to us each morning, and it is a foolish person who does not enjoy it for the miracle it is, but who instead is moody, irritable, and unpleasant. "I love you," he whispered to her tenderly, and they lay there together in bed, without making love, for the first time in their burning relationship. The flowers in the vases sighed with relief.

"So, to recapitulate," said Lieutenant Livreas, and began reading her statement to her, in his own words, using police terms. Only he still kept forgetting that intersection: Hypoxinou Street and Mesoghion Avenue. Inside his office at the Athens

Traffic Police, the smell of bear still lingered. But maybe it was the smell of the gypsy, thought Doña Rosita, who was feeling a little faint, and she took out of her purse not her scented handkerchief, but that lemon with her nail marks in it, that still, after all those days, smelled sweet.

three miraculous moments lived by Doña Rosita

the transplant

-1-

The failure of the other two notebooks, the other two stories, brought me inevitably to this third notebook, whose unlined pages mean that the narrator (that is, I) has to find on his own the imaginary line that will lead him inevitably to the station he desires. By that I mean that the lines should lead you like rails to a terminus. Indeed, the narrative journey has a beginning and an end with intermediate stops. But a page without lines might go off in any number of directions. The story might go this way, or it might go the other. But which are the stories I wanted to tell and never managed to? And what should I tell first? The stories themselves, or the story of their failure? Don't those two things add up to a single story? Aren't they both writings, texts? Therefore, in order to avoid any misunderstandings, doesn't it take the same effort to say something as to explain why you can't say it? You must think that I am joking. That I am quibbling. But no, that is not my intention at all. In order to be free of the stories I didn't tell, I have to explain what it was that prevented me. For, I fear, I am repeating myself. In the end, that too is a story.

-2-

First let me introduce myself. Who am I? I am not young. I will conceal my age, not for vanity's sake, but because I don't think I should characterize myself. Let the reader—that mythical creature whom we all pursue and whom none of us has ever found, since in all likelihood our readers are simply our fellows: writers of stories like ourselves—let the reader say how old I am. No other particular traits are needed at the moment, other than that I live in a hotel and that in my small room I have a radio, a typewriter, and a few changes of clothes. I have come here, to this strange city, to write a novel commissioned by my publisher, about a man who lives with the heart of another. It's about Don Pacifico, a man with heart trouble, who has received the transplanted heart of Doña Rosita, a woman who was killed in a car accident.

How does this man feel with the heart of this woman? I have gathered information from doctors; the novel will deal with the role the biological factor plays in a person's psychology. Doña Rosita's heart had definitely registered in its cells certain experiences or memories that pop up, every so often, in the postoperative behavior of Don Pacifico, causing him distress.

Also included will be the element of surprise, as well as humor; in short, a topical book, of which I have written quite a few (my last one about an AIDS patient was wildly successful), which is why my publisher, who goes whichever way the wind blows, but is a great guy, said: "Off you go, no time to waste, here's the topic, here's the material, go away and write. Have it back to me in a month." That is how I found myself, within a few days, transplanted here in this strange city, in this small room where I don't know what's come over me except that I can't concentrate. I write and I erase, a thing I have never done before. I just can't get into my story.

So I decided to tell another story, to get myself warmed up, the same way a composer writes an overture so that all the instruments tie in with each other, before he proceeds to the symphonic poem. In fact, I didn't have a shred of a story: someone (the hero) goes to visit a friend, a fisherman, in Crete, during the holiday of the Assumption in mid-August. The fisherman has just added one more floor to his ancestral home to rent as lodgings for tourists. He works with a Scandinavian travel agency. One day, he's left with a woman from a Norwegian group who has fallen ill. She is blond and beautiful, like a Nordic goddess. The summer goes by and the patient remains bedridden, unable to get well. The neighbors take her under their wings. The irascible, unapproachable seaman begins little by little to fall in love with her. They get married. They have two children. The mother of the blond goddess sends her everything she needs from Norway. But the goddess remains a foreigner in the village. She does not adapt to the roughness of the sun, the rocks, and the people. The following year, in mid-August, the friend comes from Crete to visit.

So? No dread, no dream, no drama. Nothing. What kind of story is that? you will ask. I asked myself the same thing.

So then I started a new story: it takes place in the transit zone of an international airport. Time: the present. Characters: She and He. The voice over the loudspeaker announces: "All flights are delayed indefinitely due to dense fog." In fact, the passengers know that the real reason is the passage of Haley's comet. He and She begin to talk to each other. They know they will never meet again. They have separate destinations. They met by chance in the transit zone. By using this symbol I wanted to say that our life is an airport transit zone, or something like that. We meet, we talk, we love each other, we fall out of sight. But who could these two people be? And what would they confess to each other? If I were He, who would She be? What would be her name? I had to do some searching. Whereas with the story about Don Pacifico, who lives with the heart of Doña Rosita, I had no problem: the topic was given, the facts were known, and the job prepaid. It was no use floundering in search of new stories when I already had my story. All I had to do was build on it.

So now, how did I fail? This is what I have been wanting to tell you. What stages did I pass through to reach the point of being overcome by panic at the thought of time going by and my not getting anything done? Just as during sex, when you can't get any pop in your pickle, you start telling stories to your partner, and she listens to you, spellbound, but when you are finished talking she asks herself, "Why did he tell me all that? Oh, yes . . . " And it is only then that she gets the picture. In the same way I, being unable to make love to my typewriter, abandoned it and took pen to snow-white paper, as I've said—and here I am telling you why I can't tell you the story I'm supposed to, the story that has been commissioned, with a signed contract and advance money in my pocket.

This isn't the first time I've gone through such a crisis. But it's the first time I've decided to record it. It is a luxury I am happy to offer myself. Because, between you and me (I can say it now), it is a frightful lie, this reader-writer pact. How am I supposed to know how a man feels with the transplanted heart of a woman? I wasn't the patient (thank God!), much less the woman killed. However, since as I said, this kind of crisis had happened to me before, I hoped to abandon myself to the flow of events, to be carried away, to be transported.

So, from the morning of the day when my crisis began, I saw the sun shining brightly outside my window. The sky was clear blue. A spring day, in other words, while the day before had been cold and rainy. I decided to go out. I had been here three days, and it had rained nonstop. Indeed, the weather outside was radiant. I didn't like it. But how could I stay cooped up? I sighed. How could I go back to my dungeon? I walked to the square, then crossed the river and stopped at a cafe for a cappuccino. The world was rejoicing. The cars were speeding along. The leaves were falling from the trees. The municipal officer was stopping cars without permits from entering the historic town center. And I was walking, telling myself I had to return to my dark room and get down to work. I saw a man in a raincoat and for a moment I imagined him as my hero. With great effort, I convinced myself to turn around and, like a dog who has been walked, return to my shell.

And so it was that as I entered, I saw her sitting on the edge of the bed. An old acquaintance, an old flame. We had split up some time ago—it had been almost a year—amidst weeping and gnashing of teeth, and I still hadn't gotten over her. She still tormented me in my sleep, she was still taking her revenge, like that song says: "I'll have revenge, you can be sure, I'll come to you while you're asleep, at night I'll haunt your dreams. . . . " Even so, our relationship was history as far as I was concerned. Rosa— that was her name—wanted to have a serious relationship, to live together, and maybe even get married; I was allergic to those kinds of relationships. But apart from that, I liked her a lot and I guess she liked me. At that moment I didn't know what to make of it. She had already filled a vase with three red roses: the trademark of our love.

"What are you doing here?" I asked. "How did you get here? How did you find me? How did you get into the room?"

Her eyes, large and luminous, were looking at me with that surprise and joy they always expressed at the sight of me. Full of light, full like the moon, full bodied—fullness always came to mind whenever I thought of Rosa—I saw on her lips, which remained shut, a single drop of saliva, one of the signs we used to use to tell each other, silently, that we wanted to make love.

"Sweetheart," I said, and threw myself on her and started to kiss her, happy that she had come to find me, but a little confused by her unexpected appearance.

"I know you're very busy," she said. "I won't stay. Here's my number. I'll be in town for a few days. I'm putting on a fashion show."

"That's great!" I said. "But stay. Stay."

"No, I'm going. I have to go. I don't want to keep you from your work. Besides, I have a few things to take care of before noon."

"How you've changed! You look more beautiful than ever!" I was saying, totally confused.

"Away from you, everyone becomes more beautiful," she replied. "I had a hard time getting over it, but I made it. I'm strong now. You have nothing to fear."

I rode down with her in the elevator and walked with her to the bar next door for a coffee. I didn't want to part with her so soon. Of course, I was also in the mood to avoid my work, but

I was genuinely glad to see her. I found out how she had discovered my hotel ("If one is interested, one can find out anything."), how she had asked for me at the front desk, how she had slipped by the receptionist and gone upstairs, having noted my room number when the receptionist had said, "He's not in." And how she had replied, "All right, I'll wait for him in the lounge," knowing from long ago that I never locked doors (she even remembered the excuse I had given her: "My manuscripts are of no value, after all."), she had given a little something to the chambermaid and had come into my room where, after putting the flowers in the vase, she had waited for my return. As I listened to her, the torrents of our ancient joy began to flow again, back from when, without the anxieties and obstacles that accumulate with time, we were living the fullness of our love. Way back, before the painful twitches that start occurring in couples that have been together for a long time, when all either of us wanted was to give ourselves to one another, endlessly and without measure. She was well dressed, as always, this time in a tight grey suit and scarf, earrings like two petrified tears, fishnet stockings, and fashionable high-heeled shoes. But she really had to go once she'd had her coffee.

"You will call me, won't you? Whenever you want. You call, so I don't disturb you. I'll be here for a week." Visibly moved, she left me at the cafe, perhaps so that I wouldn't see the tears in her eyes.

"What bliss!" I thought, as I saw her disappear around the corner. "What luck!" She had sworn never to see me again as long as she lived, and that had cut me like a knife. But I too had gotten over it. Everything is forgotten with time. The fact that she had reappeared had to mean that she would agree to my conditions of noncommitment, of an open relationship, even though in the past she had told me that with such a temporary arrangement she couldn't give herself to me body and soul. In any case, I was to find out later what had made her come to see me. At the time, I was delighted by this unexpected gift bestowed upon me in the desert. (Not that I was suffering from lack of women. In a hotel, one can find casual company. But I had loved Rosa. Her sensitivity had touched chords within me that I had forgotten; adolescent feelings buried inside me for years; the way I would cry, for no reason, when she would tell me "never again," which was something that hadn't happened to me in years.) I was living the joy of feeling joy, and I didn't know where it started or where it was taking me.

Walking back to the hotel, I looked up at the sky, which was so blue it hurt my eyes. I saw the buildings all around me, ancient, Roman, their stones charged with history, beautiful, reddish; I took a deep breath, told myself I was happy, and went up to my room, where Rosa's perfume remained lightly diffused in the air and where her three roses looked at me with their surprised little heads, as if to say: "You lucky man, you are loved by the hand that brought us to you."

It must have been around ten in the morning when I sat at my little table in front of the window, ready to start work. I turned on the radio, but I only got the news. During the three days that I had been here, the top story in the news had been organ transplants. (The Pope had only just lifted the ban in this country.) Now the patient, atop his stationary bicycle, told the journalist interviewing him that he was doing just fine, he was feeling wonderful, the stranger's heart inside him was beating as if it were his own, etc., which, of course, took care of any intention I had of writing (reality always limits the imagination).

I wanted to make my Don Pacifico, who was living with the heart of Doña Rosita, talk differently. I didn't wait for the news to end and the classical music to begin: even that can become irritating unless you are totally absorbed in your work. I turned the radio off. Music only helps you work when you don't hear it. But when you're consciously waiting to grab inspiration by the hair, any intruding sound annoys you. Silence having been re-established in my room, noises started to come in from outside. They were changing the drainpipes in the hotel courtyard, and the talking of the workers, even though it was in a foreign language, distracted me. I closed the window, shutting out the little blue I could see. That put a gag on the voices outside, but now I began to hear the footsteps in the corridor. They were carrying sacks of clean bedclothes and taking away the dirty laundry.

Clearly I was unlucky. And I wasn't being helped by external circumstances. Even so, the three roses consoled me. I knew that later on I could give Rosa a call, see her, feel reborn in the warmth of her voice. This should not be taken for love. Not at all. But since I knew that a day is only good if it starts off that way, and since this wasn't the case and I knew that a night would have to mediate to set things straight, the sweet anticipation of noon, when I would call Rosa, was a consolation for the sick man that I was.

Whenever I feel I can't express myself, when I feel pressed and pressured, I always have with me a book I love, to dive inside and take heart from. At the time, I had with me Pirandello's short stories translated into French. Of the three volumes, I had only brought along the second one, so I began a disproportionately long story, more like a novella, which was fine with me because I wanted to lose myself for a long time in my reading.

Then the cannon fire that announces noon made my window shake. I opened the window and saw that not a single cloud had come to darken the satin sky. It was as if the day insisted I go out, and I insisted on sitting and worrying in my small room. There were no noises now, it was completely calm. The workers who had been installing the drainpipes were either done for the day, or on their lunch break; in the corridor there wasn't a sound. I turned on the radio, and again I hit on the news. This time it was a Frenchman who had received a kidney transplant, talking about how wonderful he felt. I turned off the radio and sank into silence as deep as a lake.

However, this silence was not at all creative. It was not like the kind that makes fruit ripen. It was not like the silence of diving within oneself, when you find yourself rich in secret juices and you feed yourself on dreams, fertilizing your soil by discarding superfluous raw materials.

Mine was the silence of nervousness, a dissolving silence, like the kind that comes when you search with your antenna for a station and can't pick it up on the small screen of your brain. That was it: a silence with stripes, flogged by lines of interference, when you can hear the voice but you can't see the picture. I was empty, and my publisher's commission could not fill me. I had been wrong to accept, even though I believed in the beneficial role of commissions, in the fact that books are written because somebody asks for them, Maecenases in the old days, the state nowadays, since nobody can write in the abstract. In other words, I was meditating in a void, without my vegetable essences. At the same time, I could feel all around me the suffocating vice of the industrial unit that is a hotel, working away while I remained sterile at my table. Instead, I listened to the chambermaid's vacuum cleaner, which had suddenly started up in the corridor, to the plumber, repairing the faucet in the room next door. When I ordered in a coffee so as to avoid going outside into the light of the street, the bellboy who brought it up to me and set it on my table, full of high spirits, said:

"Still working, are we?"

"Still working," I replied. "What else?"

"Yesterday it almost snowed, and today the weather is so beautiful," he said, just to say something.

I didn't want to show that he was interrupting me, so I said: "That's precisely the problem."

He pretended to understand, though even I didn't know what exactly I had meant. (What problem? Whose problem? Why?) He went, leaving behind him that air of assurance that always comes with a precise job (whereas mine was intangible and nonexistent), and ruining, with his passage, the atmosphere of a mausoleum that had reigned in my small room. Poor Pirandello stood there, imprisoned forever in his white, translated prison, while I, having been awakened by the departing bellboy from the torpor of reading, was only just discovering that Pirandello had written my story, all those years ago, but in reverse.

In his story, a Scandinavian sailor falls ill during a voyage and his companions take him off the ship to a village on the coast of Sicily. He is taken in by a fisherman who also plays the role of consul, since he had picked up some words of French during the Napoleonic wars. The Scandinavian sailor is tall and blond, like a Nordic deity. He is taken care of by the whole neighborhood, while the fisherman's daughter begins, little by little, to fall in love with him. They get married. They have two children. But to the end, the blond god cannot adapt to the harshness of the sun, the rocks, the people.

One by one, I was discovering all the similarities. In my short story, the Nordic woman would give me occasion to describe the habits and customs of southern Crete. In Pirandello, it is the Nordic man who makes him describe the habits and customs of southern Sicily. (And what a master of description! How full of intensity and life are his characters and dialogues! From beneath the great Sicilian playwright an even greater novelist was revealed to me.) The same story, the same plot. I was shaken.

"You're not going to start writing a novel of manners now, are you?" I asked myself. That style of prose is dead and buried. Nowadays, people are after other things. Nowadays, it's space, and comets, like Haley's, which is going to reappear, and (I had read all this recently and it came pouring back into my head) the Soviets were getting ready to welcome it by sending two sputniks equipped with ultramodern telescopes and computers, while the French were going to send a three-meter-long test tube with an investigative photoradar, which, if it was not destroyed by the dust of unclean snow that is said to make up the tail of the comet, would send us information about the chemical composition of the universe. Nowadays, everybody is waiting with mammoth telescopes for Haley's comet, whereas when it had appeared in 1910, about the time that Pirandello's short story was written, people were terrified and thought the end of the world was at hand.

Somehow, Haley's comet, which reappears every seventy-six years, corresponded inside me with Pirandello and his short story, and I tried desperately to convince myself that between 1910 and 1986 the way we approach the same phenomenon changed. But it was no use. Perhaps it's because man is not a comet but a fixed star that, though fixed, passes like a comet through life. Only life doesn't change. Intellectual developments (psychoanalysis, sociology, and biophysics) do not help us in the least to understand the phenomenon of human existence. It is only the knowledge of the mechanics of the text, its translation so to speak, and the naïveté of the narrator in describing and analyzing his hero's reactions, that undermines our confidence. That is why the idea of a transplant excited me. It was something modern. Something that no Pirandello had ever touched because it simply did not exist in his day. Whereas the story of the Nordic goddess and the southern satyr, or, in his short story, the Nordic god and the southern siren, was outdated, and I was thankful to him for writing it so well as to rid me of my desire to write it.

Around half past one, not being able to hold out any longer, I called her. Rosa herself answered the phone. She had just gotten back from work, she said. Would she like to see me? Of course she would! Did she want me to come over? Right away. She was staying in the Parioli quarter. She gave me the address. I took a taxi and soon I was with her.

The Aldo Brandini residence was chic. As a rule, all people connected to fashion and clothes stayed here when visiting the city. In the foyer downstairs, I saw a crowd of models and photographers meeting for lunch. An atmosphere of wealth and freshness. An air of well being, merriment, and sanitized sex, that's how it seemed to me. I went up to her apartment. It was small but comfortable, with a tiny kitchen, a living room, and a bedroom. It looked out on the courtyard palm trees. Rosa looked beautiful. I was enchanted.

She was a blend of youth and maturity, the Rosa of my love. It was the first time that this symbiosis of both ages in her had struck me so vividly. Now that it had been months since I had seen her, I had acquired the proper distance to see her thus. Her face had flashes of a youth not spent, or not well spent, which allowed her a reserve of wealth, while at the same time the weariness of a life she had not lived, or that had made her suffer, that had left its heavy seal on her. Like most of the women I had been involved with, she regarded me, since I was a writer, a bit as a confessor. I knew Rosa's life, what she had been through before we met by chance at an art exhibition, and why she had attached herself to me with such a passion: she believed that she had finally met the man she had been looking for, the one who could understand as well as love her. And it had indeed been so in the beginning.

But, with time, other things count for more in a relationship: sexual habits suddenly become very important, and while two properly know that everything favors their splitting up, since their relationship is leading nowhere long-term (like living together, a necessary development after a certain point), still they are unable to split up, because meanwhile, their way of getting it on has become too powerful. If Rosa happens to read this passage, I know she will be indignant at the expression *getting it on*. Because for her, our sexual intercourse had come to signify something momentous and multifaceted, far above the mediocrity she had known in her life previously. And it was indeed so. She wasn't exaggerating, and neither am I, when I say that we had reached a degree of sexual identification that was very rare. That is precisely what brought on the problem and caused the difficulties of our separation that had cost her dearly, me somewhat less.

So then what was the meaning of her reappearance in my life? What could she want from me, when I knew that in order to forget me she had gone as far as Tierra del Fuego? I knew from friends we had in common that she had suffered terribly after our split up, and everybody had urged me to help her by never appearing in her life again. As painful as it was, I had done it. However horribly I missed her presence, I never gave a sign of life. I only made sure I met with people who knew us both, so that I could keep up with her news and, through her news, relive the sweet warmth of the good times we had had together. Of course, this happened less and less often as time went by, which was why, when I received my publisher's order to disappear into a foreign land, into a foreign city, in order to write, I accepted with pleasure: the torment of forcing myself not to see her became more bearable. If I was far away, she would be more free to circulate and perhaps to find someone else, while I would isolate myself and recover more easily. So I was very surprised that morning, when she appeared like a comet in my room. I was so happy to see her again that I didn't worry over the details of her motives. It was only now that we were together in this foreign room, both of us a little embarrassed, that these thoughts began to eat at me.

the transplant

In the bedroom, the large double bed with a foam mattress and two pillows gently touching each other was an invitation and a provocation to our old love. Rosa seemed sure of herself; she pretended to be happy to have apparently overcome her karma. She was a different person now, free of me and of my domination over her. My hallucinogenic domination, as she used to call it, since she was unable otherwise to explain the effect that I had on her. I would have been the last person, therefore, to bridge the painful rift, had it not been Rosa herself who had taken the first step, aggressive, sexual, with flowers, in my room that morning and now again in her room, where she started slowly to undress, inviting me tacitly to bed.

I wanted her. And how! Her body had been to me, at one time, worse than opium. As soon as I saw her naked, I would be seized by a sort of sexual frenzy; I wanted her unbearably, here and now. (There and then.) Her body had an impudence all its own, which was not always in accordance with her face. Her face might be talking about other things, but her body would say, "I want you. I want you to sweeten me, to soften me, to make me submit." And I would take her in my arms and together we would turn into a single rocket shooting into a space full of galaxies. She had loved our space travels so much; it was precisely their loss that had made her suffer.

I wasn't long (about an hour after the scene I have described) in understanding this strange move of Rosa's. I must say it came to me a little late because I'm an idiot where the complex psychology of a woman is concerned: I fell victim to her sexual advances, thinking that we would reach once again the apogee of our travels. But I was wrong. I was lamentably wrong. Rosa had come to see me, Rosa had sought me out, Rosa had practically asked me to bed a moment ago for one reason, apparently a very important one to her: to prove to me that she was over me. That I did not give her the same pleasure as before, that our exhilaration and our space travel belonged to a past that was irrevocably lost. She knew I would be deeply hurt by that, because it would strip me of medals I had awarded myself for her conquest. She knew (although she never told me so; we never discussed what I am now writing) that she too needed to be convinced that it was indeed so, that she was over me, that we now had an ordinary relationship, as she had had before with other men and I with other women. Nothing unique, nothing special, nothing earth-shattering like before. By proving this, she succeeded in hurting the most sensitive part of my manhood—since all men deep down are flattered when a woman loves them—and in poisoning me with the slow-acting drug of ranking our relationship together with all others.

Of course I did not understand all this at the time. When we found ourselves face to face again in bed, everything seemed to unfold according to the old scenario of our love. I wanted her and she wanted me; we gave ourselves to each other, we exchanged some of the words we used to say, as if we were taking old clothes out of a closet. But the explosion never happened, the rocket never took off, we remained on the surface of the earth, a few meters above it perhaps, but always under an inexorable terrestrial law. I had thought then that this might have been because it was the first time. Two bodies that had once loved each other shamelessly, fanatically, like neophytes of a mystical sect, could not help but suffer a slight

shock when they met again. But the same thing happened the following time. During the six days that she stayed in town, every
time we came together as lovers—and, if I'm not mistaken, there
were as many times as days—nothing happened reminiscent of that
twin flame that had set the universe on fire, its sparks like fireworks
that illuminated our darkened sky. Everything went along at an
ordinary, normal pace, without the slightest surprise.

What I am writing now is the conclusion, the summary of
all our meetings. And I am practically convinced that she did it
all for one reason: to prove to me that in fact our relationship
was over and thus to hurt me, since apparently I had hurt her so
much. As for that romantic line, "Let's stay friends," Rosa had
worded it differently: "Not only friends, but lovers too. But you
should know that love isn't what you think it is. It cannot be
ignited by the fire of the body. The body is a vessel, a tool,
endowed with an inner power greater than ourselves, since, as you
see, the very same bodies, our own, cannot reach their old records.
We are no longer Olympic champions at love, but creatures like
most others, with our feet on the ground, who carry out this func-
tion to satisfy a need." Having apparently studied my psyche well,
she knew that knowledge would hurt me. That it would kill me.
And indeed it did hurt me, it did kill me. I tried many times to
lift her up to the old heights we used to scale, like mountaineers,
hanging from taut ropes, in danger of falling to our deaths at any
moment, always to find, at the last moment, the magical flower
of our love that would save us, a miracle on the steep slope of
the most abysmal desire.

And that wasn't the worst thing. The worst thing was that
she was letting me use all the old tricks, the old passkeys with

which I used to open her most secret doors, after which she would give herself to me as to a pirate pillaging her diamond coffers, whose treasures were at once replenished. It was as if my hands, by taking her diamonds, made her give birth to newer, brighter ones, through the magical power of love.

Two lovers create their own behavioral code that, after a certain point, monitors them automatically, like a computer. All you have to do is hit the key and the equation appears on the screen. So the little hypocrite was letting me, without ever saying no—showing in fact that she was enjoying it, pretending she was participating—degrade myself by pressing all her keys according to the code and getting no result. At first, as I have said, I didn't realize what was going on. I thought that her lack of total participation was the result of trauma. I didn't know that it was her way of proving the old truth about it being the woman's participation that makes a lover omnipotent. If she is not moved by him, he resembles an automatic washer-dryer that turns when you press the button, that washes the clothes and dries them. But this procedure is formalized, industrial, and the wash does not acquire the fragrance it does when a loving hand washes it in the stream, on the smooth rock, and dries it in the unhewn light of the sun. That was exactly how she had made me feel when she left: that we had made, five or six times, however many days she had been here, a plastic, sanitized love, superficially intense but without the exhilaration and exuberance that had brought us together and carried our relationship along.

In other words, she had made me feel indigent. She had stripped me of the peacock feathers with which she herself had adorned me. She was tender with me, and joyful; she hadn't changed at all. She never complained to me about our breakup, though at the time she had called it unjust and absurd. No, never. Except once, when these words escaped her lips: "What a shame, what a shame for us both." When she said this, I didn't understand right away, and it was only later when she was saying goodbye that her words took on their real significance. It was as if she were saying: "What a shame that you destroyed the love we knew; what a shame that whatever it was that elevated us no longer exists. What a shame that we were both denied the only possibility a human being has of joining the Gods: the possibility of absolute love."

For me this was like a slap in the face, which I did not feel until later. During the days Rosa was here, something inside had been telling me that all was not well, but I had kept pulling the wool over my eyes. It'll be better tomorrow, I kept telling myself. Her pomegranate will explode. Its grains will scatter to the four corners of the earth, like before. She will become the earth again, and I her sky. She will become the sea, and I the sun that warms her. But she became, alas, neither the earth nor the sea. And I became neither the sun nor the sky. We remained within our petty, carnal burdens: Rosa and Irineos, two well-defined human beings who did not overstep the boundaries of their bodies, who did not participate in the cosmic happenings, within whom the rhythm of the world was not overthrown. Two grey partridges, not proud rock partridges, rebels of the mountain; two quails flying one meter above the clover; two aphasic pheasants; family restaurants, not diners for vagabonds; two neighborhood churches, not two country chapels drunk on their ascetic solitude, with the smell of wax hanging from ossified candle stands.

We had become the store-bought flowers in the cathedral, not the wild flowers of spring in the village church; we had become jukebox songs, not those old, rare seventy-eights that need special needles to be played.

I realized then how insignificant I was. How dependent on the other's love in order to feel love. How poor by nature in the face of self-sufficient forces. Rosa had taken her revenge in her own way, perhaps even unconsciously.

I had never considered her sly or petty. But the weight of an injury can only be thrown off, it seems, by injuring the one who caused it. In these voracious human relationships that become cannibalistic where love is concerned, Rosa, to survive, had to make me die a little, just as I had made her die in order to triumph.

Then, at last, the writing began. Every cloud has a silver lining, as the saying goes. That's pretty much what happened with me. My creative self finally got going. I have two strings to my bow, you see: when the man is hurt, the writer comes alive. When the writer Don Pacifico wins, the man Irineos loses. When the writer dies, the man survives. Rosa became Doña Rosita and I became Don Pacifico who had received her heart in a transplant and is now living with it. I had her inside me, I loved her, because with her behavior she had managed to awaken me, to make me see our relationship more clearly. What had gone wrong, what I had done wrong, that we had reached this nadir? And so, happily, because I was Don Pacifico and Rosa was Doña Rosita, I started writing and finished quickly, in less than a fortnight. Rosa's injured heart had become my own since her death. And yet, with the heart of another, how much longer would I live?

the transplant

-3-

This question—how much longer would I live?—occurred to me the day I finished the first draft. I was a wreck. I had been working fourteen hours a day, without stopping, without rereading what I wrote, advancing blindly, for I was being swept away by my passion for Rosa. I was Don Pacifico. But as soon as I finished, out of breath, I began to fear that with an artificial heart I would not be able to live much longer. After all, most transplant recipients don't live long. Six month to two years, maximum. And for the first time in my life, I was worried. How much longer do I have left then? And what does it mean to live with somebody else's heart?

I called her up, intending to tell her how happy I had been, deep down, to see her, but how a sadness deeper than the joy darkened the sun inside me. Something indistinct, something vague that I did not understand yet. I would ask her if this was perhaps the beginning of real love, and if she was experiencing the same feeling. Liberated after having written my book in one stretch, I would even invite her to come and join me for a while if she could. A man's voice spoke:

"Who's calling?"

"Have I got the right number?" I asked.

"Yes," he snapped, when I told him the number. "What do you want?"

"I'd like to speak to Rosa."

"Who's calling?"

"A friend."

"She isn't here."

"Oh, all right. Please tell her I called."

"Your name?"

"Irineos."

"Which Irineos? The bishop?"

"No. Just tell her Irineos. She'll know."

"Hang on a minute. . . ."

There was a silence. Rosa was there; he must have covered the mouthpiece with his hand while he told her my name. I waited, feeling confused, until I heard the happy, well-meaning sound of Rosa's voice on the line.

"Hello, my dear Reno. Are you back?"

"No, I'm still here in Rome."

"How's the writing going?"

"Fine. It's going fine. I'm not doing too well, though."

"But why, what's wrong?"

"Rosa . . . but what's the point of telling you? What do you care?"

"I always care about you, my dear."

But the way she said it sounded so distant, so indifferent, that I hastened to end the conversation.

"The one who answered the phone," Rosa said, "was Elias. A friend of mine. You don't know him. I just met him a few days ago. He knows you."

"But he thought I was the bishop. . . ."

"He didn't make the connection. . . . Yes, I'm doing fine. I've found my balance again."

I understood. I had to hang up.

the transplant

"I only called," I said, "to ask if you were planning to come again. That is, I'm inviting you to come again if . . ."

"I can't see it happening at the moment, my dear Reno. They're showing the Armani collection next month and . . ."

"Okay, okay, it was only an idea."

"Well, I can't see it happening. When are you coming back?"

"I don't know. I've got to go. Bye."

Her revenge was now complete, I thought to myself. We were even. How many times during our relationship had she stumbled upon female voices when calling my number? And she had pretended not to care. But deep down it had killed her. Just as she had killed me now. Still, I had the satisfaction of telling myself that this was the only way to achieve equality between the sexes, rather than sitting around and talking about it all day.

So here I am again, stranded just as I was before I started writing. Now that I've finished—although there's still a lot to be done—I'm searching for something to lean on in the outside world, an existence to hang onto. You do not eat at this abysmal solitude; it eats at you. Rosa had taken her revenge, and yet I knew she was sad, deep down. And that also ate at me.

She came to me now like an ethereal memory. Her melancholy eyes that gazed at me. Her hair, which, when she loved me, wrapped around me like a scarf. Her insistence that we must remain together, because our meeting was not a chance one. All this tormented me now, it tortured me terribly. Memories came to me of our life together, when we were living intensely, under the sword of separation, moments filled by her, tender moments, moments of total abandonment, moments when she confessed the fullness she had known with me and that would mark her for the rest of her life, so much so that she would never be able to enjoy anything else, moments of absolute sensual exaltation, and yet what had always moved me was her deep sorrow. This sadness came over me too, like self-pity, and I couldn't get out of its vicious circle. Could it be that my sadness for Rosa was pity for myself? It was only when I came to this that I began to truly understand our relationship in its entirety. I wasn't jealous that she was with another man—what was his name?—this Elias. I was glad. After having cleared things up with me, she was taking the decisive step that I had always told her she should take. But what about me? What was going to happen to me? How much longer did I have to live?

My advance money was running out and I would have to return soon. This thought darkened my horizon. Return? To whom? To do what? To hand in my manuscript? I could just as well mail it in. The world is a writer's oyster. All he needs is a language of his own that he loves, and he is the luckiest of men. He doesn't need anyone. And yet Rosa, my dreams of Rosa, to see the sun and the sea together, to listen to our favorite songs, to visit distant chapels, the world's open spaces, all these things tormented me now, now that I knew that they would never happen. She had spoken to me of Smyrna and of Salonika. Yes, I was in love, at last. At an age that I will not reveal, not because I have anything to hide or out of vanity, but so that what I say won't sound absurd: I was sixteen years old. An adolescent. And I was living the first love of my life.

The certainty of my loss made me rediscover within me all those ideals that I had forgotten about and that I had felt very intensely in the past, when I was very young. But life, that big old steamroller—heavens, what a cliché—came along and leveled them. And now these virgin, untouched sources were ruling me. I loved Rosa. I had forgotten her body; now only her face impudently remained in my mind. Her dreamy eyes, her breathless voice. Her cries during our lovemaking, which used to move me so much, now belonged to another woman, not to her.

Adolescent love does not ask to touch the ground. Taking flight is its greatest joy. To fly, not to crawl like a worm. And while the butterfly, in order to sprout wings, first goes through the chrysalis stage, the human being starts its journey on the earth with wings like a butterfly. As the years go by he turns into a worm, until the moment when he is reunited in the ground with his worm brothers and sisters. (It is only when a person lives for many years that he is able, toward the end of his life, to become a pure spirit again, and to surrender a purer soul to the Lord.)

But in my case, the exact opposite was happening. I was a butterfly soul. I was only just sprouting wings the color of Rosa, after the worm stage I had gone through with her. (Many times in the past she had accused me of neglecting the silk of the soul. She believed that I was doing myself an injustice by limiting myself to the level of the flesh and by asking only of her and not of myself for those emanations that they say come from the soul. She believed that I had other powers within me that I had made sure to mutilate over time. The tree had become deformed, in her opinion, and of course it was too late for me to change.)

And yet, thanks to her, I had changed. Thanks to her I had become who she wanted me to be. Now that I no longer had her. Would she even be interested in hearing the good news? Besides, how long would this transformation last? Wasn't there the danger, if we got back together, that I might become as I had been when she knew me, wanting to dominate her completely, to be indispensable to her, wanting . . . I had practically abolished nourishment from my life. I was living on coffee and water and a ginseng drink that gave me an instant cerebral high when I was working. Nothing else. Absolutely nothing else. I wanted my Rosa back. A Rosa of my memories. A Rosa of my own to love, and not to care about anything else. To be devoted to her the way Saint Francis was to his faith. Penniless and dressed in rags, I would be fortified by the presence of her love. I wanted to get back a Rosa who perhaps was not real, but who was the way I wanted her to be. A Rosa of my imagination.

No. Everything I knew about her told me that the Rosa of my imagination was the real one and that the other Rosa, the one I saw when I was with her, was a figment of my imagination, with whom I satisfied my sexual fantasies. And she accepted my delusion, because she loved me. Until one day, she stopped loving me, because I refused to see her for who she really was. So she left. It was only then, like another Saul on the road to Damascus, that I saw the vision, I saw the light, and I was converted.

Oh, how similar are the paths of people to trains that meet and then speed apart, without time to join together because they are placed on separate tracks! Could a train be at the same time locomotive and passenger wagon, and identical to the other train on the other track? Is that impossible?

Oh Rosa, Rosa, I kept saying to myself, like another Werther. Sweet Rosa, Rosa my love, your wrists still scarred by that attempt in the past, before you met me, oh Rosa, you who are worthy of my happiness, who made me worthy to live more

the transplant

238

broadly, more intensely, I, Rosa, who have become you, prayer book, come tonight, my dearest.

I was delirious. I had lost control. I wanted her. I was convinced of that. I had matured. Rosa, with her sad gaze of joy, her beautiful face of sadness, Rosa with the body that magnetized, with the voice that tranquilized, Rosa by the fireplace, on the beach, with the seagulls, Rosa of midday, of nighttime, of dawn, Rosa of the disco, of long ago and far away, Rosa who was earth, sky, a comet passing by earth every seventy-six years and I, with my telescope, waiting for her to pass by with her peacock's tail, waiting to respond to her deepest, most secret nature, Rosa, Rosa, don't get hurt by the sun, leave me at least the black powder of your tail, my love, Rosa, Rosa, Rosa, Rosa, I write means I want you, I love you, I am here, I want you, yes, love, Rosa is here, she is waiting for me, here she is, yes, here she is . . .

-4-

And the man went crazy. On his desk, in his small hotel room, the chambermaid found a strange piece of paper upon which he had written, like a broken record, the same phrase, over and over: "A Rosa is a Rosa is a Rosa is a Rosa is a Rosa is a Rosa . . ." as if the play on Gertrude Stein's famous words were the key to an explanation.

After his unfortunate death (they found his body floating in the Tiber, like the corpses of the resistance fighters he used to see as a boy, washed up by the River Strymon, as he describes in his books), they brought me, the press attaché at the embassy in Rome, his papers and few belongings: his radio, his typewriter, and a couple of changes of underwear. I sent the lot to Rosa, whose telephone number was written across the title page of *The Transplanted Heart*. When, later on, while on leave in Athens, I got to meet her, she spoke to me the way you would speak to a stranger you trust because at a critical moment he had done the right thing: she had greatly appreciated the fact that I had sent the manuscript not to the publisher, but to her. After having told me all kinds of things about the novel, where she had discovered countless details of their love: phrases, words, favorite meals, she began to accuse herself indirectly of having behaved harshly.

She had not realized that Don Pacifico or, as he was known, Irineos, was nothing but an immature child. He had appeared to her so heavy with experience and knowledge that she had ignored his childish fragility. She had sensed it in the beginning, but finally she had told herself that she had been mistaken and so she chose to believe (she had been wrong of course, but it was all useless now, all useless) that she was dealing with a man who undoubtedly had many personal problems, problems that he was solving, or was trying to solve, through the sex act. And so Rosa, who had never had feelings of remorse or guilt, acquired them now.

"Why did I go and pull that stunt?" she asked, sobbing, as she told me of the time when their love had filled her completely. "Why did I have to hurt him too?" But it was too late for regrets. After all, she could have died after they had broken up; she had been beside herself, looking for something to hang onto so as not to repeat what she had done when she was younger, the scars of which were still on her wrists. She could have, yes, that miserable summer when they had separated, when she herself had made the painful decision that they break up, because they just couldn't go on anymore, asking of him only not to contact her. She could have died then, and loaded him with the burden of sorrow and guilt. At least he had died happy, delirious, as his papers showed, because he had finally succeeded in falling in love, at the end of his life. He was seventy years old, you know. Old, but still capable of affecting a woman.

Afterward, Rosa wanted to enter a convent. She went through different phases, from Hinduism to Zen to the occult. She kept in touch with me. With time she got over it. Only those three flowers she had taken to his room still tormented her in her sleep. The three red roses, as scarlet as blood, that she herself had placed in the vase the chambermaid had brought her, after Rosa had given her a little something, in the hallway of the hotel, outside the door he had left unlocked, as always, because, he used to say: "Who would steal my manuscripts? Nobody reads Greek." Those roses were like three characters in search of an author to sing their praises. And the author might no longer be alive, but those flowers lived on in her memory.

-5-

That was the story I wanted to tell you, dear friends, and please forgive me any imperfections. Nowadays, people telephone each other, telegraph each other, teleprompt each other, telelove each other. *Tele* means *from afar* in ancient Greek. By virtue of this text I have come close to you. Having reached this point I would end, if only life weren't much more fictional than the best of novels. Nothing surprises us more than the continuation of life, this implacable continuation that makes our escapes into the world of fiction seem laughable. The death of the main character suits fiction writers well, because it introduces the idea of the irrevocable. Whether they start off with the death and go back over his life in the form of flashbacks, or whether they end with the death, the fact remains: the unexpected is impossible.

Likewise, the death of the author suits those who study him: it is impossible for scholars' monographs to be overturned. That is why studies, monographs, and serious analyses of a creator's work are always carried out after his death. That is when all the art historians and other researchers gather like seagulls over a sunken trawler. Otherwise, while the artist is alive, the gulls follow hesitantly, eating whatever he deigns to toss at them as he empties his nets, apprehensive of his slightest move, always ready to fall back, those gluttonous old gulls. But once the artist is dead and the trawler has sunk, along with its nets and trawls, the greyish gull researchers are no longer afraid of anything and plop whatever has been washed up from the wreck with their powerful bills. The same thing happens in novels: the death of the main character, whether at the beginning or the end of the book, gives the reader a feeling of certainty. He reads the story with the same ease with which the writer narrates it.

I repeat, however, that life is not at all like a novel. Most of the time—and that's the trouble—life goes on. She calls on you every day to prove to yourself what your life's goal is. Of course, there are escape routes, artificial gardens of Eden. But for the most part, escape is not a solution. And we have to keep on living our lives on a basis that is not at all pleasant. That is literally what was happening in my case.

Rosa's visit had released sources of energy inside me, but after she left I fell back into my familiar rut: work, work, work, then perhaps an evening out, a movie, alone, alone, alone. And then one afternoon I thought I'd go and see my friend Federico, from whom I had been concealing the fact that I was in town until I could be sure I was being productive. He was thrilled to see me, and insisted we go out to dinner that evening.

We went out. Two other Italians, also antique dealers, came along with us, as well as a woman, Ursula, who didn't seem to be with any of the three men. In fact, all three men were clearly not interested in women, but as Federico was very fond of me, it seems he had invited the young woman in an effort to play matchmaker, since, when I had visited him at his shop that afternoon, I had told him that I was traveling alone.

We went to a trattoria that looked like a movie set, with lit torches in hollows in the walls. It was an ancient Roman tomb that had been turned into a restaurant. There, Federico, who was truly happy to see me, having had a drink or two, loosened up and brought up his favorite topic, all the rage in Italy at the time: organ transplants. He started by protesting television that revealed the name and sex of the donor, which in Federico's opinion was unnecessary: the patient didn't need to know whose heart or kidney he was receiving. He went on to say that at that very moment, from one end of his oblong country to the other, from Aosta to Taormina and from Taranto to Sardinia, ambulances were carrying organs in special containers, by sea, by air, by rail, and by DHL, transversely, diagonally, vertically, and horizontally, human organs from the dead, destined for the living.

At dessert, after an abundant meal, he concluded by saying that nowadays, the way medical science has progressed, nothing is thrown away. Except perhaps the nails and the hair. His way of saying all this, by generalizing and poking fun at it, made him laugh first and then (they do say that laughter is as contagious as a head cold) his laughter spread to the others and to myself. I began to laugh hysterically, like a fool, at that "non si butta niente" ("nothing is thrown away," as they say about a good piece of beef). By the end of the evening we were all in hysterics, thinking up preposterous transplants, like, for example, a doctor friend of mine in Patras who, while we were college students, wanted to change people's heads. (Actually, he is now a successful neurosurgeon and he still cuts them open like watermelons.) The madness of one era that becomes the logic of another; isn't that what progress is?

Every phenomenon has its own place and time. In Italy, as I have said, the papal ban had just been lifted, so while up to that point Catholics had been going to other countries to receive transplants, suddenly there was a transplant boom, just as there had been a building boom in Athens when it was proclaimed the capital of the newly established Greek state. Every day, the lead item on television news programs was a successful transplant. Hospital telexes were constantly sending and receiving information about available organs: clinics were competing to see who would come first in this race against death, while the Road Safety Service set up a medical department to deal with the organs of traffic accident victims. It was only natural, therefore, that our small group, as well as all the other customers of

244

the trattoria, that extomb, would be discussing, as I could hear them doing at neighboring tables, the same current event. Everyone that is except for Ursula, the only woman in our group, who seemed to suffer because of this conversation. She laughed along with us, or at least pretended to laugh, in order not to stand out, but every so often she would say, like a chorus: "What a macabre topic!" (It is the same word in all Greco-Latin languages: macabro, macavrios, macabre.) Federico had warmed up with the wine and was now telling the story about the Carabiniero (Italians joke about the Carabinieri the way Greeks joke about the Greeks from the Caucasus), a mountain of a man, who is living with the transplanted heart of a woman and whose behavior has become effeminate (this is what amused Federico). So we laughed and laughed with the high-pitched voice of the Carabiniero on duty.

Here is a story I would tell with pleasure, I said to myself. The spark of the comic element, which I had overlooked, seemed like a lifesaver for me, trying as I was, to write in voluntary isolation, but finding only annoyance with the telegraph wire, annoyance with the telephone, annoyance with my life in general, which was scattered and disorganized and stupid. Cooped up in a hotel room, after the failure of two previous attempts, two notebooks, and now this third one, where the narration, scattered, disorganized, stupid, goes on the same way my life goes on. But I did say so in the beginning: this text speaks of the failure of the narration, not of the narration itself. That had been my plan from the start.

One might come away from an evening out with friends, especially if they are pleasant, with an entire book in one's head.

However, more often than not, one comes away escorting a woman, and while you can do whatever you want with a book, with a woman, a person distinct from yourself, after a while you might not know what to do. She attaches herself to you and becomes an imposing plane tree that cools you with its foliage and sheds its leaves poetically in the fall, but never budges.

That isn't exactly what happened with Ursula. That evening, Ursula, fed up with the stories of our little group (which, I should point out, did not pay her the slightest attention, although she was young and beautiful and not the much older, much less attractive type of woman toward whom gay men tend to gravitate), asked me if she could share a cab with me. She said she lived near my hotel; a lie, as I was to discover later, but far from an unpleasant one for me. Federico laughed as he saw us leaving together. His matchmaking had been a success.

In the taxi, I took her hand tenderly in mine.

"So you're not one of them?" she remarked slyly.

"Do I look like I am?" I asked.

"Nowadays, you never can tell. . . ."

It was clearly an invitation to find out more.

But when we arrived at the hotel, the night watchman, not the regular one, who was my friend, but his replacement, made me furious. He asked Ursula for identification papers. She had no papers on her. He insisted that he couldn't let her spend the night in my room. Not to mention that the rate of the room would have to go up.

"All right," I said. "We'll pay. What business is it of yours?" I suppose he was jealous, that dirty old Italian, because I'd landed myself with such an attractive woman, and so he was giving me a hard time.

"The police, you see . . . they don't allow us . . . the Red Brigades. . ."

Ursula told me later that she had felt more and more like a prostitute under the watchman's gaze. For my part, I kept explaining that I lived there on a regular basis, but that he didn't happen to know me because he wasn't the regular watchman. Finally, it was all settled with a Visa credit card that Ursula fortunately had in her bag and with which she paid for the room, thereby entering her name in the hotel register.

As soon as we got to my room (I had kept Rosa's three, by-then-dried-up roses as a souvenir), Ursula went into the bathroom, from where she emerged holding a pair of dirty socks.

"One can tell you're a bachelor," she said, inspecting the room. "I understand you're a writer."

"I try to be," I sighed.

"What kind of things do you write?" she asked, turning on the radio to a music program.

"Romance novels."

She leaned over the papers on my desk. She picked one up, looked at it, and let it fall like a leaf from a plane tree.

"What a shame that it's in Greek," she said. "I used to do ancient Greek in high school, but I've forgotten it all."

Then she came and sat next to me.

"Well then, let me tell you my life story."

It was daybreak when Ursula finished her story. I could hear the toilets being flushed in adjoining rooms. The first breakfast trays were coming up to my floor. People were starting to wake up. Generally speaking, tourists wake up early so they can grab the day by the scruff of the neck and see as many of the sights as they can. For the tourist, time is money. He has to take advantage of his time because he's paying for it. And most of the guests at this hotel were either groups of elderly people, miners from northern Europe, or American college brats. Every evening, next to the front desk, posters were put up announcing organized tours for the following day. Rush hour at the hotel lasted from seven to nine each morning. Then, the tree quieted down. The birds would be back again between seven and nine in the evening. That's why I never got up before nine o'clock. It was around half past seven when Ursula, exhausted, tried to lie down next to me on the single bed that was too narrow for us both.

"What do you say?" I suggested. "Shall we go out for a coffee?"

I threw some water on my face, she tidied herself up in the mirror, and we went downstairs.

My neighborhood was beautiful early in the morning. The colors of the buildings, still untouched by the harsh sunlight, were muted; the light had not yet come over the church domes to strip them. I was fine. We were fine. The old flower lady was sitting outdoors at a cafe table like a fairy tale witch, surrounded by the bags in which she arranged her possessions. She was a tall, aristocratic-looking woman who looked a bit like my grandmother from Thásos. She always sold flowers at the city's squares. I knew her from long ago. Almost twenty years. I returned to this city every so often, and the old lady was always there, in the streets and squares around the Pantheon, every evening arranging her bags, every morning arranging her flowers, and

the transplant

every time I would greet her and every time she would not rec-
ognize me. Twenty years. Some died, others left, dictatorships
were established, earthquakes, kidnappings, murders took
place; the old lady was always here. She lived in the recesses
offered to her by the churches and palazzi of the city, a little more
hunched over each time I returned, a little more bent down, her
body a little closer to closing in a circle, but always alert and ener-
getic, always with her flowers supplied to her by the cemeteries.
She seemed to me like a ghost that never dies, because it is not
alive. It only exists like a sprite, a wispy spirit that does not come
under the jurisdiction of time because it is beyond it; a Shakespearean creature, an old woman Fate, the kismet of my life.

   We were the first customers at this cafe where the old flower
lady sat, which for me was a home away from home, next door
to my hotel. Whenever I wanted to take a break, I always came
down here for a cafe *mácchiato* a coffee "dirtied" by a dash of
milk. The waiters no longer asked me what I wanted. They knew
me. Many times I would take it in a plastic cup up to my room,
where I would sip at it slowly as I wrote. That morning, they were
surprised to see I was their first customer of the day. But when
they saw my companion they understood why I hadn't kept my
regular schedule. How were they to know, I said to myself, that
a writer's life does not take place in his bed but at his writing table?
His confessional. The night watchmen were coming to drink their
first coffee, and also the ladies of the night, whom I never saw
during my usual hours. As the morning drew on, a whole world
of clerks who worked in the neighboring office buildings began
to arrive. I didn't know them either, because after nine o'clock
when I would come down, all these people were already tucked

away in some damp, sunless office, little cogs of a big machine, of the state, the banks, the companies, the slow-moving Italian bureaucracy, antiquated, unchanged since the time the small republics and kingdoms had joined and had chosen Papal Rome as their capital. These people, who carried under their arms their bags or their car radios to avoid having them stolen, constituted a different kind of army for me than the armies of tourists I was used to, with their city maps like prayer books, or umbrellas to lead the flock. Ursula and I parted company. She went to her house, where she had invited me to come that evening, and I went back to my room, where remnants of her perfume hung in the air like threads.

I found the fat cleaning lady tidying my room, puzzled that my bed was not unmade, even though I had had "company." Every morning, the fat cleaning lady, who never failed to ask me for a cigarette, would study my sheets as if they were the entrails of birds, trying to divine what kind of night I had had. She took a singular pleasure in doing my room. From the dampness of the sheets, from the little hairs like snails, from a barrette, from an earring she had once found fallen behind the bed, she would deduce my night. She would talk to me for hours. She seemed to be especially fond of me. So much so, in fact, that I was a little suspicious.

But that day, having seen me coming out with the svelte Ursula, she couldn't figure out how the bed could be untouched. She wanted to get me talking, to ask me, but she held back, either from embarrassment or because she could see I was exhausted.

"Please just leave everything as it is. I'm going to bed."

"Ah, women!" she sighed, sounding angry, and she left, after first closing the shutters.

I lay down, and the story of Ursula kept playing back in my mind like a film.

Everything revolved around a pimple on her breast that she could not identify. Was it malignant or not? In any case it was solid, not liquid. There would have to be either a needle biopsy or a surgical biopsy, which might then lead to a mastectomy. Opinions differed on that point. The needle biopsy might aggravate it, and besides, what would be the point of discovering it was benign? She might as well have surgery right from the start and be done with it. But of course that would mean going under the knife. There would be a scar left. That was Ursula's problem; nevertheless she was being brave about it. I gathered she was the kind of person who liked clear-cut solutions. She did not like problems, be they biological or emotional, to drag on in her personal life, to become cancers. That's exactly how she had severed relations with every man in her life. At some point they had all turned out to be rotten. Weak. She was looking for a man who would take her on, and all that came with her. She had found one, but he had turned out to be a mafioso. They had thrown him in the slammer. At the moment she was free, on her own, preferring solitude to cloudy and confused emotions. Since she was a frank person, she demanded the same frankness from her mate. But men, at least the ones she had come across, were cowards. The myth of the stronger sex . . .

Little by little, as she spoke to me, she started becoming another of my heroines: the woman "in transit" who meets and talks with the man in the transit zone of an airport, certain that they will never see each other again. While Ursula talked about her travels, her life, I could hear nothing but the other voice, that of my imagination, that wanted to transplant itself onto human flesh and thus pass from the nonexistence of the nebula to the existence of the tree. The tree would absorb it, it would grow, and there at last the work would exist. "Oh, what a curse it is," I said to myself, "to be a writer." To convert, like a hydroelectric station, the power of the waterfall of life that flows wastefully, plummeting stupidly down ravines. To collect it drop by drop and turn it into energy, which then becomes light in lonely light bulbs in rooms or street lamps, as they turn on with the coming of evening. Ah! The torment, the sweet torment of the imagination. At last I felt as if I were slipping gradually into a deep sleep.

I woke up around noon, shaken by a nightmare, with the boom of the Gianicolo cannon, which, at that hour, always banged its fist against my window.

I looked around me. I saw Rosa's three red roses, which I had been keeping even though they had died, in the vase with no water. The sweet figure of Rosa, forever lost, forever a dream, was inside a crystal ball. I couldn't touch her; she was like a pair of kidneys being transported in serum for transplantation into kidney patients. The nightmare that had shaken me awake at the moment the cannon was fired was the realization that I had suddenly become very poor. That I had run out of money, and that not only had I not been sent here by a publisher, but that I myself was paying for the luxury of being away from my country, which exasperated me. I loved my country and at the same time I hated it because it deprived me of the possibility of loving it while I lived in it. My country was like a woman, a beautiful adolescent in love who, after marrying me, had begun putting on weight and neglecting herself, so that even while I knew that underneath she was the same person, her appearance repulsed me. Perhaps it wasn't her fault. Maybe I was also to blame.

So in my dream I was poor. I didn't have a dime. To be exact, the few savings that I did have left would also have to be tossed onto the altar of my art, to be sacrificed to my art that nobody wanted anymore. That would be the end of my independence. Then I would have to roll up my sleeves and start making a living. As I did when I was young, when I was starting out in life, without any support, without a penny in my pocket, with a desire to change the world, to make it better. With faith in victory. But now, in my dream, I was no longer young. And even if I had the same faith, I didn't have the same courage, the same ignorance as I did then. "This parenthesis of twenty years has lasted too long," said the old flower lady in my sleep.

"Why so, my good lady?" I asked.

"Because you've known me for twenty years. I've been watching you. Now you will never see me again. I was your fate. Take these red carnations and scatter them on the grave of Panagoulis. It's been ten years since he was assassinated. Don't forget him."

I sprung up in bed. The cannon was still booming. Twelve times. But what was worse was not that I had dreamed of the old woman, but that my dream was a reality that I had repressed so as to devote myself fully to the joy of creation. And it came, deviously, like a thief in the night, out of the underground tunnels that carry our dreams, to shake me up, *because there are torture*

dreams, on racks, sacrificial altar dreams to the Thermidors of
sleep, from which you awaken with a start, only to discover that
they are anything but dreams, that they are nightmares of
irrefutable reality.

And now I, the celebrator of dreams, the author of *...And*
Dreams Are Dreams, the existentialist of dreams, had to pay the
nightmare bill of my hotel, where I had spent almost two months,
calling dream friends and dream lovers, dream interpreters and
dream critics. And it is well known that hotels always inflate their
guests' phone bills. That is how they make their money, the same
way restaurants make money from their bar, from alcoholic
drinks, and not from food. It is the same with hotels. The price
of the room is nothing compared to all the other expenses, which,
when added up, spell disaster.

I went downstairs to ask for my bill.

"Are you leaving?" asked the frosty accountant, to whom I
had given a small deposit, but who was waiting, without pressing me, since I was a resident at the hotel and had been recom-
mended by a friend of his, to see when I would finally pay him.

"I'm not leaving just yet," I explained, "but I would like to
know exactly how much I owe."

"I see you have made a lot of phone calls," he said, as if to
prepare me.

"That is precisely why . . ."

He started tapping away at the adding machine at lighten-
ing speed. It sounded like a machine gun, the same way my typewriter sounds in moments of inspiration. He was making me sick.
His cold gaze, his expertise at hitting the keys that for me translated into the blood of my veins, all this suddenly made me real-

ize the absurdity of my enterprise. To exile myself to a city, to write . . . what? When I had nothing to say, when nobody wanted anything from me, when my art of storytelling was made obsolete by the facts themselves? And as I watched him machine-gunning the interminable column of phone calls, coffees, mineral waters, never ending, like a list of heroes fallen in battle (but in which war? Who was the enemy? Under whose orders? Who were its generals?), I remembered all the times I had said to myself, in this city or elsewhere in the world where I had wandered, that all people have a specific job: one is a bellboy, the other an accountant, one is a priest, the other a trade unionist, a news agent or a hair stylist, a clerk or a politician, a cop, a stool pigeon, a fashion model, and only I and those of my kind, without even being eligible for its benefits, for whom a workers' strike would have no meaning (have you ever thought what a poets' strike would mean?), we enjoyed the luxury of having insight into a world that, alas, had never had any use for this insight but that would not have existed without it. I always felt a little out of place, a little useless, *"like classical music in a tavern."*

Now the amount I had to pay was horrific.

"Have I made a mistake?" cried out the accountant at the sight of the total, which was so huge even he could not believe it. "Did you actually make so many phone calls?"

"How much does it come to?" I asked through clenched teeth.

The amount he told me hit me like a ton of bricks. It was the kind of number one only dreams about. It unfolded like the stream of subtitles that accompany news programs for the hard of hearing. A streamer of numbers thrown at a carnival. What was I dressed up as? I saw myself as Saint Francis of Assisi and the old woman as the Holy Virgin. Her grace was abandoning me. She had been my good fate and she was leaving me.

"No, no, it can't be. Let's start *da capo* (from the beginning)," said the accountant from behind his window, while I continued to smoke more and more nervously.

But his *da capo* hit me. It was Capodistrias whom I had spent the most time studying and telephoning in the great beyond so that he could tell me what had happened before he was assassinated by Petrobey Mavromichalis in Nafplion one day on his way to church. A black dagger from the Mani.

"There must have been a mistake," said the accountant. "Technology is subject to errors, you know."

"So is *logotechny*," I started to say, but the play on words didn't work in Italian.

"It can't be, it can't be," he kept muttering. "I've been working here for years. So many people have come through this place. Celebrities calling everywhere, all over the world. And yet I've never had a bill like this before."

"Well, of course, I have been staying here for two months," I attempted.

"But there have been others who have stayed for six months. Even twelve. Take the witch. She stays here all year round. She calls her clients who live in every corner of the earth. She's never had to pay so much."

Indeed there was a witch staying in the hotel, a fat woman who looked like a fortune teller, who ran her own mail order business of herbal concoctions in little sachets, and had quite a large clientele. She did all her business over the phone, and, in fact, that is where I would invariably see her camped: outside the hotel

256

phone booths. But at least she got paid for her magic potions, whereas nobody paid me. I was phoning into a vacuum. Whenever I felt lonely I would dig up phone numbers of old friends and call them because I needed to talk. None of them ever called me. I was always the one to call. It was like a sickness, which I was now about to pay for dearly.

Naturally, the accountant came up with the same number again. I told him I would be going away for a couple of days. I would be going to France to get the money.

"No problem," he said.

In any case, our mutual friend had vouched for me. I called Ursula to cancel our appointment for that evening and to tell her that I would be calling her in a day or two, as soon as I got back.

-6-

I kept my savings in gold bars in a French bank. A film based on one of my books had been a success and had suddenly brought me a lot of money, which I had deposited into my account in Paris, where I had lived at the time. This was during the years when I could not return to Greece for political reasons. So this was money I had earned abroad and was keeping there legally. But one day, the old lady at the bank, who knew me, told me I had to immediately withdraw my money, since a new law had just gone into effect prohibiting foreigners from having more than a certain amount of cash.

"Otherwise, you will lose whatever amount exceeds the limit," she said.

"What should I do?" I asked.

"Buy shares, invest in real estate, gold . . . "

I wasn't familiar with business matters or the stock exchange, so I chose gold; it was the easiest. And I had lived off this money for the past twenty years. I remembered how, every time I went to the bank my safe deposit box became lighter rather than heavier with the passing of the years. Now I had to cash in my last gold bar, in order to pay my hotel bill and return to my base, where I had started, still without a completed manuscript. Defeated on all counts. Extinguished. And old.

No sooner said than done. It is easy to liquidate. To consolidate, now that's another matter. So I cashed in my last ingot, like one who sells a plot of land at a sacrifice because of a health problem. It was the same with me, only my sickness was of a different kind. Nevertheless I didn't relinquish my safe deposit box. I left some of my adolescent poems in it, including "The Old Plane Tree," as well as the diary my father had kept of the Asia Minor disaster. You never know, I said to myself. After all, hadn't the Bolsheviks, upon opening the safe deposit boxes of the Russian czar in 1920, found *Platonov*, an unpublished play by Chekhov? Maybe one day, upon breaking open all terrestrial safe deposit boxes, extraterrestrials would find my "Old Plane Tree." Immediately, I felt very relieved.

Financial security never gives a writer the force he needs to write powerful works. A writer, or any artist, has to live in poverty in order to always be on the side of the oppressed, to be able to listen to the innermost heartbeats of the indignant, the suffering, the wronged. And I noticed that during the years of my financial security, I had not written anything important, anything truly great.

I like being able to talk about those things that everyone usually keeps quiet about. Only Balzac mentioned such things about his characters, because he knew that without knowledge of their financial status, his reader would not be able to comprehend their behavior or their ideas, much less their emotions. And here I had labored all my life to be like him, only to succeed in becoming my own Balzac, that is to say mythifying my own experience with as much power and talent as was given me, with as much support as I could procure from a small country whose economy is absent from the world markets (no foreign bank recognizes the exchange rate for the drachma), whose language was so rich in the past and so poor nowadays (a language that is listed by foreign editors under the subcategory of Arabic dialects). I like being able to put all my cards on the table, having nothing to hide, declaring point-blank that the act of writing is a difficult act. The only problem was that all this made me anxious, and I started drinking again.

I returned, I paid my hotel bill, and I called Ursula to tell her that I wanted to see her. She was waiting for me in a strapless dress that set off her shoulders and made them look as large as wings. She was earthy, real. I kissed her on the part of her breast where she was afraid she had the malignant tumor. She caressed me, found me a little more tired than last time; she knew that what had not happened in my hotel was going to happen that evening. She had prepared a wonderful dinner. Duck à l'orange and sweet wine. For the first time in the fifteen years since I had given it up, I drank. I wanted to get drunk. To forget. I drank and we talked, we drank and we saw the bottoms of each other's glasses, the bottoms of each other's heart. We went up and down heavenly stairs with a double sob; she, filling my pockets with the money she knew I didn't have, me, kissing her breast, telling her that the pimple was nothing to worry about, that I would make it go away with the power of my love.

So I left my hotel and moved into her apartment, a modern penthouse that overlooked the Tiber. Federico was delighted when he heard, because that, he explained, was precisely why he had put us in touch with each other. He knew that we would get along well. Ursula's penthouse was split-level. I lived upstairs and she lived downstairs. Our love was abundant. She would help me, she would tell me not to worry about a thing, she was there to support me, she wanted me to write even if I didn't earn a single penny. But, gradually, I felt her presence weighing me down. She wanted to enter my life more and more deeply. On top of that, I found it tiring that we did not speak the same language. For me, my language was the sea. And a fish can't live on land. And so, one day when she was away in Florence, I packed my bags, I took my little transistor radio, my typewriter, my books, my manuscripts, my two changes of underwear, and disappeared from her house and her life, leaving her a poignant letter: "In order to write, Ursula, you have to keep your doors shut to the invaders from the outside world. You have to stop existing as *I*, as a separate individual, and become the intermediary of others. Remember what it says in the Gospel: if the seed does not fall onto good ground, it shall die; if it does not die it will bear fruit and bring forth a hundredfold. One's personal problems are nobody else's business. They cannot be made into art. They can only be got out of one's system. And the world has suffered enough from that kind of release. Nowadays, we all want to express something that is more collective, we are all concerned about the nuclear disarmament of this small planet. That is why, in order to write, you have to isolate yourself, you have to shut your doors to others, to exist within a sphere of the absolute, alone with your writing table and the universe."

And I returned here to my base, to my island that had been devastated by the summer fires. I am cultivating my garden. I am sowing clover dreams, dreams of corn that become popcorn in dream theaters, pumpkin dreams that my fishermen friends use to make the buoys for their nets. And, as the War of Independence hero Kolokotronis wrote in his diary, *"As far as I could, I did my duty to literature."* I decided to go to an orchard I had outside Nafplion. I went there, and stayed, and spent my time growing things. It pleased me to watch the small dream trees I had planted flourish. I draw water from my well, trying as much as possible to avoid artificial irrigation that would resemble Kolokotronis's *"embalmed dreams that are preserved as long as ancient aqueducts in the valleys that are now being irrigated mechanically, with palm trees of water spurting to the rhythm of a pace maker."* The water keeps flowing, watering my tomato plants.

Friends from the past come to see me every now and then. Sometimes even journalists come, to interview the writer who became a farmer. They talk to me of culture. I talk to them of agriculture. A few days ago, Rosa arrived on a yacht, traveling with some weird characters. But I liked the captain, because he was worried about the west wind. I found Rosa to be in great shape. She was happy now. She was expecting a child. Elias, her husband, was the owner of the yacht. I told her how lucky she

had been to extricate herself from me in time. Don Pacifico and
Doña Rosita . . .

I am waiting for the spring. The almond trees will
blossom this year.

-7-

Now this notebook is finished. The third one. If I had failed
with the other two, I knew from the start that I would succeed with
this one. The quality of the paper did not allow the pencil to catch
because it was smooth, shiny, expensive of course (twelve thousand lire); I knew it would lead me to the end. I have told my
story, fictitious like all stories, since the act of writing is the man-
ifestation of the imaginary with the help of real means: pencil and
paper. This third notebook, now approaching its end, determines
by the number of its pages the length of my story. What I have
written has nothing to do with me as an individual. However, I
have managed to express the difficulty of expression in a world
that keeps changing. And all ends well, since life is but a dream.